The Crystal Frontier

BY THE SAME AUTHOR

Aura

Distant Relations

Constancia and Other Stories for Virgins

Terra Nostra

The Campaign

The Old Gringo

Where the Air Is Clear

The Death of Artemio Cruz

The Good Conscience

Burnt Water

The Hydra Head

A Change of Skin

Christopher Unborn

Diana: The Goddess Who Hunts Alone

The Orange Tree

Myself with Others

The Buried Mirror

A New Time for Mexico

The Crystal Frontier

A NOVEL IN NINE STORIES

Carlos Fuentes

BLOOMSBURY

First published in Great Britain 1998

Copyright © 1995 by Carlos Fuentes
Translation copyright © 1997 by Farrar, Straus and Giroux, Inc.

First published in 1995 by Aguilar, Altea Taurus, Alfaguara, S.A. de C.V.,
Mexico, as *La frontera de cristal: Una novela en nueve cuentos*

The moral right of the author has been asserted

Bloomsbury Publishing Plc, 38 Soho Square, London W1V 5DF

A CIP catalogue record for this book is available from the British Library

ISBN 0 7475 3674 0

10 9 8 7 6 5 4 3 2 1

Printed in Great Britain by Clays Limited, St Ives plc

CONTENTS

The Crystal Frontier

A CAPITAL GIRL

For Héctor Aguilar Camín

1

"There is absolutely nothing of interest in Campazas." The Blue Guide's categorical statement made Michelina Laborde smile slightly, disturbing for a moment the perfect symmetry of her face. Her "little Mexican mask" a French admirer had called it—the perfect bones of Mexican beauties who seem immune to the ravages of time. Perfect faces for death, added the admirer, which Michelina did not like one bit.

She was a young woman of sophisticated tastes because she'd been educated that way, brought up that way, and refined that way. She was of an "old family," so even a hundred years earlier her education would not have been very different. "The world has changed, but we haven't," her grandmother, still the pillar of the household, would say. Except that there used to be more power behind the breeding. There were haciendas, demurral courts—for throwing out perfectly good lawsuits "that did not warrant legal action"—and Church blessings.

There were also crinolines. It was easier then to cover up the physical defects that modern fashions reveal. Blue jeans accentuate a fat backside or thin legs. "Our women are like thrushes," she could still hear her uncle (May he rest in peace) say. "Thin shanks, fat asses."

She imagined herself in crinolines and felt herself freer than she did in jeans. How wonderful, knowing you were imagined, hidden, that you could cross your legs without anyone's noticing, could even dare to wear nothing under your crinolines, could feel the cool, free breeze on those unmentionable buttocks, on the very interstices of modesty, aware all the while that men had to imagine it! She hated the idea of going topless at the beach; she was a declared enemy of bikinis and only reluctantly wore miniskirts.

She was blushing at these thoughts when the Grumman stewardess came by to whisper that the private jet would soon be landing at the Campazas airport. She tried to find a city somewhere in that panorama of desert, bald mountains, and swirling dust. She could see nothing. Her gaze was captured by a mirage: the distant river and, beyond it, golden domes, glass towers, highway cloverleafs like huge stone bows. But that was on the other side of the crystal frontier. Over here, below—the guidebook was right—there was nothing.

Her godfather, Don Leonardo, met her. He'd invited her after their meeting in the capital just six months earlier. "Come take a look at my part of the country. You'll like it. I'll send my private plane to get you."

She liked her godfather. He was fifty years old—twenty-five years older than she—and robust, half-bald, with bushy sideburns but the perfect classic profile of a Roman emperor and the smile and eyes to go with it. Above all, he had those dreamy eyes that said, I've been waiting a long time for you.

Michelina would have rejected pure perfection; she'd never met an extremely handsome man who hadn't disappointed her. They felt they were better looking than she was. Good looks gave them unbearably domineering airs. Don Leonardo had a perfect profile, but it was offset by his cheeks, his baldness, his age. His smile, on the other hand, said, Don't take me too seriously—I'm a sexy, fun-loving guy. And yet his gaze, again, possessed an irresistible intensity. I fall in love seriously, it said to her. I know how to ask for everything because I also know how to give everything. What do you say?

"What's that you're saying, Michelina?"

"That we met when I was born, so how can you tell me that only six months ago we—"

He interrupted her. "This is the third time I've met you, dear. Each time it seems like the first. How many more times do I get?"

"Many more, I hope," she said, without thinking that she would blush—although, since she'd just spent ten days on the beach in Zihuatanejo, no one would have been able to tell if she was turning red or was simply a little sunburned. But she was a woman who filled the space wherever she happened to be. She complemented places, making them more beautiful. A chorus of macho whistles always greeted her in public places, even in the small Campazas airport. But when the lover boys saw who was with her, a respectful silence reigned.

Don Leonardo Barroso was a powerful man here in the

north as well as in the capital. For the most obvious reasons, Michelina Laborde's father had asked Don Leonardo, the then minister, to be her godfather: protection, ambition, a tiny portion of power.

"Power!"

It was ridiculous. Her godfather himself had spelled things out for them when he was in the capital six months before. Mexico's health depends on the periodic renewal of its elites. For good or ill. When native aristocracies overstay their welcome, we kick them out. The social and political intelligence of the nation consists in knowing when to retire and leave open the doors of constant renewal. Politically, the "no reelection" clause in the constitution is our great escape valve. There can be no Somozas or Trujillos here. No one is indispensable. Six years in office and even the president goes home. Did he steal a lot? So much the better. That's the price we pay for his knowing when to retire and never say a word again. Imagine if Stalin had lasted only six years and had peacefully turned power over to Trotsky, and he to Kamenev, and he to Bukharin, et cetera. Today the USSR would be the most powerful nation on earth. Not even the king of Spain gave hereditary titles to Mexican creoles, and the republic never sanctioned aristocracies.

"But there have always been differences," interrupted Grandmother Laborde, who was seated across from her cases of curios. "I mean, there have always been 'decent' people. But just think: there are people who presume to be of the Porfirio Díaz–era aristocracy—all because they lasted thirty years in power. Thirty years is nothing! When our family saw Porfirio Díaz's supporters enter the capital after the Tuxtepec revolution, we were horrified. Who were these disheveled men from Oaxaca and these Spanish grocers and French sandal makers. Porfirio Díaz! Corcueras! Nonsense!

Limantours! An arriviste! In those days, we decent people
followed Lerdo de Tejada."

Michelina's grandmother is eighty-four years old and is
still going strong. Lucid, irreverent, and anchored by the
most eccentric of powers. Her family lost influence after the
revolution of 1910–20, and Doña Zarina Ycaza de Laborde
took refuge in the curious hobby of collecting junk, bits and
pieces of things, and, most of all, magazines. Every single
doll (male or female) that enjoyed popularity—whether it
was Mamerto the Charro or Chupamirto the Tramp, Cap-
tain Shark, or Popeye—she would rescue from oblivion, filling an entire armoire with those cotton-stuffed figures,
repairing them, sewing them up when their innards spilled
out.

Postcards, movie posters, cigar boxes, matchboxes, bot-
tlecaps, comic books—Doña Zarina collected all of them
with a zeal that drove her children and even her grandchildren to despair, until an American company specializing in
memorabilia bought her complete collection of *Today*, *Tomorrow*, and *Always* magazines for something like $50,000.
Then they all opened their eyes: in her drawers, in her ar-
moires, the old lady was stashing away a gold mine, the
silver of memory, the jewels of remembrance. She was the
czarina of nostalgia (as her most cultured grandson aptly put
it).

Doña Zarina's gaze clouded over as she looked out from
her house on Río Sena Street. If the city had been taken care
of as well as she had maintained the Minnie Mouse doll . . .
But it was better not to speak of such things. She had remained and witnessed the paradoxical death of a city that
as it grew bigger diminished, as if it were a poor being who
was born, grew, and inevitably died. She plunged her nose
back into the sets of bound volumes of *Chamaco Chico* and

did not expect anyone to hear or understand her lapidary phrase: "Plus ça change, plus c'est la même chose."

To go on being "decent" people, to maintain the style to which they were accustomed, their culture, and even—though this was pure delusion—their name in the world, the family took refuge in the diplomatic corps. In Paris, Michelina's father was assigned to accompany the young deputy Leonardo Barroso, and with each glass of burgundy, with each monstrous dinner in the Grand Véfour, with each tour of the Loire châteaus, Don Leonardo's gratitude toward the diplomatic attaché of venerable family grew, eventually extending to the attaché's wife and immediately thereafter to his newborn daughter. They didn't ask; he himself made the offer: "Let me be the kid's godfather."

Michelina Laborde e Ycaza, the young lady from the capital. You all know her because her photo's been in the society pages so often. A classic creole face: white skin but with a Mediterranean shadow—olive and refined sugar—perfect symmetry in her large black eyes protected by cloudlike eyelids and the slightest of tempests in the shadows beneath, symmetry in her straight, immobile nose, vibrant only in the disquiet of those tempests, on their disquieting wings, as if a vampire had tried to escape from the night enclosed in that luminous body. Also her cheekbones, seemingly as fragile as quail eggs behind her smiling skin, trying almost to open that skin beyond the time allotted and expose her perfect skull. And finally, Michelina's long black hair, floating, glistening, scented more from shampoo than from hair spray—the wondrous, fatal annunciation of her other, hidden soft hair. Every time, every thing divided: her upper lip, the deep comma in her chin, the separation of her skin.

Don Leonardo thought all this when he saw her grown up, and instantly he said to himself, I want her for my son.

<u>2</u>

Well-traveled, sophisticated, the young lady from the capital observed the features of Campazas without surprise. Its dusty town square and humble but proud church with broken walls and an erect carved facade that proclaimed, The Baroque came this far, to the very edge of the desert—to this point and no farther. Beggars and stray dogs. Magically supplied and beautiful markets, loudspeakers offering bargains and crooning out boleros. The empire of soft drinks: does any country consume more carbonated water? Smoke from black-tobacco cigarettes, oval and strongly tropical. The smell of sugarcoated peanuts.

"Don't be surprised at the way your godmother looks," Don Leonardo was saying, as if to draw her attention away from the ugliness of the city. "She decided to get a face-lift and even went all the way to Brazil to be done by the famous Pitanguy. When she came back, I didn't recognize her."

"I don't remember her very well." Michelina smiled.

"I almost sent her back. 'This isn't my wife. This is not the woman I fell in love with.' "

"I can't compare her," said Michelina, in an involuntary tone of jealousy.

He laughed, but Michelina again recalled old-fashioned styles, the crinolines that dissimulated the body and the veil that hid the face, making it mysterious and even desirable. In the old days, lights were low. Veils and candles . . . There were too many nuns in the family history, but few things fired Michelina's imagination more than the vocation of the cloister and, once one was safe inside it, the liberation of the powers of imagination—the freedom to love anyone, desire anyone, pray to anyone, confess anything. When she was twelve, she wanted to enter some old colonial convent, pray a lot, flagellate herself, bathe in cold water, and pray some more: "I always want to be a girl. Blessed Virgin, help me. Don't turn me into a woman."

The chauffeur honked as they came to an immense wrought-iron gate, the kind she'd seen outside studios in movies about Hollywood. Correct, her godfather said, around here they call our neighborhood Disneyland. People in the north love to make wisecracks, but the fact is, we have to live somewhere, and nowadays you need protection, no way around it. You've got to defend yourself and your property.

"What wouldn't I give to leave the doors wide open the way we used to here in the north. But now even the gringos need armed guards and police dogs. Being rich is a sin."

Before: Michelina's gaze wandered from her memory of Mexican colonial convents and French châteaus to the real vision of this group of walled mansions, each one half fortress, half mausoleum, mansions with Greek capitals, columns, and svelte statues of gods wearing fig leaves; Arabian mosques with little fountains and plaster minarets; reproductions of Tara, with its neoclassical portico. Not a single tile, not one adobe brick—only marble, cement, stone, plaster, and more wrought iron, gates behind gates, gates within gates, gates facing gates, a labyrinth of gates, and the inaudible buzz of garage doors that opened with a stench of old gasoline, involuntarily urinated by the herds of Porsches, Mercedes, BMWs that reposed like mastodons within the caves of the garages.

The Barrosos' house was Tudor-Norman, with a double roof of blue slate, exposed timbers, and leaded glass windows everywhere. The only things missing were the Avon River in the garden and Anne Boleyn's head in some trunk.

The Mercedes stopped and the driver tumbled out running. He resembled a small cube with the face of a raccoon, a swift die dressed in navy blue who buttoned his jacket as he hurried to open the car door for the *patrón* and his goddaughter. Michelina and Don Leonardo got out. He offered her his arm and led her to the entrance. The door opened. Doña Lucila Barroso smiled at Michelina (Don Leonardo had exaggerated—the lady looked older than he) and hugged her; behind stood the son, Marianito, the heir, who never traveled, who went out infrequently, whom she'd never met but whom it was high time she did meet, a very withdrawn young man, very serious, very formal, very fond of reading, very given to hiding out on the ranch to read day and night—it was high time he went out a bit, he'd already turned twenty-one. That very night the young lady from the capital and the provincial, the goddaughter and the son, could go out dancing on the other side of the border, in the United States, half an hour away from here, dance, get to know each other, learn about each other. Of course. What could be more logical?

<u>3</u>

Marianito came home alone, drunk, crying. Doña Lucila heard him stumbling on the stairs and thought the impossible thought: a thief. Leonardo, there's a robber in the house. It's impossible—the guards, the gates. The godfather, in his bathrobe, ran and found his son kneeling and puking on a landing. He helped him to his feet, hugged him. A knot formed in the father's throat, the son stained the beautiful Liberty of London robe with vomit. The father helped him to his dark bedroom, which had no lamps. The boy had asked that it be that way, and the father had made jokes:

You must be a cat. You see in the dark. You'll go blind. How can you read in the darkness?

"What happened, son?"

"Nothing, Dad, nothing."

"What did she do to you? Just tell me what she did to you, son."

"Nothing, Dad, I swear. She didn't do anything to me."

"Wasn't she nice?"

"Very nice, Dad. Too nice. She didn't do anything to me. I was the one."

He was the one. It made him ashamed. In the car, she tried to make pleasant conversation about books and travel. At least the car was dark, the driver silent. The discotheque wasn't. The noise was unbearable. The lights, harsh, terrible, like white knives, chased him, seemed to look for him, only him, while even the shadows respected her, desired her, shrouded her with love. She moved and danced wrapped in shadows—beautiful, Dad, she's a beautiful girl.

"Not half good enough for you, son."

"You should have seen how everyone there admired her, how jealous they were of me for being with her."

"We all feel good when that happens, right, Mariano? We feel on top of the world when people envy us because of the woman we have, so what happened? What happened? Did she treat you bad?"

"No, she's got the best manners—too good, I'd say. She does everything well, and you can see right away she's from the capital, that she's traveled, that she's got the best of everything. So why didn't the disco lights chase her instead of me?"

"But she let you, right?"

"No, I walked out. I took a gringo taxi. I left the Mercedes and the driver for her."

"No, I didn't say *left*, I said *let*—she let you do what you wanted, right?"

"No, I bought a bottle of Jack Daniels and drank it right down. I felt as if I was dying. I took a gringo cab, I tell you. I came back over the border. I can't be sure I know what I'm telling you."

"She humiliated you, isn't that so?"

He told his father she hadn't, or perhaps she had: Michelina's good manners did humiliate him. Her compassion offended him. Michelina was like a nun in an Yves St. Laurent habit; instead of a surplice she carried one of those Chanel evening bags, the ones with a gold chain. She danced in the shadows, she danced with the shadows, not with him—him she turned over to the slashes of the strobe lights, dawn, frozen, where everyone could see him better and laugh at him, feel repulsion, ask that he be thrown out. He ruined parties. How could they have let him in? He was a monster. He only wanted to get together with her in the shadow, take refuge in the individuality that had always protected him. I swear, Dad, I didn't want to take advantage of her, I only asked her for the thing she was giving me, a touch of pity, in her arms, with a kiss—what could a kiss mean to her? You give me kisses, Dad, I don't scare you, do I?

Don Leonardo patted his son's head, envying the boy his bronzed, lion-colored hair. He himself had gone bald so early. He kissed him on the forehead and helped him settle down in bed, rocked him as he did when Mariano was a little boy, did not bless him because he didn't believe in that stuff, but was on the verge of lulling him to sleep with a song. It seemed ridiculous to sing him a lullaby. The truth was, he only remembered boleros, and all of them talked about humiliated men and hypocritical women.

"You screwed her, right? Tell me you did."

<u>4</u>

The welcome party for Michelina was a complete success, especially because Doña Lucila ordered the men of the house—Don Leonardo and Marianito—to make themselves scarce.

"Go out to the ranch and don't come back until late. We want a party just for us girls, so we can relax and gossip to our heart's content."

Leonardo girded his loins. He knew Michelina wouldn't be able to take the drivel that pack of old bitches spewed whenever they got together. Marianito was in no condition to travel, but his father said nothing to Lucila; anyway, the kid never let himself be noticed. He was so discreet, he was a shadow . . . Don Leonardo went alone to have dinner with some gringos on the other side of the border. Dinner at six o'clock in the afternoon, how crude. When he got back, the party was in full swing, so he put his finger over his lips to tell the young Indian servant to say nothing. It didn't matter: the boy was a Pacuache who didn't speak Spanish, which was why Doña Lucila had hired him, so the ladies could say whatever they liked without eavesdroppers. Besides, this little Indian boy was as slim and handsome as a desert god, made not of white marble but of ebony instead, and when the highballs had gone to their heads, the ladies would collectively undress him and make him walk around naked with a tray on his head. They were soul sisters, completely uninhibited, or did the ladies in the capital think that just because they were from the north they had to be hicks? No way! With the border a mere step away, you could be in a Neiman Marcus, a Saks, a Cartier in half an hour. What right did these women from the capital have to brag, when they were condemned to buy their clothes at Perisur? Okay now, keep it down—Doña Lucila put her finger to her lips—here comes Leonardo's goddaughter. They say she's really conceited, that she's traveled a lot, and that she's very chic (as they say), so just be yourselves, but don't offend her.

Michelina was the only one who didn't have a face-lift. She sat down, smiling and amiable, among the twenty or so rich and perfumed women, all of them outfitted on the other side of the border, bejewelled, most with mahogany-tinted locks, some wearing Venetian fantasy glasses, others watery-eyed trying out their contact lenses, but all liberated. And if this girl from the capital wanted to join them, fine, but if she turned out to be a tight-ass, they'd just ignore her . . . This was the girls' gang, and they drank supersweet liqueurs because they got you stoned faster and were tastier, as if life were an eternal dessert (desert? dessert? *postre? desierto?*). They would drink sweet anise on ice, a so-called nun, a cloudy drink that got you drunk fast. (Oh, Lucilita, how I'm screwing up—and it's only my first little nun . . .) Like drinking the sky, girls, like getting drunk on clouds. They began singing: You and the clouds have driven me crazy, you and the clouds will be my death . . .

They all laughed and drank more nuns and someone told Michelina to loosen up, that she really looked like a nun sitting there in the middle of the room on a puff covered in lilac brocade, all symmetrical. But isn't your goddaughter crooked anywhere, Lucilita? Hey, she's only my husband's goddaughter, not mine. Anyway, what perfection, her eyes along one line, her nose another straight line, her chin cleft, her lips so . . . ! Some laughed because they were sorry for Lucila, staring at her and blushing, but Lucila let it all go by, turned inward; their comments rolled off her like water off a duck, as if nothing had happened. They were here celebrating the absence of men—well, except for that little Indian boy who doesn't count. And there's my husband's goddaughter, who's oh so refined and courteous. Now, don't make her uncomfortable. Let her be just as she is and let us be the way we are. After all, we all came from the convent, don't forget. All of us went to school with the nuns and one day we all got liberated, so don't make Michelina feel funny. But come on, we're all back in the convent, Lucilita, said a lady whose glasses were encrusted with diamonds, all alone, without men, but sure thinking about them!

This set off a verbal Ping-Pong game about men, their evils, their cheapness, their indifference, their adeptness at avoiding responsibility (work the usual pretext), their fear of physical pain (I'd like to see a single one of those bastards give birth just once), their limited sexual skill (so how could they not look for lovers?). Hey, hey, what do *you* know, Rosalba? Don't be a bunch of jerks now—all I know is what you all tell me, and me, well, I'm a saint, my saint. And they sang a little again, and then they started laughing at men once more ("Ambrosio's gone nuts: he makes the maid shave under her arms and wear perfume. Can you beat that? The poor bitch's going to start thinking she's someone"; "He makes out that he's so generous because we have a joint account in New York, but I found out about the secret account in Switzerland. I got the number and everything. I seduced the lawyer. Let's see that wiseass Nicolás pull a fast one on me"; "They all think we shouldn't get the cash until they kick off. You've got to know all the bank accounts and have access to all the credit cards just in case they dump you"; "In one shot, I ripped off my first husband's Optima card for $100,000 before he knew what hit him"; "We have to watch porno films together for that little thing to happen"; "First it's 'The president called me,' then it's 'The president told me, confided in me, distinguished me with an embrace.' 'So why don't you marry him?' I said.") But they didn't have the nerve to strip the Pacuache with Michelina there. She went along politely with their laughter, toying with her pearl necklace and nodding sweetly at the jokes the women made; her position—not distant yet not right in among them—was perfect, though she was fearful it would all end in the usual group embrace, the great unbosoming of feelings, the sweat, the tears, the repentance, the desire, vibrant and suppressed, the terrible admission: there is absolutely nothing of interest in Campazas for anyone, outsider or native, city person or northerner. Lord, how they wanted to get in the Grumman and fly off to Vail right now. But why? Just to run into more dissatisfied Mexicans, horrified at the idea that all the money in the world isn't worth shit because there's always something more, and more, and more, something unattainable—to be the queen of England, the sultan of Brunei, be a piece like Kim Basinger or have a piece like Tom Cruise. They started giggling, imitating the movements of skiers, but they weren't on the Colorado slopes but in the desert of northern Mexico, which suddenly exploded in the firmament at sunset and passed through the leaded windows of the Tudor-Norman mansion, illuminating the faces of the twenty women, painting them satanic red, blinding the contact-lens wearers, and forcing all of them to look at the daily spectacle of the sun disappearing amid the fire, carrying their treasures into the underworld, exhibiting them one last time on the bald mountains and rocky plains, leaving only the prickly pears as the crowns of the night, carrying everything else away: life, beauty, ambition, envy, fortune. Would the sun rise again?

All eyes concentrated on the sunset. Except those of two people.

Leonardo Barroso watched everything from behind a scarlet curtain.

Michelina Laborde e Ycaza watched him until he saw her.

Their eyes met at the exact instant when no one had any interest in seeing where the young lady from the capital was looking or finding out if Leonardo had returned. The twenty women silently watched the sunset as if, in tears, they were attending their own funerals.

Then the northern troupe came in, banging drums and playing trumpets and guitars, and the place filled with men wearing Stetsons and short jackets. The spell was broken and all the women howled with pleasure. No one even noticed when Michelina excused herself, walked to the curtain, and, among its thick folds, found her godfather's burning hand.

5

Only Lucila heard with what a desperate sound, with what a screech of burning rubber, the Lincoln convertible pulled out of the garage. But she paid no attention because, no matter how fast it went, the car would never reach the limits of the red horizon. To Mrs. Barroso, that seemed like a very neat poetic idea—"We shall never reach the horizon"—but she had no words to communicate it to her pals, who, in any case, were all drunk. Perhaps she only imagined the engine's noise, which might have been nothing more than the echo of the guitar in her crazed head.

Leonardo was not drunk. His horizon did have a limit: the border between Mexico and the United States. The night air cleared his head even more, clarified both his ideas and his eyes. He drove with only one hand on the wheel. With his other hand, he squeezed Michelina's. He told her he regretted having to say it to her, but she should understand that she would have anything she wanted. He didn't want to brag, but she would get all the money, all the power; now she was seeing only the naked desert, but her life could be like that enchanted city on the other side of the frontier: golden towers, crystal palaces.

Yes, she said, I know, I accept it.

Leonardo slammed on the brakes, exiting the straight desert highway. In the distance, the monuments of cathedral-like stone, which seemed now like fragile paper silhouettes, watched over them.

He looked at her as if he, too, could read in the dark. The girl's eyes shone brightly enough. At least Marianito and she would have that in common, the gift of penetrating the darkness, of seeing into the night. Perhaps without that penumbra he wouldn't have clearly seen what he recognized in his goddaughter's eyes. Daylight would surely have dazzled his vision. Night was necessary for seeing clearly the soul of this woman.

Yes, she said, I know and accept.

Leonardo held onto the Lincoln's steering wheel as if it were the rock of his most intimate being. He was money. He was power. The desired love, he realized, was his own.

"No, not me."

"You," Michelina said. "You are what I want."

She kissed him with those perfect lips, and against his beard, earlier shaved close but stubbly at that hour, he felt the depth of Michelina's cleft chin. He sank into the open mouth of his goddaughter, as if all light had no other origin but that tongue, those teeth, that saliva. He closed his eyes to kiss and saw all the light of the world. But he never let go of the wheel. His fingers had a voice and shouted to get closer to Michelina's body, to dig among her buttons, to find and caress and stiffen her nipples, the next symmetry of that perfect beauty.

He kissed her for a long time, exploring the girl's perfectly formed, uncleft palate with his tongue, and then God and the devil, once again allies, made him feel he was kissing his own son, that the father's tongue cut itself and bled in the jagged cleft of the palate, broken like a coral reef, that the smoothness of Michelina's mouth had been brutally replaced by his son's swollen, irritated, reddish carnality, wounded, smeared with mucus, dripping thick phlegm.

Is that what she felt when he screwed her last night without wanting to confess it? Why was she telling him now that she wanted him, the father, when it was obvious she was here to seduce the son incapable of seducing anyone? Wasn't she here to conclude the family pact, to acknowledge the unlimited protection the powerful politician Leonardo Barroso gave to the impoverished Laborde e Ycaza family, to thank him for a few marvelous days in Paris—wines, restaurants, monuments? Was that what made working, getting rich, worthwhile? Paris was the reward, and now she was Paris; she incarnated the world, Europe, good taste, and he was offering her the complement to her elegance and beauty, the money without which she would quickly cease to be elegant and beautiful and become merely an eccentric aristocrat like her ancient grandmother, bent over the collectible curios of the past.

He invited her to conclude the pact. He became her godfather in order to single out her family. Now he was offering her his son in matrimony. The gold seal.

"But I've already got a boyfriend in the capital."

Leonardo stared fixedly until he lost his own eyes in the desert.

"No more."

"I'm not lying to you, godfather."

"Everything and everyone has a price. That punk was more interested in money than in you."

"You did it for me, didn't you? You love me, too, isn't that true?"

"You don't get it. You just don't get it."

Together with his promise, the invisible line of the frontier passed through his head. He was well-known in the luxury hotels on the other side; they never asked him for identification or baggage and simply rented him the most luxurious suite for a night or a few hours, making sure there was a basket of fruit and a bottle of champagne in the room before he stepped out of the elevator. A sitting room. A bedroom. A bathroom. The two of them showering together, lathering each other up, caressing . . .

Leonardo turned the key in the ignition, started the car, and headed back to Campazas.

<u>6</u>

Grandmother Doña Zarina agreed with her granddaughter. Michelina would be dressed for her marriage in the old-fashioned way, in authentic clothes the old lady had naturally been collecting for generations. The girl could choose.

A crinoline, said the young woman, I've always dreamed of wearing a crinoline so everyone could wonder about me, could imagine me, and not know clearly what the bride was like. In that case, the grandmother said cheerfully, you'll need a veil.

One night, she tried on her wedding outfit, the crinoline and the veil, and went to bed to sleep alone for the last time. She dreamed she was in a convent, strolling through patios and arcades, chapels and corridors, while the other nuns, locked in, peered out like animals through the bars on their cells, shouted obscenities at her because she was getting married, because she preferred the love of a man to wedding Christ. They insulted her for violating her vows, for leaving her religious order, her social class.

Michelina tried to escape from her dream, whose space was identical to that of the convent, but all the nuns, crowded in front of the altar, blocked her way. The black maids tore the habits off the sisters, stripping them naked to the waist, and then the nuns screamed imploringly for the whip to suppress the devil in the flesh and to give an example for Sister Michelina. Others immodestly menstruated on the tiled floor, then licked their own blood and marked crosses on the icy stone. Others lay next to the prostrate, bleeding, wounded, thorn-pierced Christs, and here Michelina's dream in Mexico City fused with Mariano's in the lightless bedroom in Campazas. The boy, too, dreamed of one of those dolorous Christs in Mexican churches, more dolorous than their Virgin Mothers, the Son laid out in a crystal coffin surrounded by dusty flowers, He Himself turning to dust, disappearing on His homeward journey to the spirit, leaving only the evidence of a few nails, a lance, a crown of thorns, a rag dipped in vinegar . . . how he longed to leave behind the miseries of this ephemeral body!

That was only for Christ, and how Mariano envied Him! If the suffering, mocked, wounded Christ had been left in holy peace, why not him? All he wanted was to live on his parents' ranch, reading all day with no other company than the Indians, who were natural and indifferent to the perversions of nature, Indians some called Pacuaches and others "erased Indians." Like him: invisible Indians, beings who copied that great canvas of imitations and metamorphoses, the desert. Was he more confined, more isolated out there on the desert ranch than his family was in Disneyland, out of touch as they were with Campazas, with the nation, ignoring everything that occurred outside their high walls, consuming only imported things, watching only cable television? Why was he denied his solitude, his isolation, when he was indifferent to theirs? He who read so much, things that were so beautiful, worlds as perfect as his imagination could desire, infinitely new pasts, futures foretold and already, already enjoyed.

He dreamed of a hare.

A hare is a wild quadruped with long ears and a short tail.

Its fur is reddish, and its offspring are born hairy.

Its feet are longer than those of the rabbit. It runs very quickly because it is very timid.

It does not dig, as other members of the species do. It makes nests, seeking out a stable, warm, respected space where it will be left in peace.

It's a mammal. It's born from milk, desires it again, wants to suckle in darkness, to be sucked, in a nest with no surprises and no one to watch it enjoy itself.

There wasn't a woman in the world who could tolerate his desire. Mariano only wanted, finally, to live physically where he'd always wanted to live by will and where he'd always lived in spirit. On a ranch. With little money, many books, and a few "erased Indians" as silent as he. Alone, because where in the world was there a woman who could eclipse all space but the bedroom, where space and presence coincided. Was Michelina such a woman? Would she respect his solitude? Would she liberate him forever from ambition, inheritance, social obligations, the need to make public appearances?

It wasn't his fault that inside his mouth there lived a

blind, hairy, swift, and voracious hare, nesting permanently on his tongue.

7

On her wedding day, Michelina entered the living room of the Tudor-Norman mansion wearing her beautiful old dress, her crinoline, flat-heeled white velvet slippers, and a heavy white veil that completely hid her features. And above the veil, a crown of orange blossoms. She was on the arm of her father, the retired ambassador Don Herminio Laborde. Michelina's mother was unwilling to make the trip north (gossip had it that she disapproved of the marriage but lacked the means to stop it). The grandmother, old as she was, would have made the trip with pleasure.

"I've seen every type of crossbreeding imaginable, and one more, even if it's between a tigress and a gorilla, much less between a dove and a rabbit, isn't going to shock me."

Her ailments kept her from traveling; somehow, though, she was present in the crinoline, in the veil . . . Doña Lucila spent a whole month in Houston outfitting herself as if she were the bride, and today she looked like something from a pastry shop. She embodied the wedding cake itself: triangular like a cream pyramid, she was crowned with a cherry hat, her hair a caramel delight, her face a huge, smiling meringue, her breasts a wave of crème Chantilly. And then the dress: draped over her like a burial shroud, it had all the tones of blackberry jam spread over marzipan.

But she did not offer her arm to her son, Mariano. No, it was Leonardo Barroso himself who wrapped Mariano's shoulders in a big embrace. The young man was simply dressed: a beige suit, a blue shirt, and a string tie. Doña

Lucila did not lean on her son until the party, the gathering of a multitude of friends, acquaintances, curiosity seekers, all there to attend the wedding of the son of one of the most powerful men, et cetera. Properties, customs offices, real estate deals, wealth and power provided by control over an illusory, crystal border, a porous frontier through which each year pass millions of people, ideas, products—in short, everything (sotto voce: contraband, drugs, counterfeit money, et cetera).

Was there anyone who didn't have something to do with or didn't depend on or hope to serve Don Leonardo Barroso, tsar of the northern frontier? What a shame about his son. There has to be a balance in this life. The son humanizes the father. But the young lady from the capital sold herself, don't tell me otherwise. Human beings are bought, Don Enrique. Put it this way: the buying and selling are humanized, Don Raúl.

Although in those years every possible concession had been made to the Catholic Church, Don Leonardo Barroso maintained his liberal Jacobinism, the old tradition of nineteenth-century Mexican reform and revolution: "I'm a liberal, but I respect religion."

In their bedroom (to the horror of Doña Lucila), he had a reproduction of Picasso's *Guernica* instead of the Sacred Heart of Jesus. "What ugly scrawls! A child could draw better than that." Luckily, by then they were sleeping in separate bedrooms, so they each had their own icons over the bed: Pope Paul VI and Jesus, united in their vision of sacrifice, death, and redemption. Don Leonardo never entered a church and held the civil part of the nuptial ceremony in his own house—of course, where else? Even so, the bride's outfit infused the act with a mysterious severity, sacred rather than ecclesiastical.

"Think she's a witch?"

"No, man, just one of those snooty bitches from the capital who come up here to make us look like hicks."

"Is that the latest fashion?"

"For moths, yes, the very latest."

"They say she's a real knockout."

The guests fell silent. The judge said the usual things and read an abbreviated version of Melchor Ocampos's epistle: Obligations, Rights, Mutual Support. All shared, in sickness and in health, joy and suffering—the bed, time, the times. Bodies. Stares. The witnesses signed. The bride and groom signed. Don Leonardo lifted Michelina's veil and brought Mariano's face close to that of his bride. Michelina could not supress an expression of disgust. Then Leonardo kissed the two of them. First, he held his son's face in his hands and brought those lips so esteemed by Michelina, so sexy and so fickle, close to his son's mouth, kissed him with the same intensity Michelina attributed to the father's eyes: I fall in love seriously, I know how to ask for everything because I also know how to give it.

The lips separated, and Don Leonardo caressed his son's head, kissed him on that disgusting mouth, Normita, while Doña Lucila turned pale and wished she were dead, and then, showing off his daring and his personality—not for nothing is he Leonardo Barroso—with his son's drool still on his lips, he raised again the lowered veil of the bride—a real beauty, Rosalba, you were right!—and gave her a long and terrible kiss that frankly, my dear, had absolutely nothing of the father-in-law (or godfather, for that matter) in it.

What a morning, I tell you, what a morning! I wouldn't have missed it for the world! Campazas will never be the same after this wedding!

8

The Lincoln convertible, this time with its top up, rapidly crossed the cold, silent evening desert, filling it with the noise of tires and motor, frightening the hares, which leapt far away from the straight highway, the uninterrupted line to the frontier—crossed the desert in order to break the illusory crystal divider, the glass membrane between Mexico and the United States, and continue along the superhighways of the north to the enchanted city, temptation in the desert, illuminated, brilliant, with a Neiman Marcus, a Saks, a Cartier, and a Marriott, where a luxury suite awaited the bride and groom: champagne and baskets of fruit, a sitting room, spacious closets, a king-size bed, lots of mirrors in which to admire Michelina, a pink marble bath tub in which to bathe with her—her buttocks were larger than they seemed, her legs thinner, like a thrush's—oh, woman of tempestuous eyes, immobile little nose, and nervous nostrils through which night escapes from you, parted lips, moist, through which my tongue gets lost without finding coral reefs or stalactite caves or ruined Gothic vaults—there is only the tickle of your cleft chin, my precious, the announcement of your other duplicities. Those I know I caress slowly so that nothing fades between us, so that everything lasts amid expectation, surprise, the desire for more and more, yes, Godfather, give me more, nothing can separate us now, Godfather, you said so, remember? Every time you see me I want it to be the first. Oh, Leonardo, it's that I fell in love with your eyes because they said so many things.

"I know how to ask for everything because I also know how to give everything. What do you say to me, capital girl?"

"That same thing, Godfather, that . . ."

Through the half-opened window came a song sung by Luis Miguel, "I need you, need you a lot, I don't know you . . ." How could Leonardo and Michelina know that that music was coming from an "erased" Indian village, Pacuaches, where Mariano read books and listened to music and went into ecstasy guessing which birds were singing at four o'clock in the morning. That morning, a jet crossed the heavens, and the birds fell silent forever. She was no longer there . . .

2

PAIN

For Julio Ortega

1

Juan Zamora asked me to tell this story while he kept his back turned. What he means is that he wants to have his back to the reader the whole time. He says he's ashamed. Or, as he puts it himself, "I'm in pain." "Pain" as a synonym for "shame" is a peculiarity of Mexican speech, comparable to saying "senior citizens" for "old people"—so as not to offend—or saying "He's in a bad way" to soften the idea that someone's illness is terminal. Shame causes pain; sometimes pain causes shame.

So Juan Zamora will not offer you a view of his face over the course of this story. You'll be able to see only the nape of his neck, his back. I won't say "his ass," because that, too, is a loaded term in Mexico. Especially in the sense of "offering" your ass to someone, the lowest act of cowardice, a yielding or a type of abject courtesy. That's not the case with Juan Zamora. He wears a big university sweatshirt, size XXL, decorated in front with the emblem of the university in question, the kind of sweatshirt that hangs down to your thighs (though he wears it tucked into his jeans). No, Juan Zamora insists I tell you he won't be offering anything. He only wants to emphasize that his shame is equal to his pain. He doesn't blame anyone. It is true that he touched a world and that the world touched him.

But after all, everything that happened passed through him and happened inside him. This is what counts.

The story takes place during the time of the Mexican oil boom, at the end of the 1970s and beginning of the 1980s. Right from the start, that explains part of the pain-shame identification Juan Zamora is talking about. Shame because we celebrated the boom like a bunch of nouveaux riches. Pain because the wealth was badly used. Shame because the president said our problem now was to administer our wealth. Pain because the poor kept on getting poorer. Shame because we became frivolous spendthrifts, slaves of vulgar whims and our comic macho posturing. Pain because we were incapable of administering even our shame. Pain and shame because we were no good at being rich; the only things appropriate for us are poverty, dignity, effort. In Mexico, there have always been corrupt authoritarian figures with too much power. But they are forgiven everything if they are at least serious. (Is there one corruption that's serious and another that's frivolous?) Frivolity is intolerable, unforgivable, the mockery of all those who've been screwed. That's the source of the pain and the shame of those years when we were millionaires for a day, then woke up broke, out in the street, tears of laughter pouring down our faces before we began to laugh with pain.

Juan Zamora has his back to you. When he was twenty-three, he got to study at Cornell, thanks to a scholarship. He was a dedicated pre-med student at the National Preparatory School and then at the National University, and he swears to you that that would have been enough for him if his mother hadn't got it into her head that during the Mexican boom period it was necessary to do some postgrad work at a Yankee university.

"Your father never knew how to take advantage of an opportunity. He was Don Leonardo Barroso's administrative lawyer for twenty years and died without a penny to his name. What could he have been thinking about? Well, not about you or me, Juanito, you can be sure of that."

"What did he say to you?"

"That honesty is its own reward. That he was an honorable professional. That he wasn't going to betray Mario de la Cueva and his other professors at the law school. That he'd been taught that law is an honorable profession. That you cannot defend the law if you're corrupt yourself. 'But it's not illegal, Gonzalo,' I'd say to your father, 'to accept a payment for doing favors. It's no crime drawing a matter to the attention of Minister Barroso. Everyone in government gets rich but you!'

" 'That's called a bribe, Lelia. It's a triple deception, besides being a lie. If the matter develops, it looks as if I was paid to move it along. If it fails, I look like a crook. In either case, I deceive the minister, the nation, and myself.'

" 'A little public-works contract, Gonzalo, that's all I'm asking you to request. You get your commission and bye-bye. No one will find out. With that money we could buy a house in Anzures. And get out of Colonia Santa María. We could send Juanito to a gringo university. What I mean is, the boy's a very good student and it would be a shame for him to go to waste with that riffraff at the National University.' "

Juan tells me to say that his mother recounted those things with a bitter smile on her face, a grimace that her son had only seen, from time to time, on cadavers he studied at school.

His father, Gonzalo Zamora, CPA, had to die for his widow to ask a single favor from Don Leonardo Barroso: would he see if he could get a scholarship for Juanito to study medicine in the United States? With great elegance, Don Leonardo said, Why, of course, he would be delighted to take care of it—why, that's the least the memory of good old Zamora deserved, such an honest lawyer, such a diligent functionary.

2

I'm following Juan Zamora, the Mexican student with his gray sweatshirt, through the sad streets of Ithaca, New York. I have no idea what he's looking for since there's so little to see here. The main street has barely any stores, two or three very bad restaurants, and immediately after that come mountains and gorges. Juanito feels—almost—as if he's in Mexico, in San Juan del Río or Tepeji, places he'd visited from time to time on holiday to breathe the air of forests and gorges, far from the pollution of the capital. The gorge in Ithaca is a deep and forbidding ravine, apparently a seductive abyss as well. Ithaca is famous for the number of suicides committed by desperate students who jump off the bridge spanning the gorge. One joke says that no professor will fail a bad student, for fear he'll dive into the chasm.

Since there isn't much to see around here on Sunday, Juan Zamora is going back to the house where he's living. It's a beautiful place of pale pink brick with a blue slate roof, surrounded by a well-kept lawn that becomes gravel around the house and extends into a tangled, thin, and somber woods behind it. Ivy climbs up the pink brick.

The seasons make up for Ithaca's lack of charm. Now it's late fall, and the forest is denuded, the trees on the mountainsides look like burned toothpicks, and the sky comes two or three steps down to communicate to all of us the silence and pain of God in the face of the fleeting death of the world. But winter in Ithaca gives a voice back to nature, which takes revenge on God by dressing in white, scattering frozen dust and snow stars, spreading large ivory mantles like sumptuous sheets on the earth—and an answer to heaven. Spring explodes, rapid and agonizing, in handfuls of splendid roses that perfume the air and leave a flash of forgotten things before summer takes over, heavy, sleepy, and slow, unlike the swift spring. Idle and lazy summer of stagnant waters, pesky mosquitoes, heavy, humid breathing, and intensely green mountains.

The gorge, too, reflects the seasons, but it also devours them, collapses them, and subjects them to the implacable death of gravity, a suffocating, final embrace of all things. The gorge is the vertigo in the order of this place.

Alongside the gorge, there is a munitions factory, a horrifying building of blackened brick with obscene chimneys, almost an evocation of the ugliness of the Nazis' "night and fog." The pistols produced by the Ithaca factory were the official side arm of the army of El Salvador, which is why officers and men there called them "itaquitas"—little Ithacas.

Juan Zamora asks me to tell all this while he turns his back on us because he was received as a guest in the residence of a prosperous businessman who in former years was connected with the munitions factory but now prefers to be an adviser to law firms negotiating defense contracts between the factory owners and the U.S. government. Tarleton Wingate and his family, in the days when Juan Zamora comes to live with them, are excited about the triumph of Ronald Reagan over Jimmy Carter. They watch television every night and applaud the decisions of the new president, his movie-star smile, his desire to put a halt to excessive government control, his optimism in declaring that a new day is dawning in America, his firmness in stopping the advances of Communism in Central America.

Wingate is a likable giant with fewer wrinkles on his fresh, juvenile face than an old saddle. His dull, sandy-colored hair contrasts with the platinum blond of his wife, Charlotte, and with the burnished, reddish-chestnut hair of the daughter of the house, Becky, who is thirteen. When the Wingates all sit down to watch television, they kindly invite Juan to join them. He doesn't understand if they are pained when terrible pictures of the war in El Salvador appear— nuns murdered along the roadside, rebels murdered by paramilitary death squads, an entire village machine-gunned by the army as the people flee across a river.

Juan Zamora turns his back to the screen and assures them that in Mexico they applaud President Reagan for saving us all from Communism, just as much as people do here. He also tells them that Mexico is interested in growing and prospering, as they can clearly see in the massive development of the oil industry by the government of López Portillo.

The gringos smile when they hear that, because they believe that prosperity is an inoculation against Communism. Juan Zamora wants to ask Mr. Wingate how his business with the Pentagon is going but decides he'd better keep quiet. What he insinuates first and then emphatically declares is that his family, the Zamoras, are adapting perfectly to Mexico's new wealth because they have always had lands, haciendas—the word has great prestige in the United States, where they pronounce the silent *h*—and oil wells. He realizes the Wingates don't know that oil is the property of the state in Mexico and are amazed at everything he tells them. Dogmatically but innocently, the Wingates believe that the expression *free world* is synonymous with *free enterprise*.

They have received Juan with pleasure, as part of a tradition. For a long time, foreign students have been hospitably taken into private homes near campuses in the United States. It surprises no one that rich young Latin Americans seek out such homes as extensions of their own and use them to accelerate their assimilation of English.

"There are kids," Tarleton Wingate assures him, "who have learned English spending hours in front of a TV set."

They all watch Peter Sellers's movie *Being There*, where the protagonist knows nothing except what he learns watching television, which is why he passes as a genius.

The Wingates ask Juan Zamora if Mexican television is good, and he has to answer truthfully that it isn't, that it's boring, vulgar, and censored, and that a very good writer, widely read by young people, Carlos Monsiváis, calls it "the idiot box." That seemed hilarious to Becky, who says she's going to tell it to her class—the idiot box. Don't put on intellectual airs, Charlotte tells her daughter; "egghead" she calls her, smiling as she tousles her hair. The redhead protests, don't tangle my hair, I'll have to fix it again before I baby-sit tonight. Juan Zamora is amazed at how gringo children work from the time they are young, baby-sitting, delivering papers, or selling lemonade during the summer. "It's to teach them the Protestant work ethic," Mr. Wingate says solemnly. And him? How did you ever grow up without television? Becky asks. Juan Zamora understands very well what Mr. Wingate is saying. Being rich and aristocratic in Mexico is a matter of land, haciendas, farm laborers, an elegant lifestyle, horses, dressing up as a *charro*, and having lots of servants—that's what being wealthy means in Mexico. Not watching television. And since his hosts have exactly the same idea in their heads, they understand it, praise it, envy it, and Becky goes out to earn five dollars as a babysitter. Charlotte puts on her apron to cook dinner, and Tarleton, with a profound sense of obligation, sits down to read the number-one book on the *New York Times* best-seller list, a spy novel that happens to confirm his paranoia about the red menace.

<u>3</u>

If the city of Ithaca is a kind of suburban Avernus, Cornell University is its Parnassus: a brilliant cream-colored temple with modern, sometimes almost Art Deco lines and vast green and luminous spaces. Given the abrupt nature of the terrain, the campus is linked by beautiful terraces and grand stairways. Both lead to places that are centers of the life of the Mexican student Juan Zamora. One is the student union, which tries to make up for all of Ithaca's shortcomings with books, a stationery store, movies, theater, clothing, mailboxes, restaurants, and places to meet. Moving among those spaces, his back toward us, Juan Zamora tries to connect with the place. He takes special notice of the extreme sloppiness of the students. They wear baseball caps they don't even take off indoors or when they greet women. They rarely shave completely. They drink beer straight from the bottle. They wear sleeveless T-shirts, revealing at all hours their hairy underarms. Their jeans have torn knees, and at times they wear them cut off at the thigh and unraveling. They sit down to eat with their caps on and fill their mouths with hamburgers, french fries, and an entire menu pulled out of plastic bags. When they really want to be informal, they wear their baseball caps backward, with the visors cooling the napes of their necks.

One day, an athletic boy, blond, with pinched features, ordered a plate of spaghetti and began to eat it with his hands, by the fistful. Juan Zamora felt an uncontrollable revulsion that obliterated his appetite and forced him for the first and perhaps only time to criticize a fellow student. "That's disgusting! Didn't they teach you how to eat at home?" "Of course they did. My family's pretty rich, for your information." "So why do you eat like an animal?" "Because now I'm free," said the blond through a mouthful of pasta.

Juan Zamora arrived at Cornell not in a sports coat and tie but in blue jeans, a leather jacket, a sweater, and loafers. While alive, his father resigned himself to this scruffiness: "We used to wear suits and ties to class at law school . . ." Little by little, Juan assumed a more casual wardrobe—sweatshirt, Keds—but he always maintained (with his back turned) a minimal properness. He understood that the shabby disguise worn by the students was a way of equalizing social classes, so no one would ask about family background or economic status. All equal, equalized by sloppiness, the T-shirts, baseball caps, sneakers. Only in his refuge—the residence of the Wingate family—could Juan Zamora say, with impunity and with universal approval, even impressing them: "My family is very old. We've always been rich. We have haciendas, horses, servants. Now with the oil, we'll simply live as we always have, but with even more luxury. If only you could visit us in Mexico. My mother would be so happy to receive you and thank you for your kindness to me."

And Charlotte would sigh with admiration. She was the first platinum-dyed white woman Juan Zamora had ever seen wearing an apron. "How polite Spanish aristocrats are! Learn, Becky."

Charlotte never called Juan Zamora Mexican. She was afraid of offending him.

4

The other space in the life of the Mexican student was the school of medicine, especially the amphitheater, built on Greek lines and as white as snow, but solid and crowning a hill as if intentionally, so that the smells of chloroform and formaldehyde would not contaminate the rest of the campus. Here the outlandish student outfits were replaced by the white uniform of medicine, although at times hairy legs and (almost always) blackened Keds would appear at the bottoms of the long clinic gowns.

Men and women, all in white, gave the place the air of a religious community. Young monks and nuns passed through its sparkling corridors. Juan thought chastity would be the rule in this order of young doctors. Besides, the white uniform (unless the hairy legs stuck out) accentuated the generational androgyny. Some girls wore their hair very short, while some boys wore it very long, so at times it was difficult to tell from behind what sex a person was.

Juan Zamora had had a couple of sexual relationships in Mexico. Sex was not his strong suit. He didn't like prostitutes. His female classmates at the National University were very demanding, very devouring and distracting, talking about having families or being independent, about living this way or that, about succeeding, and they talked with a decisiveness that made him feel out of place, guilty, ashamed of not being, ever, yet, all he could be. Juan Zamora's problem was that he confused each step of his life with something definitive, finished. Just as there are young people who let things flow and leave everything to chance, there are others who think the world ends every twenty-four hours. Juan was one of the latter. Without admitting it, he knew that his mother's anguish about their modest means, his father's upright pride, and his own uncertainties about his father's morality gave him a feeling of perpetual distress, of imminent doom that was mocked by the gray, implacable flow of daily life. If he had accepted that tranquil march of days, he might perhaps have entered a more or less stable relationship with a girl. But girls saw in Juan Zamora a boy who was too tense, frightened, insecure. A young man with his back turned, in pain.

"Why are you always looking behind you? Do you think someone's following us?"

"Don't be afraid to cross the street. There are no cars coming."

"Listen, stop ducking. No one's swinging at you."

Now, at Cornell, he put on his white robe and carefully washed his hands. He was going to perform his first autopsy, he and another student. Would it be a man or a woman? The question was important because it applied as well to the cadaver he would be studying.

The auditorium was dark.

Juan Zamora felt his way to the barely visible autopsy table. Then his back rubbed against someone else's. The two of them laughed nervously. In a flash, the blinding, implacable lights went on, like some vengeful Jehovah, and the janitor apologized for not getting there on time. He always tried to be more punctual than the students, he exclaimed, laughing, ashamed.

Which one would Juan Zamora look at first? The student or the cadaver? He looked down and saw the body covered by a sheet. He looked up and found that a very blond person with long hair and not very wide shoulders was looking away from him. He looked down again and uncovered the cadaver's face. It was impossible to know if the cadaver was a man or woman. Death had erased not only its time but its sexual personality. The only thing certain was that it was old. It was made of wax. You always had to think that the cadavers were made of wax. It made them easier to dissect. This one's eyes weren't closed tightly, and Juan was shocked to think they were still crying. But the thin nose stuffed with cotton balls, the rigid jaw, the sunken lips were no longer the cadaver's or ours. Death had stripped the individual of pronouns. It was no longer he or she, yours or mine. The other gloved hand held out a scalpel to him.

They worked in silence. They were masked. The blond person working with him, small but decisive, knew the guts of a dead person better than Juan did and guided him in the incisions he would have to make. He or she was an expert. Juan dared to look into the eyes opposite his own. They were gray, that hazel-tinted gray that sometimes appears in the most beautiful Anglo-Saxon eyes, where the unusual color is almost always accompanied by dreamy eyelids, depths of desire, fluidity, but also intensity.

Isolated by the latex, the masks, the robes, their gloved hands touched with the same feeling as when a man wears a condom. Only their eyes saw each other. Now Juan Zamora faces us, he turns to look at us, pulls off his mask, reveals his mestizo face, young, dark, with prominent, chis-

eled bones, his skin like some dessert—brown sugar, cinnamon candy, *café con leche*—his smooth, firm chin, his thick
lower lip, his liquid black eyes that find the hazel-gray eyes.
Juan Zamora no longer has his back turned. Instinctively,
passionately, he turns his face toward us, he brings it close
to the lips of the other, they join in a liberating, complete
kiss that washes away all his insecurities, all his solitude, all
his pain and shame. The two boys urgently, tremulously,
ardently kiss in order to conquer death, if not for all time,
then at least for this moment.

<u>5</u>

Jim was twenty-two, thin and refined, serious and studious,
interested in politics and art: the other students called him
Lord Jim. His blond head, his hazel-tinged eyes, and his
small physique were accompanied by good muscles, good
bones, a nervous agility, and, especially, extremely agile
hands and long fingers. He would be a great doctor—Juan
Zamora would say—though not because of his fingers and
hands but because of his vocation. He was a little bit—Juan,
despite the distance, orders us to say—like Juan's father,
Gonzalo, a dedicated man, solid, though not worthy of compassion.

The two young men, a contrast of light and dark, looked
good together. At first they attracted attention on campus,
then they were accepted and even admired for the obvious
affection they showed for each other and the spontaneous-
ness of their relationship. In terms of love, Juan Zamora
finally found himself satisfied, his feelings identified; at the
same time, he was surprised. He really had had no idea about
his homosexual tendencies, and to feel them revealed in this
way, with this man, so completely and so passionately, with

such satisfaction and understanding, filled him with a calm pride.

They continued studying and working together. Their conversation and their life had an immediacy, as if Juan Zamora's problem—the fear that each day would be the last, or at least the definitive, day—had become, thanks to Lord Jim, a blessing. For several weeks, there was no before and no after. Shared pleasure filled their days, kept other concerns and other times at bay.

One afternoon, as they were working together on an autopsy, Jim asked Juan for the first time about his studies in Mexico. Juan explained that he'd studied in the University City but that occasionally he'd passed through the old School of Medicine, located in the Plaza de Santo Domingo. It was a very beautiful colonial building that had housed the offices of the Inquisition. Lord Jim responded with a nervous laugh: it was the first time Juan had left him for a time that was not only remote but even forbidden and detested by the Anglo-Saxon soul. Juan persisted. There were no women doctors in Mexico until 1873, and the first one, Matilde Montoya, was allowed to do autopsies only in empty auditoriums, with the cadavers fully clothed.

Jim's nervous laugh was a small break in the tension or the distance (were they the same thing?) which that simple reference to the Holy Inquisition had introduced into the way they were together, the first irruption of a past into a relationship that the two boys lived only for the present. Juan Zamora had the ungraspable but desolating feeling that at that precise moment an even more dangerous perspective was also opening—the future. They slowly covered the cadaver of a beautiful girl who'd committed suicide and whose body no one had claimed.

Juan Zamora carefully timed his meetings with Lord Jim for the afternoons so he could return to the Wingates on time, have dinner with them, watch television, and make comments. Reagan was beginning his dirty secret war against Nicaragua, which was starting to annoy Juan Zamora, though he did not understand why. Tarleton, on the other hand, celebrated Reagan's decision to put a limit to Marxist expansion in the Americas. Perhaps that was the reason for the growing coolness of Charlotte and Tarleton Wingate and for the rather comic confusion of Becky, who was dispatched to her room as soon as Juan appeared, as if his mere appearance announced a plague. Did Juan Zamora look like a guerrilla and a Sandinista?

Of course, the Mexican student understood immediately that rumors of his homosexual association had filtered down from Parnassus to Suburbia—the community was small. But he decided not to give in and to go on normally, because his relationship was exactly that, normal, for the only people who had anything to say about it—he and Jim.

Jim was sensitive, he had good antennae, and he noticed a certain nervous malaise in his lover. He knew it had nothing to do with their relationship. In Jim's dormitory bed, wrapped in each other's arms, Juan tried to excuse himself because that afternoon he had not been able to perform. Jim, caressing Juan's head as it rested against his shoulder, told him it was normal, it happened to everyone. Both of them were doctors and were well acquainted with the stereotyped ideas surrounding sexual activity of all kinds, from masturbation, which supposedly drove adolescents insane, to the perfectly normal use of pornographic material by older people. But the myths of homosexuality were the worst. He understood. The Wingates would not tolerate a gay couple. It wasn't the racial or the social difference that bothered them. But Juan never played the role of rich boy with Jim. He said nothing. Jim wasn't interested in the past.

Juan tried to kiss Jim, but Jim stood up, naked, enraged, and said it was he who couldn't stand the repugnant Puritanism of these people, their disgusting disguise of goodness and their perpetual, inviolable sanctity in politics and sexuality. He turned to Juan in a fury.

"Do you know what your landlord, Mr. Tarleton Wingate, does for a living? He inflates the budgets of companies doing business with the Pentagon. Do you know how much Mr. Wingate charges the air force for lavatories for its planes? Two hundred thousand dollars each. Almost a quarter of a million dollars so someone can shit comfortably in midair! Who pays the expenses of the Defense Department and the earnings of Mr. Wingate? I do. The taxpayer."

"But he says he adores Reagan because he's eliminating government and lowering taxes."

"Just ask Mr. Wingate if he wants the government to stop defense spending, stop saving failed banks, or stop subsidizing inefficient farmers. Ask him and see what he says."

"He'd probably call me a Communist."

"They're a bunch of cynics. They want free enterprise in everything, except when it comes to weapons and rescuing thieving financiers."

It's hard for Juan Zamora to accept Jim's statements, accept something that breaks his rule about ingratiating himself with the Wingates, being accepted by them and, through them, by American society. But the criticism is coming from his lover, the being Juan loves most in the world, and his lover proclaims it in an implacable, angry tone, not caring how anyone, even Juan, reacts.

The Mexican student had feared something like this,

something that would break their perfect, cloistered inti-
macy, the self-sufficiency of lovers. He hates the world, the
busybody world, the cruel world, which gains nothing by
poking its nose into the lives of lovers except that—the ma-
licious pleasure of distancing them from each other. Could
they ever enjoy the same sense of fullness they experienced
before this little incident? Juan was confident they could, and
he multiplied the proofs of his affection and loyalty to Lord
Jim, his little pamperings, his attention. Perhaps the desire
to reconstruct something so perfect it had to crack one day
was all too obvious.

6

Once again they are together, wearing their white masks,
their gloves, dissecting another woman's body, this time an
old one's. Lord Jim asks Juan to remember that place, the
palace of the Inquisition in Mexico that became the medical
school. He's amused by the idea of the same building's being
used for torture one day and to bring relief to bodies the
next. The Mexican student subtly changes the subject and
tells him about the Plaza de Santo Domingo and the ancient
tradition of the "evangelists," old men with old typewriters
who sit in the doorways and type out the dictation of the
illiterates who want to send letters to their parents, lovers,
friends.

"How do they know these scribes are reliable?"

"They don't. They have to have faith."

"Confidence, Juan."

"Right."

Jim took off his mask and Juan gestured for him to be
careful—they had to take precautions. Once before, the first
time, they had kissed next to a cadaver, but the bacteria of

the dead have killed more than one careless doctor. Jim gave him a strange look. He asked Juan to tell him the truth. About what? About his family, his house. Jim knew what people said around the university, that Juan was the scion of a rich family, hacienda owners, and so forth. Juan had never told Jim that, because they never talked about the past. Now Jim asked him to send a spoken letter, as if he, the gringo, were the "evangelist" in the plaza and Juan the illiterate.

"It's all lies," said Juan. His back was turned once again, but he spoke without hesitation. "Pure lies. We live in a very modest apartment. My father was a very honorable man who died penniless. My mother always threw it in his face. She'll die reproaching him. I feel pain and shame for the two of them. I feel pain for my father's useless morality, which no one remembers or values and which wasn't worth shit. On the other hand, people certainly would have celebrated him if he'd been rich. I'm ashamed that he didn't steal, that he was a poor devil. But I'd be just as ashamed if he were a thief. My dad. My poor, poor dad."

He felt relieved, clean. He'd been faithful to Lord Jim. From now on, there wouldn't be a single lie between them. He thought that and fleetingly he felt ill at ease. Lord Jim could be sincere with him as well.

"Explain to me 'pain and shame,' as you call them— which would be something like 'pity and shame' in English," said the American.

"My mother causes me pain, always complaining about what never was, heartsick about her life, which she should accept because it will never be different. I'm ashamed of her self-pity, you're right, that horrible sin of inflicting pain on yourself all day long. Yes, I think you're right. You've got to have compassion to cover the pain and shame you feel toward others."

He squeezed Lord Jim's hand and told him they shouldn't talk about the past because they understood each other so well in the present. The American shot him a strange look that he almost associated with the dead woman who would not resign herself to closing her eyes, the woman they never finished dissecting.

"I feel awful saying this to you, Juan, but we have to talk about the future."

The Mexican student made an involuntary but dramatic gesture, two swift and simultaneous, though repeated, movements, one hand raised to his mouth, as if he were begging silence and another extended forward, denying, stopping what was coming.

"I'm sorry, Juan. It really pains me to say this. It even shames me. You understand that no one controls his destiny absolutely."

7

Juan turned his back—this time literally—on Cornell. He stopped studying and courteously said good-bye to the Wingates, who were surprised and upset, asking him why, did it have anything to do with them, with the way they'd treated him? But there was relief in their eyes and secret certainty: this had to end badly. He hoped to see them again someday. He would love to take them on a tour of the hacienda on horseback. Look me up if you come to Mexico.

The American family felt relieved but also guilty. Tarleton and Charlotte discussed the matter several times. The boy must have noticed the change in his hosts' attitude when he started to go out with Jim Rowlands. Had they broken the rules of hospitality? Had they allowed themselves to succumb to irrational prejudice? They certainly had. But prejudices could not be removed over night; they were very old, they had more reality—they did—than a political party or a bank account. Blacks, homosexuals, poor people, old people, women, foreigners: the list was interminable. And Becky— why expose her to a bad influence, a scandalous relationship? She was innocent. And innocence should be protected. Becky listened to them whisper while they imagined she was watching television, and she tried to keep a straight face. If they only knew. Thirteen years old and in a private school. How could they blame anything on her? What was money for? Day after day, all day, every day, the litany of the Me Generation was entitlement to every caprice, every pleasure; there was only one value: Me. Weren't her parents that way? Weren't they successful because they were that way? What did they want from her? For her to be a Puritan from the days of the Salem witch hunts? Then the girl immersed herself in what was happening on the screen so she wouldn't hear the voices of her parents, who didn't want to be heard, and she asked herself a question that confused her greatly: How can you enjoy everything and still seem a very moral, very puritanical person? Her blood tickled her, her body was changing, and Becky was anguished not to have answers. She hugged her stuffed rabbit and dared to ask him: What about you, Bunny, do you understand anything?

Up in the clouds, Juan, en route to Mexico City in his tourist-class seat on Eastern Airlines, tried to imagine a future without Lord Jim and accepted it with bitterness, desolation, as if his life had been canceled. The bad thing was to have admitted first the past, then the future. It was the painful act of leaving the moment when they loved each other without explanations, possessors of a single time, a single space, the Eden of a loving youth that excluded parents, friends, professors, bosses. But not other lovers.

Suspended in midair, Juan Zamora tried to remember everything, the good and the bad, once more and then to cancel it forever, never again think about what happened. Never again feel hatred, pain, shame, compassion for the past his poor parents lived. And never feel pity, shame for himself or for Lord Jim, for the future they were both going to live, separated forever: Juan Zamora's desolate future, Lord Jim's happy, comfortable, secure one, his marriage having been arranged since God knows when, since before he knew Juan. That was what the families of the rich professional class did in Seattle, on the other side of the continent, where it was expected that a young doctor with a future would marry and have children—things that would inspire respect and confidence. And anyway, in the Anglo-Saxon tradition a homosexual experience was an accepted part of a gentleman's education—there wasn't an Englishman at Oxford who hadn't had one, he'd say, if something about them should leak out. Cornell and Seattle were far apart, the country was immense, loves were fragile and small.

"And we rich people, I'll tell you by quoting a good writer, are not like other people," said Lord Jim, pounding in the final nail.

Juan remembered Jim's being angry only once, over Tarleton Wingate's hypocrisy. That's the Lord Jim he wanted to remember.

He pressed his burning head against the frozen window and turned his back on everything. Below, the Cornell gorge seemed insignificant to him, it didn't say anything to him, was not for him.

8

Four years later, the Wingates decided to take a vacation in Cancún. They stopped over in Mexico City so Becky could visit the marvelous Museum of Anthropology. Becky, now seventeen, was rather colorless even though she imitated her mother by dyeing her hair blond. Very curious, even liberated, she found herself a little Mexican boyfriend in the hotel lobby, and they went to spend a day in Cuernavaca. He was a very passionate boy, which seemed to annoy the driver, an angry, insecure man who tried to terrify tourists by taking curves at top speed.

It was Becky who encouraged her parents to pay a surprise visit on Juan Zamora, the Mexican student who'd lived with them in 1981. Did they remember him? How could they not remember Juan Zamora? And since Tarleton and Charlotte Wingate were still ashamed about the way in which Juan left their house, they accepted their daughter's idea. Besides, Juan Zamora himself had invited them to visit him.

Tarleton called Cornell and asked for Juan's address. The university computer instantly provided it, but it was not a country address. "But I want to see a hacienda," said Becky. "This must be his town house," said Charlotte. "Should we call him?" "No," Becky said excitedly, "let's surprise him." "You're a spoiled brat," answered her father, "but I agree. If we call him, he might figure out a way not to see us. I have the feeling he was angry when he left us."

The same driver who brought Becky to Cuernavaca now drove her along with her parents. The driver had a huge mocking smile on his face. If they'd only seen her the day before, kissing her face off with that low-life slob. Now, quite the young lady, the hypocrite, with that pair of distin-

guished gringos—sometimes even weirder things happen—
searching for an impossible place.

"Colonia Santa María?" asked the driver, almost laughing. Leandro Reyes, Tarleton read on the chauffeur's license
and noted mentally—just in case. "This is the first time anyone's ever asked me to take them there."

They crossed the densest urban spaces, spaces swirling
around them noisy as a river made entirely of loose stones;
they cut through the brown crust of polluted air; and they
also crossed the time zones of Mexico City, disordered, anarchic, immortal—time overlapping its past and its future,
like a child who will be father to his posterity, like a grandson who will be the only proof that his grandfather walked
through these streets; they moved steadily north, along Mariano Escobedo to Ejército Nacional, to Puente de Alvarado,
and Buenavista station, beyond San Rafael, which was increasingly underneath everything, uncertain if under con-
struction or in collapse. What is new, what's old, what is
being born in this city, what's dying—are they all the same
thing?

The Wingates looked at one another, shocked, pained.

"Perhaps there's been a mistake."

"No," said the driver. "This is it. It's that apartment
house right over there."

"Maybe it would be better if we just went back to the
hotel," said Tarleton.

"No," Becky practically shouted. "We're here. I'm dying
of curiosity."

"In that case, you can go in by yourself," said her
mother.

They waited a while outside the lime-green building.
Three stories high, it was in dire need of a good coat of
paint. Clothes were hanging on the balconies to dry, and

there was a TV antenna. At a soft-drink stand by the entrance, a red-cheeked girl wearing an apron but also sporting a permanent was busy putting bottles in the cooler. A wrinkled little old man in a straw hat poked his head out the door and stared at them curiously. On either side, a repair shop. A tamale vendor passed by shouting, Red, green, with chile, sweet, lard. The driver, Leandro Reyes, went on and on in English about debts, inflation, the cost of living, devaluations of the peso, pay cuts, useless pensions, everything messed up.

Becky reappeared and quickly got back in the car. "He wasn't there, but his mother was. She said it's been a long time since anyone's visited her. Juan's fine. He's working in a hospital. I made her swear she wouldn't tell him we were here."

9

Every night, Juan Zamora has exactly the same dream. Occasionally he wishes he could dream something else. He goes to bed thinking about something else, but no matter how hard he tries, the dream always comes back punctually. Then he gives up and concedes the power of the dream, turning it into the inevitable comrade of his nights: a lover-dream, a dream that should adore the person it visits because it won't allow itself to be expelled from that second body of the former student and now young doctor in the social security system, Juan Zamora.

Night after night, it returns until it inhabits him, his twin, his double, the mythological shirt that can't be taken off without also pulling off the dreamer's skin. He dreams with a mixture of confusion, gratitude, rejection, and love. When he wishes to escape the dream, he does so by intensely desiring to be possessed again by it; when he wants to take control of the dream, his daily life appears with the bitter smile of all of Juan Zamora's dawns, sequestering him in the hospitals, ambulances, and morgues of his urban geography. Kidnapped by life, hostage of the dream, Juan Zamora returns each night to Cornell and walks hand in hand with Lord Jim toward the bridge over the gorge. It's fall, and the trees again look as bare as black needles. The sky has descended a bit, but the gorge is deeper than the firmament and summons the two young lovers with a false promise: heaven is down here, heaven is here, face up, breathing underbrush and brambles; its breath is green, its arms spiny. You have to earn heaven by giving yourself over to it: paradise, if it does exist, is in the very guts of the earth, its humid embrace awaiting us where flesh and clay mix, where the great maternal womb mixes with the mud of creation and life is born and reborn from its great reproductive depth, but never from its airy illusion, never from the airlines falsely connecting New York and Mexico, Atlantic and Pacific, in fact separating the lovers, breaking the marvelous unity of their perfect androgyny, their Siamese identity, their beautiful abnormality, their monstrous perfection, casting them to incompatible destinies, to opposite horizons. What time is it in Seattle when night falls in Mexico? Why does Jim's city face a panting sea while Juan's faces nervous dust? Why is the coastal air like crystal and the air of the plateau like excrement?

Juan and Jim sit on the bridge railing and look at each other deeply, to the depth of the Mexican's black eyes and the American's gray ones, not touching, possessed by their eyes, understanding everything, accepting everything, without rancor, without illusions, disposed nevertheless to have everything, the origin of love transformed into the destiny of love with no possible separation, no matter how daily life may split them apart.

They look at each other, they smile, they both stand at the edge of the bridge, they take each other by the hand, and they jump into the void. Their eyes are shut but they know that all the seasons have gathered to watch them die together—winter scattering frozen dust, autumn mourning the fleeting death of the world with a red and golden voice, slow, lazy, green summer, and finally another spring, no longer swift and imperceptible but eternal. A gorge replete with roses, a soft, fatal fall into the dew that bathes them as they still hold hands, their eyes closed, Lord Jim and Juan, brothers now.

10

Juan Zamora, that's right. He asked that I tell you all this. He feels pain, he feels shame, but he has compassion. He's turned his face toward us.

3

SPOILS

For Sealtiel Alatriste

Dionisio "Baco" Rangel became famous when he was just a kid, when competing on the radio program *Junior Professors* he unhesitatingly gave out his recipe for Puebla-style marrow tarts.

A discovery: gastronomic knowledge can be a source not only of fortune but of magnificent banquets, transforming the need to survive into the luxury of living. This fact defined Dionisio's career, but it gave him no higher goal.

His ascent from mere appetite to culinary art and from there to a well-paid profession was attributable to his love of Mexican cuisine and disdain for cuisines of lower status, like that of the United States of America. Before he was twenty, Dionisio had taken as an article of faith that there were only five great cuisines in the world: Chinese, French, Italian, Spanish, and Mexican. Other nationalities had dishes of the first quality—Brazilian *feijoada*, Peruvian chicken soup with chiles, Argentine beef were excellent, as were

North African couscous and Japanese teriyaki—but only Mexican cuisine was a universe unto itself. From Sinaloa's *chilorio*, with its little cubes of pork well seasoned with oregano, sesame, garlic, and fat chiles, to Oaxaca's chicken with mountain herbs and avocado leaves, the *uchepo* tamales of Michoacán, Colima's sea bass with prawns and parsley, San Luis Potosí's meatloaf stuffed with cheese, and that supreme delicacy which is Oaxaca's yellow mole—two so-called wide chiles, two *guajillo* chiles, one red tomato, 250 grams of green *jitomatillos*, two tablespoons of coriander, two leaves of *hierbasanta*, two peppercorns—Mexican cuisine was for Dionisio a constellation apart that moved in the celestial vaults of the palate with its own trajectories, its own planets, satellites, comets, meteors. Like space itself, it was infinite.

Called upon, also in short order, to write for Mexican and foreign newspapers, to give courses and lectures, to appear on television and to publish cookbooks, Dionisio "Baco" Rangel, at the age of fifty-one, was a culinary authority, celebrated and well-paid, nowhere more so than in the country he most disdained for the poverty of its cuisine. Having appeared all over the United States of America (especially after the success of *Like Water for Chocolate*), Dionisio decided this was the cross he would have to bear in life: to preach fine cooking in a country incapable of understanding or practicing it. Excellent restaurants could of course be found in the big cities—New York, Chicago, San Francisco, and New Orleans (whose tradition would have been inexplicable without the lengthy French presence there). But Dionisio challenged the lowliest cooks in Puebla or Oaxaca to approach without a sense of horror the gastronomic deserts of Kansas, Nebraska, Wisconsin, Indiana, or the Dakotas where they would seek in vain for *espazote*, *ajillo* chile, *huitlacoche*, or *agua de jamaica* . . .

For the record, Dionisio said he wasn't anti-Yankee in this matter or in any other, even though every child born in Mexico knew that in the nineteenth century the gringos had stripped us of half our territory—California, Utah, Nevada, Colorado, Arizona, New Mexico, and Texas. The generosity of Mexico, Dionisio would habitually say, shows in its not holding a grudge for that terrible despoiling, although the memory lingered on, while the gringos didn't even remember that war, much less know its unfairness. Dionisio spoke of "the United States of Amnesia."

From time to time he thought humorously about the historical irony that caused Mexico to lose all that territory in 1848 through abandonment, indifference, and a sparse population. Now (the elegant, well-dressed, distinguished silver-haired critic smiled roguishly), we were on the way to recovering it, thanks to what could be termed Mexico's chromosomal imperialism. Millions of Mexicans worked in the United States, and thirty million people in the United States spoke Spanish. But at the same time, how many Mexicans spoke decent English? Dionisio knew of only two, Jorge Castañeda and Carlos Fuentes, for which reason both seemed suspicious to him. For the same reason, the exclamation of the Spanish bullfighter Cagancho seemed admirable to him: "Speak English? God help me!" Since the gringos had screwed Mexico in 1848 with their "manifest destiny" so now Mexico would give them a dose of their own medicine, reconquering them with the most Mexican of weapons, linguistic, racial, and culinary.

And Rangel himself, how did he communicate with his English-speaking university audiences? In an accent he learned from the actor Gilberto Roland, born Luis Alonso in Coahuila, and with a profusion of literal translations that delighted his listeners:

"Let's see if like you snore you sleep."

"Beggars can't carry big sticks."

"You don't have a mom or a dad or even a little dog to bark at you."

All this just so you'll understand with what conflicted feelings Dionisio "Baco" Rangel carried out, twice a year, the tours that took him from one U.S. university to another, where the horror of sitting down to dinner at five in the afternoon was nothing compared with the terror he felt when he realized what, at an hour when Mexicans were barely finishing their midday meal, was being served at the academic tables. Generally, the banquet would begin with a salad of fainting lettuce crowned with raspberry jam; that touch, he'd been told several times in Missouri, Ohio, and Massachusetts, was very sophisticated, very gourmet. The well-known rubber chicken followed, uncuttable and unchewable, served with tough string beans and mashed potatoes redolent of the envelope they had just recently abandoned. Dessert was a fake strawberry shortcake, more a strawberry bath sponge. Finally, watered-down coffee through which you could see the bottom of the cup and admire the geological circles deposited there by ten thousand servings of poison. The best thing, Dionisio told himself, was a furtive sip of the iced tea served at all hours and on any occasion; it was insipid, but at least the lemon slices were tasty. Rangel sucked them avidly so he wouldn't come down with a cold.

Was it because they were cheap? Was it because they lacked imagination? Dionisio Rangel decided to become a Sherlock Holmes and investigate what passed for "cuisine" in the United States by secretly carrying out an informal survey of hospitals, mental asylums, and prisons. What did he discover was served in all those places? Salad with raspberry jam, rubbery chicken, spongy cake, and translucent coffee. It was, he concluded, a matter of generalized institutional food, exceptions to which would probably be surprising, if not memorable. Professors, criminals, the insane, and the sick set the tone for U.S. menus—or was it perhaps that the universities, madhouses, jails, and hospitals were all supplied by the same caterer?

Dionisio smiled as he shaved after his morning bath—his best ideas always came to him then. Rubbing Barbasol onto his cheeks, he imagined a historical explanation. National cuisines are great only when they arise from the people. In Mexico, Italy, France, or Spain, you need have no fear when you walk into the first roadside restaurant, the humblest bistro, the busiest *tavola calda*, because you're certain of finding something good to eat there. It's not the rich, Rangel would say to anyone who cared to listen, who dictate culinary taste from above; it's the people, the worker, the peasant, the artisan, the truck driver who, from below, invent and consecrate the dishes that make up the great cuisines. And they do it out of intimate respect for what they put in their mouths.

Patience, time, Dionisio would explain in his classes, standing in front of an uncomprehending herd of young people with chewing gum in their mouths and baseball caps on their heads. You need time and patience to prepare a *lapin faisandé* in France, need to let the rabbit spoil to the point when it attains its tastiest, most savory tartness (ugh!); you need love and patience to prepare a *huitlacoche* soufflé in Mexico, using the black, cancerous corn fungus that in other, less sophisticated latitudes is fed to the hogs (yuck!).

By the same token, you can't have time or patience when you're trying to fry a couple of eggs in a covered wagon and you're attacked by redskins and must pray for the cavalry to arrive and save you (whoopee!). Dionisio would be speaking to dozens of Beavis and Butt-head wanna-bes, the offspring of Wayne's World, legions of young people convinced that being an idiot is the best way to pass through the world recognized by no one (in some cases) or everyone (in others). Masters always of an anarchic liberty and a stupid natural wisdom redeemed by an imbecility devoid of pretensions or complications. Knowing consisted in not knowing. The depressing lesson of the movie *Forrest Gump*. To be always available for whatever chance may bring . . .

How could the successors of Forrest Gump understand that, when a single Mexican city, Puebla, can boast of more than eight hundred dessert recipes, it is because of generations and generations of nuns, grandmothers, nannies, and old maids, the work of patience, tradition, love, and wisdom? How, when their supreme refinement consisted in thinking that life is like a box of chocolates, a varied prefabrication, a fatal Protestant destiny disguised as free will? Beavis and Butt-head, that pair of half-wits, would have finished off the nuns of Puebla by pelting them with stale cake, the grandmothers they would have locked in closets to die of hunger and thirst, and of course they would have raped the nannies. And finally, a favor of the highest order for the leftover young ladies.

Baco's students stared at him as if he were insane and sometimes, to show him the error of his ways and with the air of people protecting a lunatic or bringing relief to the needy, would invite him to a McDonald's after class. How were they going to understand that a Mexican peasant eats well even if he eats little? Abundance, that's what his gringo students were celebrating, showing off in front of this weird Mexican lecturer, their cheeks swollen with mushy hamburgers, their stomachs stuffed with wagon-wheel pizzas, their hands clutching sandwiches piled as high as the ones Dagwood made in his comic strip, leaning as dangerously as the Tower of Pisa. (There's even an imperialism in comic strips. Latin America gets U.S. comics but they never publish ours. Mafalda, Patoruzú, the Superwise Ones, and the Burrón family never travel north. Our minimal revenge is to give Spanish names to the gringo funnies. Jiggs and Maggie become Pancho and Ramona, Mutt and Jeff metamorphose into Benitín and Eneas, Goofy is Tribilín, Minnie Mouse becomes Ratoncita Mimí, Donald Duck is Pato Pascual, and Dagwood and Blondie are Lorenzo and Pepita. Soon, however, we won't even have that freedom, and Joe Palooka will always be Joe Palooka, not our twisted-around Pancho Tronera.)

Abundance. The society of abundance. Dionisio Rangel wants to be very frank and to admit to you that he's neither an ascetic nor a moralist. How could a sybarite be an ascetic when he so sensually enjoys a *clemole* in radish sauce? But his culinary peak, exquisite as it is, has a coarse, possessive side about which the poor food critic doesn't feel guilty, since he is only—he begs you to understand—a passive victim of U.S. consumer society.

He insists it isn't his fault. How can you escape, even if you spend only two months of the year in the United States, when wherever you happen to be—a hotel, motel, apartment, faculty club, studio, or, in extreme cases, trailer—fills up in the twinkling of an eye with electronic mail, coupons, every conceivable kind of offer, insignificant prizes intended to assure you that you've won a Caribbean cruise, unwanted subscriptions, mountains of paper, newspapers, specialized magazines, catalogs from L. L. Bean, Sears, Neiman Marcus?

As a response to that avalanche of papers, multiplied a thousandfold by E-mail—requests for donations, false temptations—Dionisio decided to abandon his role as passive recipient and assume that of active transmitter. Instead of being the victim of an avalanche, he proposed to buy the mountain. Why not acquire everything the television advertisements offered—diet milkshakes, file systems, limited-edition CDs with the greatest songs of Pat Boone and Rosemary Clooney, illustrated histories of World War II, complicated devices for toning and developing the muscles, plates commemorating the death of Elvis Presley or the wedding of Charles and Diana, a cup commemorating the bicentennial of American independence, fake Wedgwood tea sets, frequent-flyer offerings from every airline, trinkets left over from Lincoln's and Washington's birthdays, the tawdry costume jewelry purveyed by the Home Shopping Channel, exercise videos with Cathy Lee Crosby, all the credit cards that ever were . . . all of it, he decided, was irresistible, was for him, was available, even the magic detergents that cleaned anything, even an emblematic stain of *mole poblano*.

Secretly, he knew the reasons for this new acquisitive voraciousness. One was a firm belief that if, expansively, generously, he accepted what the United States offered him—weight-loss programs, detergents, songs of the fifties—it would ultimately accept what he was offering: the patience and taste to concoct a good *escabeche victorioso*. The other was a plan to get even for all the garbagey prizes he'd been accumulating—again, passively—by going on television and competing on quiz shows. His culinary knowledge was infinite, so he could easily win and not only in the gastronomic category.

Cuisine and sex are two indispensable pleasures, the former more than the latter. After all, you can eat without love, but you can't love without eating. And if you understand the culinary palate you know everything: what went into a kiss or a crab *chilpachole* involved historical, scientific, and even political wisdom. Where were cocktails born? In Campeche, among English sailors who mixed their drinks with a local condiment called "cock's tail." Who consecrated chocolate as an acceptable beverage in society? Louis XIV at Versailles, after the Aztec drink had been considered a bitter poison for two centuries. Why in old Russia was the potato prohibited by the Orthodox Church? Because it wasn't mentioned in the Bible and therefore had to be a creation of the devil. In one sense the Orthodox clergy were right: the potato is the source of that diabolical liquor vodka.

The truth is, Rangel entered these shows more to become known among larger audiences than to win the washing machines, vacuum cleaners, and—*mirabile visu!*—trips to Acapulco with which his successes were rewarded.

Besides, he had to pass the time.

A silver-haired old fox, an interesting man, with the looks of a mature movie star, Dionisio "Baco" Rangel was, at the age of fifty-one, something of a copy of that cinematic model personified by the late Arturo de Córdova, in whose films marble stairways and plastic flamingoes filled the background of neurotic love scenes featuring innocent fifteen-year-old girls and vengeful forty-year-old mothers, all of them reduced to their proper size by the autumnal star's memorable and lapidary phrase: "It doesn't have the slightest importance." It should be pointed out that Dionisio, with greater self-generosity, would say to himself as he shaved every morning (Barbasol) that he had no reason to envy Vittorio De Sica, who moved beyond the movies of Fascist Italy, with their white telephones and satin sheets, to become the supreme neorealist director of shoeshine boys, stolen bicycles, and old men with only dogs for company. But still, how handsome, how elegant he was, how surrounded by Ginas, Sophias, and Claudias! It was to that sum of experience and that smoothness of appearance that our compatriot Dionisio "Baco" Rangel aspired as he stored all his American products in a suburban warehouse outside the border city of San Diego, California.

The problem was that girls no longer flocked to our autumnal star. The problem was that his style clashed badly with theirs. The problem was that as he stared at himself in the mirror (Barbasol, no Brilliantine, no brilliant ideas) he had to accept that after a Certain Age a star must be circumspect, elegant, calm—all so as not to succumb to the maximum absurdity of the aged Don Juan, Fernando Rey, in Buñuel's *Viridiana*, who possesses virgins only if he dopes them up first and then plays them Handel's *Messiah*.

"Unhandel me, sire."

Dionisio had therefore to spend many solitary hours, on his lecture tours and in television studios, wasting his melancholy on futile reflections. California was his inevitable zone of operations, and there he spent a season passing time in Los Angeles observing the flow of cars through that headless city's freeway system, imagining it as the modern equivalent of a medieval joust, each driver a flawless knight and each car an armor-covered charger. But his concentrated observation aroused suspicion, and the police arrested him for loitering near the highways: Was he a terrorist?

American oddities began to command his attention. He was pleased to discover that beneath the commonplaces about a uniform, robotic society devoid of culinary personality (article of faith), there roiled a multiform, eccentric world, quasi-medieval in its corrosive ferment against an order once imposed by Rome and its Church and now by Washington and its Capitol. How would the country put itself in order when it was full of religious lunatics who believed beyond doubt that faith, not surgery, would take care of a tumor in the lungs? How, when the country was full of people who dared not exchange glances in the street lest the stranger turn out to be an escaped paranoid authorized to kill anyone who didn't totally agree with his ideas, or a murderer released from an overcrowded mental hospital or jail, or a vengeful homosexual armed with HIV-laden syringes, a neo-Nazi skinhead ready to slit the throat of a dark-skinned person, a libertarian militiaman prepared to finish off the government by blowing up federal buildings, a country where teenage gangs were better armed than the police, exercising their constitutional right to carry rocket launchers and blow off the head of a neighbor's child?

Sliding along the streets of America, Dionisio happily gave to that single country the name of an entire continent, gladly sacrificing in favor of a name with lineage, position, history (like Mexico, Argentina, Brazil, Peru, Nicaragua . . .) that name without a name, the ghostlike "United States of America," which, his friend the historian Daniel Cosío Villegas said, was a moniker like "The Neighborhood Drunkard." Or, as Dionisio himself thought, like a mere descriptor, like "Third Floor on the Right."

A good Mexican, Dionisio conceded all the power in the world to the gringos except that of an aristocratic culture: Mexico had one, paying the price, it was true, with abysmal, perhaps insurmountable inequality and injustice. Mexico also had conventions, manners, tastes, subtleties that confirmed her aristocratic culture: an island of tradition increasingly whipped and sometimes flooded, though, by storms of vulgarity and styles of commercialization that were worse, because grosser, cheaper, more disgusting, than those of North Americans. In Mexico even a thief was courteous, even an illiterate was cultured, even a child knew how to say hello, even a maid knew how to walk gracefully, even a politician knew how to behave like a lady, even a lady knew how to behave like a politician, even the cripples were acrobats, and even the revolutionaries had the good taste to believe in the Virgin of Guadalupe.

None of that consoled him in his ever longer moments of middle-aged tedium, when classes were over, when the lectures had come to an end, the girls had left, and he had to return to the hotel, the motel . . .

It was perhaps these curious shelters that led Dionisio "Baco" Rangel to his latest way of amusing himself in California. He spent weeks sitting outside the places that most tested his patience and good taste—McDonald's, Kentucky Fried Chicken, Pizza Hut, and, abomination of abominations, Taco Bell—so he could count the fat people who came to and left from those cathedrals of bad eating. He was armed with statistics. Forty million persons in the United States were obese, more than in any other country in the world. Fat—seriously fat—people: pink masses, souls lost under rolls and rolls of flesh, to the point of rendering characteristics like eyes, noses, mouths, even their sexes ephemeral. Dionisio watched a 350-pound woman pass by and wondered where her vein of pleasure might be. How, among the multiple slabs along her thighs and buttocks, would you get to the sanctum sanctorum of her libido? Would her male counterpart dare ask, Honey, could you just fart so I can get my bearings here? Dionisio laughed to himself at his vulgarity, celebrated and forgiven, because every Hispanic aristocrat owes something to the scatology of that great poet Don Francisco de Quevedo y Villegas. Quevedo connects our spirit and our excrement: we will be dust, but dust in love. He justifies our enjoyment of the huge dose of profanity that existence offers us, and our compiling, as Quevedo did in the seventeenth century and no one until Kundera did in the twentieth, praises of the asshole's grace and disgrace.

The parade Dionisio observed owed more to Fernando Botero and his adipose crews of immense courtesans than to Rubens, who never imagined obese priests, swollen children, generals about to burst . . . Forty million fat gringos? Was it just the effect of bad food? Why did this happen in the United States and not in Spain, Mexico, or Italy, despite the pork sausages, tamales, and tagliarini that fleshed out those cuisines? In each potbelly that went by Dionisio suspected the presence of millions of paper and cellophane bags zealously safeguarding, in the void that precedes the flood, hundreds of millions of french fries, tons of popcorn, sugar cakes frosted with nuts and chocolate, audible cereals, mountains of tricolored ice cream crowned with peanuts and hot caramel sauce, hamburgers of toughened dog meat, thin as shoe soles, served between tombstones of greasy, insipid, inflated bread, the national American host, smeared with ketchup (This is my blood) and loaded with calories (This is my body) . . . Spongy buttocks, hands moist and transparent as gelatin, pink skin holding in the mass of pus, blood, and scales . . . He watched them pass.

And nevertheless, as Dionisio "Baco" Rangel observed the massive parade of fat women, he began to feel, perversely, inexplicably, a sexual itch. This was like his experience when he had his first erection at thirteen—something sweet, unexpected, and alarming. No, not the first time he masturbated, something he did rationally, as an act of will, but the first flowering of his sex, shocking, unthinkable before it actually happened . . . The first semen spilled by the young man, eternally, at that moment, the first man, Adam, a man adrift in semen.

The intuition profoundly disturbed the solitary, itinerant

gourmet. True, in Mexico there was no dearth of distinguished ladies of fifty and even forty willing to accompany him to eat at Bellinghausen, to have dinner at the Estoril, to attend one of the concerts at the Historic Center festival organized by Francesca Saldívar, or even to hear lectures by his two old colleagues from the *Junior Professors* radio show, José Emilio Pacheco and Carlos Monsiváis. True, some of those ladies were also happy to sleep with him from time to time, but it was too late in the day to learn their little habits or instruct them in his. And none of them had any way of knowing that nothing excited him so much as a woman's hand on the back of his neck, just as he had no way of knowing which of them liked to have their nipples nibbled and which didn't (ouch! that hurts!). The death of his friend Marcelo Chiriboga, a specialist in fat women, deprived him of the pleasure of comparing notes with that wise, ignored, and sensual Ecuadorian novelist, who now, at the right hand of God, would be reciting the well-known prayer that came from the ancient Inca capital conquered by Sebastián de Benalcázar: "While on earth, Quito, and when in heaven, a tiny hole to see Quito." At this point, all Dionisio wanted was a tiny hole to see the tiny hole of some chubby woman.

Thus did the parade of fat women have its singular, entirely novel effect on Dionisio. He began by imagining himself in the arms of one of these immense women, lost in a leafiness like that of a forest of fleshy ferns, searching for secret jewels, diamond-hard points, hidden velvet, mother-of-pearl smoothness, invisible moistures of The Fat Woman. But Dionisio, being Dionisio (a discreet, elegant, recognized Mexican gentleman), did not dare to act simply on the impulse of his imagination and his body, to approach the obese object of his desire and thereby leave himself open to rejection or even—with luck—acceptance. Rejection, no matter how brutal, would be less painful than her consent to an afternoon of love: having never made love to a fat woman, he didn't know which end to work from, what he should say, what he shouldn't say, what the erotic protocol was when dealing with the *very* obese.

For instance, how could he offer them something to eat without, perhaps, offending them? What love talk would a fat woman expect that wouldn't diminish or mock her? Come here, my little honey, what cute little eyes you have? "Little" would be offensive, but your great big eyes, your huge tits—augmentatives were equally verboten. Afraid he'd lose his unaffected style and, with it, his effectiveness, Dionisio resigned himself to not making a pass at any of the fat women leaving the Kentucky Fried Chicken, but the very abundance of those women whom he desired for the first time made him think—by way of obvious association—about food, about compensating for the erotic impossibility with culinary possibility, about eating what he couldn't screw.

He was in a commercial neighborhood north of San Diego, perusing the Yellow Pages in search of a restaurant that wasn't too vile. An O Sole Mio guaranteed him week-old pasta camouflaged by a Vesuvius tomato sauce. A Chez Montmartre promised horrible food and haughty waiters. A Viva Villa! would condemn him to detestable Tex-Mex with a moustache. He chose an American Grill, which would at least make excellent Bloody Marys and which, from outside, looked clean, even shiny, in its aggressive display of chrome tables, leather seats, a nickel-plated bar, and mirrors—a quicksilver labyrinth, in fact, designed so a diner could see his reflection without looking away from his dinner partner. Or could look at himself the whole time to compensate for the tedium of the food.

He sat down, and a handsome blond young man, dressed like a waiter from the 1890s, offered him a menu. Dionisio had chosen a secluded corner with a view of a skating rink, but shortly two cross bald men bent with age though still energetic, wearing seersucker caps, white cardigan sweaters, and blue pants, took the table next to his. They sat down noisily, shuffling their Nikes.

"Let's see. To start off . . ." Dionisio read over the menu.

"Show me the proof," said one of the bristling old men.

"I don't have to. You know it isn't true," said his companion.

"A shrimp cocktail."

"You didn't make a dime on that deal."

"I don't know why I go on arguing with you, George."

"No sauce. Just some lemon."

"I told you you'd lose your shirt."

"I told you, I told you, I'll tell you—don't you know any other songs?"

"What is the soup of the day?"

"You don't know a thing."

"I could see it coming a long way off, Nathan. Don't say I didn't warn you."

"Vichyssoise."

"I'm telling you, you don't know anything."

"I don't know anything? Do you know that half the merchant ships in World War Two were lost?"

"Prove it. You just made that up."

"A steak, but right away."

"Wanna bet?"

"Sure. I always win when I bet against you. You're ignorant, George."

"Medium."

"Do you know what gravity is?"

"No, and neither do you."

"It's a magnetic force."

"No, skip the green stuff. Just the steak."

"Let's see now. Is there gravity right at the edge of the ocean?"

"No, it's zero there."

"Whoa! That's real learning. No one's going to pull a fast one on you."

"Put up or shut up."

"Don't worry, I'll take the bet."

"No, son, I don't like baked potatoes, with or without sour cream."

"We still have to charge you for it."

"Charge me, but don't put it on the same plate with the steak."

"Look, they're going to fire me if I don't. It's the rule."

"Okay, okay, put it on the same plate."

"They were going to charge you for it anyway. The steak costs twenty-two-ninety with or without potato."

"Fine."

"George, you know a little about a lot, but you don't know anything important."

"I know a bad deal when I see one, a deal that'll end in failure, Nathan. You can't deny I know that."

"Well, I don't know anything, but I'm an educated man."

"Facts, Nathan, facts."

"Are you listening to me?"

"With the patience of a saint."

"I don't know why we keep talking to each other."

"A green salad."

"After everything else?"

"Yes, my boy, salad comes at the end."

"Are you a foreigner?"

"Yes, I'm a really strange foreigner with really strange quirks—like having salad after everything else."

"In America, we eat it first. That's the normal way."

"Are you listening to me, George?"

"Give me facts, Nathan."

"Do you know that the annual earnings of the publishing industry in America are the same as the earnings of the hot dog industry? Did you know that?"

"Where did you get that? Are you trying to insult me?"

"Since when have you become a book publisher?"

"I'm not. I make hot dogs, as you know perfectly well, Nathan. Are you listening to me?"

"And lemon meringue pie. That's all."

"Wanna bet?"

"Are you listening to me?"

"Give me proof."

"You don't know anything."

"I don't know why we're still eating together."

"Bet."

"I'll make a bet. Is there gravity on the moon?"

"Facts, facts."

"I told you that deal was headed for failure. No doubt about it. You're broke, George."

The one named George gave out a hoarse, tumultuous sob that didn't seem possible coming from that impassive face.

There is no fascination that doesn't also contain its pinch of repulsion. We scold ourselves when we allow ourselves to be seduced by the eye of Medusa, but in the case of this pair of dried-out, bald, long-nosed, arthritic, argumentative old codgers armed with unlit phallic cigars—No smoking, please—repulsion overcame fascination. Dionisio impatiently began to play with a bottle of sauce, rubbing it more and more nervously as the endless debate between George and Nathan went on and on, like insomnia, utterly engrossing for the two old men, unbearable for Dionisio. To save himself from them, the Mexican gastronome began to think about women as he rubbed the bottle, and as he rubbed it, he noticed what it was: Mexican sauce, jalapeño chile sauce. Suddenly, magically, something was unleashed from within, a volcano bursting the ancient crust over its crater and vomiting lava the more the man named after Bacchus rubbed it.

Except that it wasn't chile sauce that came out of the bottle but a man, diminutive but recognizable by his *charro* suit, his mariachi hat, and his Zapata-style moustache.

"*Patrón*," he said, revealing his hairy head, "you've saved me from a yearlong imprisonment. No gringo would open me up. Thank you! Your wish is my command!" concluded the tiny *charro*, caressing the pistol he was carrying on his hip.

For a moment, Dionisio "Baco" Rangel remembered the joke about the shipwrecked man who's spent ten years on a desert island and one day sets free the genie in a bottle. When the genie asks him what he wants, the man asks for a really great mama. And what he gets is Mother Teresa.

Dionisio decided to be frank with the little *charro* from the bottle, who looked just like a character in Abel Quezada's cartoons.

"A woman. No—several women."

"How many?" asked the little *charro*, ready, it seemed, to populate a harem if necessary.

"No," explained Dionisio. "One for each course I ordered."

"Served with each course, master, or instead of each?"

"That I leave to you," said Dionisio "Baco" Rangel, the universal Mexican who is, was, and shall be our protagonist. He said it indifferently, accustomed as always to the unusual. "Like the dish being served, with the dish being served . . ."

The little *charro* made a magician's wave, shot into the air, and disappeared. In his place, there appeared, simultaneously, the waiter and a thin woman with dark, lank hair and bangs, starved-looking, bony as Popeye's girlfriend or Modigliani's models, the total opposite of the fatties Dionisio had so perversely dreamed of. She was armed with a Diet Coke, which she drank by the teaspoonful as she gazed at Dionisio with eyes at once bored, ironic, and tired. The same eyes, with infinite weariness, explored the American Grill as she wondered out loud, in a drawl as long as the Mississippi, what she was doing there and whom she was with. He said he'd asked the genie in the bottle for a woman. He didn't manage to surprise her. Suppressing a yawn, the anorexic gringa answered that she'd asked for the same thing. There's no luck worse than sharing luck with someone else. She'd asked for a man—she smiled with immense fatigue, infinite hunger—leaving everything to chance because every choice she'd made in the past was a poor one. She'd let someone else choose for her. She was available, completely available.

"I'm a terrible lover," she said, almost with pride. "I'm just warning you. But I never take any blame. The man is always the one to blame."

"That's true," said Dionisio. "There are no frigid women. There are only impotent men."

"Or enthusiasts," ruminated the skinny woman. "I can't stand enthusiastic lovemaking. It takes all the sincerity out of it. But I can't stand sincerity either. I can only put up with men who lie to me. Lies are the only mystery in love."

She yawned and said they should postpone their sexual encounter.

"Why?"

"Because the only important thing about sex for me is being able to erase all trace of my sexual partner. All this is very tiring."

Dionisio reached his hand out to touch the skinny woman's. She pulled hers back with repugnance and laughed a cabaret laugh.

"How do you act in private, when no one's watching?" asked the Mexican. She showed her teeth, drank a teaspoon of Diet Coke, and disappeared.

The shrimp cocktail also disappeared. For an instant, Dionisio wondered if he'd eaten it while he'd chatted with the anorexic New Yorker. (She had to be from New York; it was too pat, vulgar, predictable for her to be from California. At least boredom and fatigue in New York have literary foundations and don't result from the climate.) Or, thinking he was eating a shrimp cocktail, had he eaten the gringa who had so carefully avoided looking him in the eye? (Was she trying to avoid being discovered or even guessed at?) He couldn't bear the curiosity of knowing if he'd eaten with her or eaten her or if everything might end up—he trembled with pleasure—in a mutual culinary sacrifice . . .

He heard the *charro*'s shot, the waiter placed the vichyssoise on the table, and opposite him, eating the same thing, appeared a woman, fortyish, but obviously and avidly enamored of her childhood, with a Laura Ashley dress and a red chignon crowning her Shirley Temple curls. These odd accessories could not distract Dionisio from the repertoire of grimaces accompanying the words and noisy soup slurping of this old Shirley counterfeit, who between slurps and grimaces managed to express only excitement and shock: how

exciting to be sitting there eating with him, how shocking to
know a man so romantic, so sophisticated, so, so, so . . .
foreign. Only foreigners excited her—it seemed unbelievable
to her that a foreigner would notice her, she who lived only
on dreams, dreaming about impossible, shocking, exciting
romances, all her life dreaming of being in the arms of Ronald Colman, Clark Gable, Rudolf Valentino . . .

"Do you ever dream about Mel Gibson?"

"Who?"

"Tom Cruise?

"Who's he?"

No, she had no complaints about life, she went on, making her faces, rolling her eyes, shaking her curls like a luxury
floor mop, raising her eyebrows to her topknot, nodding her
head like a porcelain doll—and also hissing like a snake,
clucking like a hen, howling like a she-wolf before confessing
that when she went to bed she sang lullabies and recited
Mother Goose, though through her mind (everything was
shocking, exciting, unheard of) passed horrible catastrophes,
air and sea disasters, highway mayhem, terrorist acts, muti-
lated bodies, so the lullabies and pretty verses were to ex-
orcise the horrors—did he, an obviously foreign, exciting,
sophisticated, wonderful, wonderful, wonderful gentleman
understand?

As she spoke the word *wonderful*, this Alice in Blunder-
land, blond and pink, faded into a haze. The soup, too, had
disappeared. Dionisio gazed at the empty bowl, disconsolate.
Again the *charro*'s shot rang out, the waiter served the steak,
and an extremely beautiful and elegant woman appeared, in
a black tailored suit, with pearls at her neck and bracelets
on her wrists, perfectly coiffed and made-up and showing a
considerable amount of cleavage. She stared at him in silence.

Dionisio cut his meat without saying a word and raised a bloody morsel (he'd requested medium) to his mouth. At that precise instant she began to speak. But not to him. She spoke into a cellular telephone which she held in one hand while she touched the divide between her breasts with the gesture of a woman perfuming that crevice of pleasure before going out to dinner.

"I'm making an exception and eating sitting down, you understand? I never have time to sit down; I eat standing up. This seems abnormal to me."

"But what's so strange—" interrupted Dionisio, before realizing that the woman was talking not to him but to her telephone.

"Miss? You think I miss you?"

"No, I never said—" Dionisio decided to make a mistake. Damnation.

"Listen," said the beautiful woman in the black tailored suit showing a considerable amount of cleavage, her breasts barely hidden by the (appropriately) double-breasted jacket. "I get my faxes at one number. I don't have a name or address. I don't need secretaries. My computer is with me wherever I am. I have no place. No, I don't have time either. I'm proving it to you, stupid. What does it matter to me that in Holland it's midnight if it's three p.m. in California and we're here working . . . ?"

"On a snatch, I mean, a snack." Dionisio corrected himself but the beauty ignored him, just barely touching herself behind an ear, again as if she were putting on perfume, as if her fingers were a bottle of Chanel.

"Just think, I don't even need a doctor anymore. You know my bracelet? Well, let me tell you, it's not just some frivolous piece of jewelry. It's my portable hospital. Anywhere I happen to be, it can do a cardiogram, check my blood pressure, and even tell me my cholesterol without wasting time."

Dionisio wondered if this beautiful woman was really a nurse in disguise. A hospital would have rewarded her efficiency, but it was haste, not efficiency, that mattered most to this divine creature. Dionisio began to doubt she was speaking to someone in Holland, but there was certainly no way in hell she was speaking to him. Was she talking to herself?

"So listen, with no time, no address, no name, no place, no office, no vacation, no kitchen, what am I left with?"

Her voice broke; she was going to cry. Dionisio panicked. He wished he could hug her or at least stroke her hand. She was becoming more hysterical by the minute. For the first time, she looked at him, telling him she was Sally Booth, thirty-six years old, a native of Portland, Oregon, voted in high school most likely to succeed, three husbands, three divorces, no children, occasional lovers, farther and farther away, love by telephone, long-distance orgasms, love with security, without problems, no body fluids, safe. I won't go to a hospital, I'm going to die at home . . .

Abruptly interrupting her emotional flow, her instant biography, she squeezed Dionisio's hand and said, "What is money good for? To buy people. We all need accomplices."

And on that note, she disappeared like the first two, and Dionisio sat there staring at an empty plate where only the juicy traces of a rare steak survived (even though he had explicitly ordered medium).

"You could have been more cruel and less beautiful," said the Symbolist poet whom Dionisio, to his sorrow although also for his intermittent pleasure, carried within him.

But this time his portable Baudelaire never left the suitcase; the little *charro*'s pistol went off again, and the blond waiter unexpectedly set down before him a lemon sherbet that Baco identified as the *trou normand* of French cuisine, the "Norman hole" that cleanses the palate of the main courses and prepares it for new tastes. He was astounded that the American Grill in a commercial center on the outskirts of San Diego would know anything about such subtleties, but he was even more taken aback to find, when he looked up, a woman before him. Without being beautiful, she was radiant—that he saw instantly. Her face, devoid of makeup, both needed and didn't need cosmetics—they were irrelevant. Everything in her immaculate face had meaning. Her eyebrows, with their blond pallor, were like the meeting place of sand and sea; her lips, appropriately thin, were appropriately furrowed by an insinuation of imminent maturity she didn't deign to disguise; her hair was pulled back and gathered in a bun, her first gray hairs of no importance to her, floating like lost clouds over a field of honey; her eyes, her eyes of a deep gray, the gray of good cashmere, of morning rain, as gray as an unexpected encounter, intelligent, slate and chalk, announced her special nature—they were eyes that changed color with the rain. They looked past Dionisio's shoulder toward the television screen.

"I always wished I could play for a baseball team," she said, smiling, as Baco, lost in the eyes of his new woman, let his lemon sherbet melt away. "It takes a special kind of art to make those low catches."

"Like Willie Mays," Dionisio interposed. "He really knew how to pull out those low catches."

"How do you know that?" she said with genuine amazement, genuine fondness.

"I don't like American cooking, but I do admire American culture—sports, movies, gringo literature."

"Willie Mays," said the un-made-up woman, rolling her

eyes up toward heaven. "It's funny how someone who does things well never does them just for himself. It's as if he did them for everyone."

"Who are you thinking of?" asked Dionisio, more and more ravished by this *trou normand* of a woman.

"Faulkner. I'm thinking of William Faulkner. I'm thinking about how a single genius can save an entire culture."

"A writer can't save anything. You're mistaken there."

"No, it's you who are mistaken. Faulkner showed the southerners that the South could be something other than violence, racism, the Ku Klux Klan, prejudice, and rednecks."

"All that came into your head from watching television?"

"It really does intrigue me. Do we watch television because things happen there, or do things happen so they can be seen on television?"

He went on with the game. "Is Mexico poor because she's underdeveloped, or is she underdeveloped because she's poor?"

Now it was her turn to laugh.

"You see, people used to watch Willie Mays play, and the next day they read the paper to make sure he'd played. Now you can see the information and the game at the same time. You don't have to verify anything. That's worrisome."

"You mentioned Mexico," she said, questioningly, after a moment in which she lowered her eyes, doubtful. "Are you Mexican?"

Dionisio nodded affirmatively.

"I love and don't love your country," said the woman with the gray eyes and the clouds crowning her honey hair. "I adopted a Mexican girl. The Mexican doctors who gave her to me didn't tell me she had a serious heart problem. When I brought her here, I took her in for a routine checkup and was told that if she wasn't operated on immediately she wouldn't last another two weeks. Why didn't they tell me that in Mexico?"

"Probably so you wouldn't change your mind and would go ahead with the adoption."

"But she could have died, she could have . . . Oh, Mexican cruelty, the abuse, the indifference toward the poor—what they suffer. Your country is a horror."

"I'll bet the girl's pretty."

"Very pretty. I really love her. She's going to live," she said, her eyes transfigured, just before she disappeared. "She's going to live . . ."

Dionisio could only stare at the melted sherbet he'd had no time to eat; the *charro* genie, impatient to carry out his orders and disappear, had fired his pistol again, and a cute woman appeared with curly hair and a flat nose, nervous, jolly eyes, dimples, and capped teeth. She gave him a big smile, as if she were welcoming him onto a plane, school, or hotel. It was impossible to know what it meant—appearances are deceiving. Her features were so nondescript she could have been anything, even a bordello madam. She wore jogging clothes, a light-blue jacket and sweatpants. She never stopped talking, as if Dionisio's presence were irrelevant to her compulsive discourse, which had neither beginning nor end and seemed directed to an ideal audience of infinitely patient or infinitely detached listeners.

The salad appeared, accompanied by the waiter's scornful gesture and his muttered censure: "Salad is eaten at the beginning."

"Think I should get a tattoo? There are two things I've never had. A tattoo and a lover. Think I'm too old for that?"

"No. You look as if you could be between thirty and—"

"When you're a kid, that's when having tattoos is good. But now? Imagine me with a tattoo on my ankle. How am I going to show up at my own daughter's wedding with a tattoo on my ankle? Even worse, how am I going to go—someday—to my granddaughter's wedding with a tattoo on my ankle? Maybe it would be better if I had a tattoo on my boob—that way only my lover would see it in secret. Now that I'm about to get a divorce, I was lucky enough to meet this in-cred-ible man. Where do you think his territory is?"

"I don't know. Do you mean his house or his office?"

"No, silly. I mean how much territory he covers professionally. Guess! I'd better tell you: the whole world. He buys nonpatented replacement parts. Know what those are? All the parts for machinery, for household appliances, TVs, where no rights have to be paid. What do you think of that? He's a genius! Even so, I suspect he may be a homosexual. I don't know if he'd know how to bring up my kids. I toilet trained them very early. I don't understand why friends of mine toilet trained their kids so late or never bothered . . ."

Dionisio quickly ate the salad to get rid of the soon-to-be-divorced lady, and with his last bite, she vanished. Did I cannibalize her or did she cannibalize me? wondered the food critic, overcome by a growing sense of anguish he could not identify. Was all this a gag? It was a fog.

And it was not cleared away by the arrival of dessert, a lemon meringue pie whose female counterpart Baco was afraid to see, especially because at the beginning of this adventure he'd watched the fat women pass by, desiring them platonically. He was right to be afraid. Seated opposite him, he saw when the noise of the *charro*'s shot had faded, was a monstrous woman who weighed 650 if she weighed a pound. Her pink sweatshirt announced her cause: FLM, the Fat Liberation Movement. She couldn't cross her Michelin man arms over her immense tits, which moved on their own inside her sweatshirt and fell like a flesh Niagara Falls over the barrel of her stomach, the only obstacle blocking one from contemplation of her spongy legs, bare from the thighs down, indifferent to the indecency of her wrinkled shorts. Her moist hands, loathsome, rested on Dionisio's. The critic trembled. He tried to pull his hands free. Impossible. The fat woman was there to catechize him, and resigned to his fate, he prepared himself to be good and catechized.

"Do you know how many million obese people we have in the USA?"

"As a matter of fact, I do."

"Don't even guess, my boy. Forty million of what others pejoratively call fat people. But I'm telling you, no one can be discriminated against for their physical defects. I walk the streets telling myself, I am beautiful and intelligent. I say it in a low voice, then I shout it, I am beautiful and intelligent! Don't force me to be perverse! That gets their attention. Then I make our demands. Obese is beautiful. Weight-loss programs should be declared illegal. Movies and airlines should install special seats for people like me. We've had enough of buying two tickets just so we can travel in comfort."

She raised her voice, hysterical.

"And nobody make fun of me! I'm beautiful and intelligent. Don't make me be perverse. I was cook on a ship registered in San Diego. We were coming from Hawaii. It was a freighter. One day I was walking on deck eating ice cream and a sailor got up, pulled it out of my hand, and threw it overboard. 'Don't get any fatter,' he said, laughing his head off. 'Your fat disgusts all of us. You're ridiculous.' That night, down in the kitchen, I put a laxative in the soup. Then I walked through the passageways shouting over the moans of the crew, 'I'm beautiful and intelligent. Don't mess with me. Don't make me be perverse.' I lost my job. I hope you'll want me. Is it true? Here I am . . . listen . . . what's wrong with you?"

Dionisio liberated his hands and swallowed the pie so the fat woman would disappear. But she understood his contempt and managed to shout: "You were tricked, you jerk! My name is Ruby, and I'm involved with a Chilean novelist named José Donoso. I will only be his!"

Dionisio stood up in horror, left an outrageous hundred-dollar bill on the table, and ran from the American Grill. Once again he felt that terrible anguish, felt it turn into a feeling of something lost, of something he had to do, though he didn't know what.

He stopped running when he came to the window of an American Express office. A dummy representing a typical Mexican, in a wide sombrero, huaraches, and the clothes of a peon, was leaning against a cactus, taking his siesta. The cliché infuriated Dionisio. He stormed into the travel agency and started to shake the dummy. But the dummy was made not of wood but of flesh and blood, and exclaimed, "Damn it to hell, they don't even let you sleep around here."

The employees were shouting, too, telling him to leave their "pee-on" alone, let him do his job, we're promoting Mexico. But Dionisio pushed him out the door, took him by the shoulders, shook him, and asked him who he was, what he was doing there. And the Mexican model (or model Mexican) respectfully removed his sombrero.

"There would be no way for you to know it, but I've been lost here for ten years."

"What are you saying? Ten what? What?"

"Ten years, boss. I came over one day and got lost in the shopping mall and never got out. And then they hired

me here to take siestas in windows, and if there's no work,
I can sneak in and sleep on cushions or beach chairs. There's
more than enough food—they just leave it, they throw it
away. If you only saw—"

"Come, come with me," said Dionisio, taking the peon
by the sleeve, electrified by the word *food*, awake, alert to
his own emotions, to the memory of the woman with gray
eyes, the woman who adopted the Mexican girl, the woman
who read Faulkner—that's the one he should have chosen.
Providence had arranged things. None of the other women
mattered, only that one, that sensitive little gringa, who was
strong, intelligent. She was his, had to be his. He was fifty-
one and she was forty—they'd make a fine couple. What was
this perverse game all about? The *charro* genie, his kitschy
alter ego, that bastard, that picturesque asshole, that skirt
chaser, that total opposite of his Symbolist, Baudelairean,
French alter ego, was also his double, his brother, but the
little guy was Mexican and was always pulling a fast one,
teasing him, offering him the moon but handing him shit,
devaluing his life, his love, his desire. The genie didn't tell
him that when he ate a steak or a shrimp cocktail or a lemon
meringue pie he was also eating the woman who was the
incarnation of each dish, and here he was, delirious, going
mad, dragging a poor hungry man through a California mall
until they reached the restaurant called the American Grill
and he was illuminated, convinced now it was all true. He'd
eaten everything but the lemon sherbet: she was alive, she
had not been devoured by his other Aztec ego, his pocket-
sized Huitzilopochtli, his national Minimoctezuma.

"Sorry," said the waiter who'd taken care of him, "we
throw away the leftovers. Your melted sherbet went down
the drain a while ago."

Saying it evidently gave him pleasure, and he licked his

down-covered lips. Ready to weep with sadness, Dionisio screamed. He was still dragging the peon along by the hand, and lost in the labyrinth of consumerism, the Mexican became alarmed and said, I've never gotten beyond this place, this is where I get lost, I've been captive here for ten years! But Dionisio paid no attention and pushed him into the rented Mustang. The peon suffered the tortures of the damned as they raced through the tangled nets of highways, the vertebrae of a cement beast, sleeping but alert. They arrived at the storage center north of the city.

Here Dionisio stopped.

"Come along. I need you to help me."

"Where we going, boss? Don't take me away from here! Don't you realize what it costs us to enter Gringoland? I don't want to go back to Guerrero!"

"Try to understand. I have no prejudices."

"It's that I like all this—the shopping center where I live, the television, the abundance, the tall buildings . . ."

"I know."

"What, boss? What do you know?"

"None of this we're seeing here would exist if the gringos hadn't stolen all this land from us. In Mexican hands, this would be a huge wasteland."

"In Mexican hands—"

"A big desert, this would be a big desert, from California to Texas. I'm telling you this so you won't think I'm unfair."

"Okay, chief."

Almost no one saw them. They abandoned the Mustang in the Colorado desert, south of Death Valley. The peon lost for ten years in the mall had not lost his ancestral talent for carrying things on his back. He was the descendant of bearers—bearers of stones, corn, sugar cane, minerals, flowers, chairs, birds . . . Now Dionisio loaded him up with a pyramid of electrical appliances, machines to make you thin, limited-edition CDs of Hoagy Carmichael, Cathy Lee Crosby exercise videos, plates commemorating the death of Elvis, and cans, dozens of cans, the entire world in cans, metal gastronomy. Dionisio, meanwhile, gathered in his arms the catalogs, subscriptions, newspapers, specialized magazines, and coupons; and the two of them, Baco and his squire, the Don Quixote of fine cuisine and the Mexican Rip Van Winkle who slept away the Lost Decade in a shopping mall, made their way south, toward the border, toward Mexico, scattering along the U.S. desert, along earth that once belonged to Mexico, the vacuum cleaners and washing machines, the hamburgers and Dr. Peppers, the insipid beers and watery coffees, the greasy pizzas and frozen hot dogs, the magazines and coupons, the CDs and the confetti made of electronic mail. Heading toward Mexico with nothing gringo, exclaimed Dionisio, tossing all the accumulated objects into the air, onto the earth, into the burning sun, until the Mustang exploded in the distance, leaving a cloud as bloody as a mushroom of flesh. Everything, get rid of everything, Dionisio said to his companion. Get rid of your clothing, just as I'm doing, scatter everything in the desert—we're going back to Mexico, we're not bringing a single gringo thing with us, not a single one, my brother, my double. We're returning to the fatherland naked. You can already see the border. Open your eyes wide—do you see, do you feel, do you smell, can you taste?

From the border came the unmistakable scent of Mexican food, an unstoppable smell.

"It's the Puebla-style marrow tarts!" exclaimed Dionisio "Baco" Rangel jubilantly. "Five hundred grams of marrow! Two chiles! Smell it! Cilantro! It smells of cilantro! Let's get to Mexico, to the frontier, let's go, brother. Let's arrive there as naked as the day we were born, return naked from the land that has everything to the land that has nothing!"

The recipe for Puebla-style marrow tarts consists of 500 grams of marrow, a cup of water, two chiles, 600 grams of dough, 3 teaspoons of flour, and oil to cook it all in.

4

THE LINE OF OBLIVION

For Jorge Castañeda

I'm sitting. Outside. I can't move. I can't speak. But I can hear. Only I don't hear anything. Maybe because it's night. The world is asleep. Only I am awake. I can see. I see the night. I watch the darkness. I try to understand why I'm here. Who brought me here? I feel as if I'm waking from a long artificial sleep. I'm trying to figure out where I am. I would really like to know who I am. I can't ask, because I can't speak. I'm paralyzed. I'm mute. I'm sitting in a wheelchair. I feel it rock a bit. I touch the rubber wheels with the tips of my fingers. Every so often it moves forward a little. Every so often it seems to go backward. What I fear most is its turning over. To the right. To the left. I'm starting to get my bearings again. I'm dizzy. To the left. I laugh a little. To the left. That's my downfall. That's my ruin. Going to the left. I've been accused of that. Who? Everyone. It makes me laugh, I don't know why. I have no reason to laugh. I think my situation is horrible. All fucked up. I don't remember who I am. I should make an effort to remember my face. I just realized something absurd: I've never seen my own face. I should invent a name for myself. My face. My neck. But that turns out to be harder than remembering, so I'll pin my hopes on memory. Memory, not imagination. Is remembering easier than imagining? I think it is for me. But I was saying, I'm afraid of tipping over. Rolling doesn't scare me much. Going backward, though, that does frighten me. I can't see where I'm going. I don't have eyes in the back of my head. If I'm going forward, at least I have the illusion that I'm controlling something. Even if I roll into the abyss. I'll see it as I fall. I'll see the void. Now I realize I can't fall into the abyss. I'm already there. That's a relief. Also a horror. But if I can fall no farther, does that mean I'm somewhere flat? My eyes are the most mobile part of me. I try to look straight ahead, then from side to side. First to the right. Then to the left. I see only darkness. I look up, straining my poor stiff old neck. Am I in a safe place? I don't see any stars. The stars have gone away. In their place a grimy sheen covers the sky. It's darker than darkness. Is there light anywhere? I look down at my feet. A blanket covers my knees. What a nice detail. Who, in spite of everything, felt compassion for me? My scuffed shoes stick out from beneath the fringe of the blanket. Then I see what I should see. I see a line at my feet. A luminous stripe, painted a phosphorescent color. A line. A boundary. A painted stripe. It shines in the night. It's the only thing shining. What is it? What does it separate? What does it divide? I have nothing but this line to orient me. And yet I don't know what it means. Nothing says anything to me tonight. I can neither move nor speak. But the world has become like me. Mute and immobile. At least I can look. Am I looked at? Nothing identifies me. When the sun rises, maybe I can figure out where I am. With

luck, I'll figure out who I am. I think of something: if someone found me abandoned in this blind, open place where
there is only a painted line shining on the ground, how
would that person identify me? I look at as much of myself
as I can. It's easiest to see my lap. Just tip my head down. I
see the blanket on my knees. It's gray. It's got a hole. Right
over my right knee. I try to move my hands to cover it up,
hide it. My hands are rigid on the rubber wheels. If I try
hard to stretch out my crippled fingers I can figure out that
the wheels are wheels. Now, I know I said the line on the
ground is artificial. How do I know that? Maybe it's natural,
like a gorge, a ravine. But maybe I'm an artificial being, an
imaginary presence. I scream out to my memory to return
and save me from destructive imagination. Where the fringe
on the blanket ends I can see my shoes. I've already said
they're old, scuffed, banged up. Like a miner's boots. I cling
to that association. Am I imagining or remembering? Miner.
Excavations. Tunnels. Gold? Silver? No. Mud. Only mud.
Mud. I don't know why, but when I say "mud" I want to
cry. Something terrible stirs in my stomach when I say
"mud," when I think "mud." I don't know why. I don't
know anything. I love my old shoes. They're hard but they're
comfortable. They have hooks and eyes. They're like boots.
A little higher than my ankles. To give me confidence. Even
if I can't walk. My shoes keep me steady. Without them, I'd
fall over. I'd fall on my face, go to pieces. I'd flop to one
side. Left? Right? That's the worst thing that could happen
to me. I'm already in the abyss. To fall to one side is what
I fear most. Who'd help me up? I'd be on the ground in a
real mess. My nose would smell the line. Or the line would
devour my nose. My shoes rest firmly on the footrests of the
chair. The chair rests on the ground. Not too firmly. I can't
possibly move. But the chair could roll and tip over. I'd fall

to the ground. I've already said that. But now I'll add something new. I'd cling to the ground. Is that my fate? The fluorescent line mocks me. It keeps the ground from being ground. The ground has no boundaries. The line says there are. The line says the earth has been split. The line makes the earth into something else. What? I'm so alone. I'm so cold. I feel so abandoned. Yes, I'd like to fall to the ground. Descend to the ground. Fall into its deepness. Into its real darkness. Into its sleep. Into its lullaby. Into its origin. Into its end. To start over. To finish for good. All at once. To fall into my mother—that's it. To fall into the memory of what I was before being. When I was loved. When I was desired. I know I was desired. I need to believe it. I know I'm in the world because I was loved by the world. By my mother. By my father. By my family. By those who were going to be my friends. By the children I was going to have. I say this and stop, horrified. I have spoken forbidden things. I sneak off, I hide in my thoughts. I can't bear what I've just said. My children. I can't accept it. The idea horrifies me. Disgusts me. I look at the line on the ground again and regain my cold comfort. I can't reunite with the earth, because the line stops me. The line tells me that the earth is divided. The line is something different from the earth. The earth stopped being earth. It turned into the world. The world is what loved me and brought me from the earth where I slept, one with the earth and with myself. I was taken from the earth and placed in the world. The world called to me. The world wanted me. But now it rejects me. Abandons me. Forgets me. Flings me back to the earth. But even the earth doesn't want me. Instead of opening up a protective abyss, it sets me on a line. At least an abyss would embrace me. I'd enter the true total darkness that has neither beginning nor end. Now I look at the earth and an indecent line splits it. The line possesses its own light. A painted, obscene light. Totally indifferent to my presence. I am a man. Aren't I worth more than a line? Why is the line laughing at me? Why is it sticking its tongue out at me? I think I woke from a nightmare and will fall back into it. The meanest objects, the most vile things will live longer than I. I will pass. But the line will remain. It's a trap to keep the earth from being earth and from receiving me. It's a trap for the world to hold onto me without loving me. Why does the world not love me? Why does the earth still not accept me? If I knew those two things, I'd know everything. But I know nothing. Perhaps I should be patient. I should wait for sunrise. Then two things will surely happen. Someone will approach me and recognize me. Hello there, X, he'll say. What are you doing here? Don't tell me you spent the night here? Alone, out in the open? Don't you have a home? And your children? Where are they? Why aren't they taking care of you? That's what I'm thinking. That's what I'm saying. And I howl. Like an animal. I scream as if I were imprisoned in a fragile crystal glass and my screaming could shatter it. The sky is my glass. I howl like the wolves to frighten away a single word. Children. I prefer to go quickly to my second possibility. The sun will rise and I'll recognize where I am. That will soothe me. That, perhaps, will give me the strength to take charge, to take the wheels in my hands and head off in a precise, known direction. Where? I haven't the slightest idea. Who's waiting for me? Who will protect me? These questions make me think the opposite. Who hates me? Who abandoned me here in the middle of the night? I lower the volume on my howl. No one. No one recognizes me. No one waits for me. No one abandoned me. It was the world. The world forsook me. I stop howling. Does no one love me? The questions are pure possibilities. Which means that I'm not dying yet. I'm imagining possibilities. Does death cancel all possibilities? I imagine I recognize and am recognized. I want to know where I am. I want to know who I am. I want to know who put me here. Who abandoned me at the line, in the night. If I keep asking about all this, it means I'm not dead. I'm not dead, because I'm not renouncing possibility. But no sooner do I think that than I start thinking there are many ways of being dead. Perhaps I've imagined only some of them, and this is just one. I'm sitting mute and paralyzed in a wheelchair in the middle of the night and in an unknown place. But I don't believe I'm dead. Could that be an illusion? Do we go on thinking as long as we're alive? Could that be the real death? I don't believe so. If I were really dead, I'd know that it was death. That consoles me. Since I don't know what death is, I must still be alive. And if I'm alive, it's because I imagine death in many ways. At the same time, I must be very close to it because I sense my possibilities running out. First I tell myself I'm passing on. I don't dare name my death. It frightens me. I'm just passing through, I say pleasantly, so no one gets scared. Many people appear before me to say yes, yes you're just passing through, that's all. And one day you'll have passed through. You'll be dead. They smile in the darkness when they say that. The people. It relieves them. If I don't die, because I'm only passing through, they won't die either. They'll have passed away. I find the idea repugnant. I reject it. I search for something to deny it. Something to deny its horrible hypocrisy. Let no one say of me, "X passed on." I prefer the voice inside me that says, "X already died." I've already died. I like that better. I hope they say that about me when I'm really dead, when I truly die. It's as if I was waiting for death and finally the day came. *Ya se murió.* But it's also as if death had been waiting for me forever, with open arms. He's already dead. That's why he was born.

That's why we made him, loved him, nurtured him, taught him to walk. So he would die. Not simply so he could pass on just like that. No. We nurtured him so he'd die. I hope that's clear. I've just had a great idea, as if thinking these two things—he just passed on, he's already died—were the same as thinking everything. One voice comes from one side of the line and says to me, "You're passing away." Another comes from the other side and says to me, "You've already died." The first voice, the one from the side that isn't mine, behind me, speaks in English. "He passed away," it says. The other, facing me, on my side, says, in Spanish, "Ya se murió." He bought the farm. He kicked the bucket. He's gone west. He's pushing up daisies. "He's already died." Who? No one says that to me. No one gives me back my name. Painfully I tilt my head back. I've already said that. My neck is stiff. It's very old. As they say, a chicken neck doesn't cook at the first boil. Suddenly, as if my ideas called them forth, the stars shine in the night. Then I do something totally unexpected, mysterious. I manage to lift an arm. I cover my eyes with my hand. I drop it to my knees. I have no idea why I do that. And no idea how I manage to do it. But when I open my eyes and look at the sky, I locate the polestar. I feel a great sense of relief. To see it, to identify it—for an instant I am back in the world. The polestar. Its presence and its name come to me. Clear, sharp. There they are, the star and the pole. They don't move. Eternally they announce the beginning of the world. Above and behind me is north. But instead of announcing the beginning the way I wanted, the voice of the star says to me, "You are going to pass away." I will pass away. I am dust and to dust will I return. I am the master of dust. Mr. Dust. I am mud and to mud will I return. I will be the master of mud. Mr. What . . . ? This time I don't scream. I clutch the wheels. I scratch them, furious and bewildered. I'm on the verge of knowing. I don't want to know. A horrible intuition tells me I do know. I'm going to suffer. I stop looking at the North Star. Instead I look at the darkness in the south. Downward. Toward my feet. "You're going to die now," the half-light says to me. It speaks in Spanish. And I answer. I manage to speak. I say something. A prayer learned long ago. In Spanish. Blessed be the light. And the Holy Cross. And the Lord of Truth. And the Holy Trinity. That comforts me enormously. But it also makes me want to urinate. I suddenly remember that, when I was little, every time I prayed I felt like going to the bathroom. The way some people pee when they hear the sound of water, I have to attend to my bladder when I pray. No sooner said than done. The Holy Trinity. Wee-wee starts to flow. I'm ashamed of myself. It's going to stain my trousers. I look down at my lap, expecting a moist stain around my open fly. But nothing's wrong, even though I'm sure I just urinated. Again I move my right hand with difficulty. I stick it in my fly. I don't find my underpants or the opening that would allow me to touch my obscenely gray pubic hair, my wrinkled dick, my balls that have grown to elephant size. None of that. I find a diaper. No mistaking it. Satiny and waterproof, thick and cushioned. Someone's put a diaper on me. I feel relief and shame. Relief because I know I can pee and shit as I please without worrying. Shame for the same reason: I'm being treated like a baby. Someone thinks I'm a helpless baby. Someone's put a diaper on me and abandoned me in a wheelchair next to a line painted on the ground. If I poop, who's going to smell my shit? Will someone come help me? That would be humiliating. I prefer to go on thinking I've been abandoned and no one will come for me. No one will change my diaper. I've been abandoned. The diaper forces me to repeat that. I am the abandoned child, the foundling. The orphan. Whose orphan? I'm tempted to move the wheels of my invalid's chair. I've already explained why I don't. I'm afraid of rolling. Falling. On my face. Toward the south. On my back. Toward the north. Not to the right. Better to the left. But that word disturbs me, I've already said so. I try to avoid it. Just as I avoid the idea of mud, the notion of having children, the need to speak English. But the little word overwhelms me. Left. If I let it in, I'll let in all the others. Name. Mud. Children. Death. Language. I repeat it and I see myself, miraculously, in the precise spot where I am. Only now standing up. Now on foot. Now young. And accompanied. I'm on the line. I'm facing an armed group. Police. They wear short-sleeve khaki shirts. T-shirts underneath. Even so, the sweat from their chests and armpits stains their shirts. Americans. They stand on one side of the line. Behind me is an unarmed group. Wearing overalls. Shoes like mine. Straw hats. They have tired faces. Faces that show they've traveled a long way in arid places. They have dust on their eyelashes, ringing their mouths, in their moustaches. They look as if they've been buried alive. And brought back to life. Just saying that brings a name to mind with the same force as the polestar. Lazarus. I speak in his name. I argue. I defend. Shots ring out. The men of dust fall. Then people I should know and love surround me. They surround me to protect me from the bullets. They protect me but they rebuke me. Agitator. Who asked you? Don't butt in. You're placing us in danger. It's not right. Go home. Accept things as they are. You're endangering all of us. Your wife. Your children. Especially your brother. My brother? Why my brother? Why am I here if not to defend my brother? Look at him. He's almost stopped breathing. He's covered with dust. He's just come out of the grave. His name's Lazarus. That's my brother. I defend him here, at the line. Lazarus. They laugh at me. You look like a fighting cock on your line. A well-pecked cock, more dead than alive. Your brother is the real cock. It's his line, not yours. Don't endanger him. Between us we're going to wear you down until you give up. We're going to show you that your display of bravery is useless. We're going to move you off the line, you little rooster. We're going to wear you down, you old bird. No matter what you do, the world won't change. Those you call your brothers will keep coming. When their arms are wanted, they'll cross the line and no one will bother them. Everyone will look the other way. But when they're no longer needed, they'll be rejected. They'll be beaten up. They'll be killed in the streets in broad daylight. They'll be kicked out. The world won't change. You won't make it change. You're a drop of water in an ocean of self-interest that rolls on in huge waves, with or without you. It's your brother who moves the world. He's the owner of the whole line, from sea to sea. He creates wealth. He draws water from stones. He makes the desert bloom. He makes bread from sand. He can change the world. Not you, you poor devil. Not you, you old fool with your diaper and your wheelchair, sitting on the very line where you were a brave young man long ago. A man of the left. A brave young man of the left. A brave young man of the left with bright eyes. You aren't your brother. You have no name. You scream. You howl again. You see. You hear. You scream. You do it because you discover that it gives you strength, lets you move your crippled arms a little. Who are you? The nocturnal chorus attacks and insults me, and I wish I knew who I was so I could answer them: I am not No One, I am Someone. I click my teeth for joy. Now I know. The label in my jacket. It says there who I am. That's where my name is. My wife always wrote my name on the label in my jackets. You go to those meetings, she'd say, and you take off your jacket and talk in your shirtsleeves. Afterward, no one knows whose jacket is whose. And you come home in shirtsleeves. You get a chill. But in fact you haven't got the money to buy another jacket. Let me write your name on the label on the inside pocket, next to your heart. My name. My heart. Her. I remember her. First I remembered my real brothers. I quickly forgot my phony brother. But I remembered them in fragments, in a half-light. I should remember her whole, as she was, loving and loyal. She was a beautiful woman, strong and good, like a rock, but she smelled like a bakery. She smelled of bread. She tasted like lettuce. She was strong and blessed and fresh. She protected me. She held me in her arms. She gave me courage. She would write my name on the jacket label next to my heart. "So you don't lose it, next to your heart." Now I raise my painful hand to that place, my empty hand, the good hand of my body split in half. I find nothing. There's no patch. No name. No heart. No label. They ripped it out, I scream to myself. They ripped out my name. They stripped me of my heart. They abandoned me without a name in the middle of the night at the line. I hate them. I must hate them. But I prefer to love her. She, too, is absent, like me. But if that's true, why don't we find each other? If we're both absent, we should meet. I hunger for her, for her company, her sex, her voice, her youth, and her old age. Why aren't you with me, Camelia? I stop. I look at the stars. I look at the night. I'm shocked. The world returns to me. The earth throbs and it summons me. I spoke the name of the woman I love. That was enough for the world to return to life. I spoke the first name in my solitude, a woman's name, a name I adore. I say and think all that and in my head the doors of a memory of water open. It's a response to the dryness that surrounds me. I smell dry earth. A stony place. Mesquite. Cactus. Thorns. Thirst. I smell an absence of rain, a distant storm. The only thing that rains is Camelia's name. Camelia. It rains on my head. It's a flower, a drop, gold. I caress that name with my eyes. I let it roll through my closed eyelids. I capture it between my lips. I savor it. I swallow it. Camelia. Her name. I bless it. And I curse it. Why weren't the others like her? Why were the others ungrateful, greedy, cruel? I detest Camelia's name because it opens the door to the names I don't want to remember. I feel shame when I think that. I can't reject Camelia's name. It's like murdering her and killing myself. Then I realize that the woman's name demands a sacrifice of me. It pulls me out of myself. Until the moment when I said the name Camelia, I'd been talking only of myself. I don't know my own name and don't need it. If I talk to myself I don't need a name. My name is for others. I talk to myself and don't need to name myself. Other people are other people. I am not "Julio," "Héctor," "Jorge," or "Carlos." My dialogue with myself is internal, integral, unbroken. The thinnest scalpel could not separate the two voices of the "I" that is the "I" speaking with myself. The others are the others. The rest. Superfluous. But I say "Camelia," and Camelia answers me. Now I'm not talking to myself. Now you're talking to me. And if you're talking to me, I have to talk to the others. I must name the rest. Now I have to name everything so as to be able to name her. She says, Name all of them so you can name me. I do name her: Camelia. I remember her: my wife. I have to remember them: my children. My resistance is enormous. It's monstrous. I don't want to give them their names. We'd rather be alone, Camelia and I. Why did we have them? Why did we have them baptized, confirmed; why did we praise them, kiss them, make sacrifices to bring them up? So that one day they'd say to me, Why weren't you like your brother, our uncle? Why did you have to be poor and wretched? Why did you wear yourself out fighting for lost causes? How can you expect us to respect you? Why did you have to be poor and wretched? *Pochos*, I called them, denaturalized Mexicans, worst of the worst. Don't be one of the enemies. They laughed at me. It's worse on the other side: Mexico's the enemy. On the Mexican side, there's more injustice, more corruption, more lies, more poverty. Be thankful we're gringos. That's what my son said to me. He's harder and more bitter. My daughter tried to be gentler. No matter how you look at it, Papa, from this side of the border or the other, there's injustice and you aren't going to fix it. And you can't make us copy you. Hardheaded old man. Old sucker. They're right in the gringo schools here when they say there's a sucker born every minute. We didn't put a gun to your head so you'd have us and bring us up. We don't owe you anything. You're a drag. If you were at least politically correct. You embarrass us. A Communist. A Mexican. An agitator. You gave us nothing. It's your obligation. Fathers are only good for giving. Instead you took things away from us. You forced us to justify ourselves, to deny you, to affirm everything you aren't so we could be ourselves. Be someone. Be from the other side. Don't get upset. Don't get that expression on your face. If you grow up on the border, you have to choose: this side or the other. We chose the North. We're not suckers like you. We adapted. Would you rather we wore ourselves out like you? You ruined our mother's life. But you're not going to ruin ours. Angry old man. Nasty old man. Have you forgotten your own violence? Your monstrous fury, your colossal rage? How you were gradually extinguished, disarmed in the mere presence of youth. If they're young, you forgive them everything. If they're young, you worship them. If they're young, they're always right. I feel surrounded by a world—North and South, both sides—that venerates the young. Before my eyes pass advertisements, images, offers, temptations, window displays, magazines, television—all promoting young people, seducing young people, prolonging youth, disdaining old age, discarding old people, to the point that age seems a crime, a sickness, a misery that cancels you out as a human being. I quickly raise a barrier against this avalanche of dazzling, blinding multicolored lights that split, spread out, scatter. I close my eyes. I duplicate the night. I people it with ghosts. Groping, I return to the earth. It is like my blind gaze. It is black. This time the dark part of the world we call earth receives me. It's full of another kind of light. There is an old man in the light. Barefoot. Wearing peasant clothes. But with a vest. On the vest a watch chain glitters. I approach him. I kneel. I kiss his hand. He strokes my head. He speaks. I listen attentively, with respect. He tells the oldest stories. He tells how everything began. He says there were two gods who created the world. One spoke, the other didn't. The one who didn't speak created all the mute things in the world. The one who spoke created men. We do not resemble the silent god. We cannot understand him. He is everything we aren't, says the old man, who strokes my head and is my father. We venerate him and know what he is only because he isn't what you and I are. God is only what we are not. I mean that, thanks to him, we only know what he is not. But the second god risks being like us. He gives us the power of speech. He gives us names. He dares to speak and listen. We can answer him. We don't venerate him as much, but we love him more. Name and speak, son—you, too, should speak and name things. Venerate the creator god, but speak with the redeemer god. Don't lock yourself inside yourself. Perfection is not solitude. Imperfection is community but also possible perfection. The old man who was my father gave me a bit of bitter peyote to chew and asked me to speak, name, take risks. Be like the god who gave us speech. Not like the god who left us mute. Mute as I am this instant, father, I try to respond. But my father is already gone, smiling, saying good-bye with one hand raised. He's gone far away. He's from a time that has nothing to do with mine. A time with no ambition to be different. A time of braziers and the *comal* for making tortillas. Time of smoke, of sudden dawns and watchful nights. Time of masks, doubles, spirits. Time of the Nahuatl language. Time when lives were one with the prickly pear and mesquite. How different from my own time of learning to read and write, of taking medicine, receiving the land, replacing *huizache* with pavement, looking at ourselves in shopwindows, buying newspapers, knowing who is president, immersing ourselves in the articles of the constitution. And how different from the time of my children, of refrigerators and television, days without nature, nights lit up, food untouched by human hands, envy of other people's property, desire to believe in something but failure to find anything, desire to know all but knowledge only of nothing, conviction we know it all, and alarm at what a bare, ignorant foot can know. They're right to be different. But I loved my father, I respected him and despite everything tried to find his redeeming, speaking, garrulous god. But now I find I'm like the mute god. As abandoned and solitary as he, with no name, no father. I kiss your hands again and again. I don't ever want to stop. I want to love. I want to venerate. I don't want to speak. I don't want to remember. And I understand that I've been left here—abandoned, anonymous—as a challenge to remember who I am. But if I don't know, how will anyone else know? My father asked me to do two things: remember and name. How will I speak if I can't? I was left mute. The attack left me speechless and paralyzed. I can barely move one hand, one arm. There we are: I don't speak, but I do remember. I try desperately to compensate for lack of speech with memory. Doesn't my father know what happened to me? How can he ask me to speak, name, communicate? The old idiot, can't he see that I'm a ruin, older than he was when he died? I bite my tongue. I'm a respectful man. I believe in respect for the elderly. Not like my children. Or is it a law of life to despise old people secretly like this? The old fogey, you heard them say. The mummy. Ready for the junk heap. Methuselah. Useless fossil, a burden, he's not leaving us a thing, he makes us earn a living at hard labor, and on top of that we've got to go on supporting him. Who has the time or patience to bathe him, dress him, undress him, put him to bed, wake him up, sit him down in front of the TV all day so just by chance he's amused and learns something, so he looks at something else instead of staring at us as if we were the TV set—or something alive and nearby but unbearable? Why wasn't he like his brother, our uncle? Twenty years younger, his brother understood everything our father couldn't fathom or scorned. You don't share poverty. First, you have to create wealth. But wealth trickles down little by little in droplets. That's a fact. Be patient. But equality is a dream. There'll always be dumb people and smart people. There'll always be the strong and the weak. Who eats whom? Wealth honestly come by doesn't have to be distributed among the lazy. Those who are poor because they want to be. There is no ruling class. There are superior individuals. Now I secretly laugh at my children. When they went to my younger brother for help, he told them the same thing they tell me and everyone else. I made my money the hard way. There's no reason I should support a family of lazy fools.

Chips off the old block. You're the children my brother deserved. You want to live on charity. For your own good, I tell you to stand on your own two feet. Don't expect anything from me. From sea to shining sea. From the Pacific to the Gulf. From Tijuana to Matamoros. A dead part of my brain returns the way my old father wanted to return, laden with names. All along the frontier I hear the name of my powerful brother. But his real name is Contracts. His name is Contraband. His name is Stock Market. Highways. Assembly plants. Whorehouses. Bars. Newspapers. Television. Drug Money. And an unfair fight with a poor brother. A struggle between brothers for the destiny of our brothers. Brothers Anonymous. What's my name? What's my brother's name? I can't answer as long as I don't know the name of each and every one of my anonymous brothers. Why do they cross the border? We have different rationales in each instance, he and I. He: Because of Mexico's impoverishing statist policies. I: Because the gringo market lures these people. He: We have to create jobs in Mexico. I: We have to pay better wages in Mexico. He: The gringos have the right to defend their borders. I: You can't talk about free markets and then close the border to workers who respond to demand. He: They're criminals. I: They're workers. He: They come to a foreign country, they should show some respect for it. I: They're returning to their own land; we were here first. They aren't criminals. They're workers. Listen, Pancho, I want you to work for me. Come over here, I need you. Listen, Pancho, I don't need you anymore. Get out. I've just turned you in to Immigration. I never signed a contract with you. When I need you I make a contract with you, Pancho; when I don't I turn you in, Pancho. I beat you up. I hunt you down like a rabbit. I cover you with paint so everyone will know you're illegal. My boys are going to set

packs of white cannibals out to kill you, you undocumented
Mexican Salvadoran Guatemalan. No, I scream, no, you
can't do that and talk about justice. That's what I fought for
all my life. Against my brother. For my brothers. And against
us, my children exclaimed. Against our well-being, our assimilation into progress, into opportunity, into the North.
Against our own uncle, who could not protect us. You
wouldn't allow it. You condemned yourself and you condemned us. What do we have to thank you for? Our poor
mother was a saint. She put up with everything you did. We
have no reason to. You gave us nothing but bitterness. We'll
pay you back in kind. Cripple. Paralytic. Whom will you live
with? Whom are you going to pester and drive to despair
now? Who's going to get you up, put you to bed, clean you,
dress you, undress you, feed you spoonful by spoonful, take
you out in your wheelchair, sit you in the sun so you don't
shrivel up? Who's going to wipe the snot off your nose,
brush your teeth, smell your gases, cut your nails, wipe your
ass, clean the wax out of your ears, shave you, comb your
hair, put deodorant on you, fasten your bib when you eat,
make sure the drool doesn't drip down your chin, who?
Who's got the time, will, and money to help you? Me, your
son who has to cross the border every day at dawn to work
at Woolworth's? Me, your daughter who got a job as a fore-
lady in an assembly plant on this side? Your grandson who
doesn't even remember you, who makes burritos in a Mexican restaurant on the gringo side? Your granddaughter who
also works in the assembly plant? Do you think they don't
see your brother in the newspapers, saying, doing, traveling,
with rich men, beautiful babes? Our children, your grandchildren, who barely made it through high school on the
American side and only want to enjoy the music, clothes,
cars, universal envy you left them out of ineptitude, out of

generosity toward everyone but your own? Those sentences echo in my head. They resound like loose stones in a swift and swirling river. I wish the river would grow calm as it enters the sea. Instead, it smashes against the sandbar of its own waste. It accumulates sediment, garbage, mud. Mud you are and to mud you will return. Mud. Muddy. My muddy brother Leonardo. Leonardo Muddy. My name. My own. I don't have it. It was torn from me. I can't be admitted to a hospital. Or even a home. My name is on the blacklists. Here and there. I've been stripped of my rights. Agitator. Communist. Entry denied. Not even charity for this disturber of the peace. Let his own people take care of him. My labels were ripped out. A diaper was pinned on me. I was seated in this chair. I was abandoned at the line. The line of oblivion. The place where I don't know my name. The place where I am but am not. The vague intermediate zone between my life and my death. We're sorry, we can't let him in here. Or here. You understand. Charges were brought against him. He's not trustworthy. He's a marked man. He's got the worst political history. He's not loyal. Here or there. He's a red. Let the people take care of him. Or the Russians. Don't let him compromise our workers. Here or there. Confederation of Mexican Workers. American Federation of Labor. Freedom, yes. Communism, *no*. Democracy, well, let's see. They would have killed me. And it would have been a good thing. Cowards. They've abandoned me to chance. To the elements. To anonymity. I heard them: If we leave him without a name, he'll be taken in, someone will feel sorry for him. His very name is cursed. And he spatters it on the rest of us. He's our yellow star. The cross of our calvary. We're doing him a favor. If nobody knows who he is, they'll feel compassion for him. They'll take him in. They'll give him the care we neither can nor want to give him. Let someone else deal with him. Hypocrites. Sons of bitches. No, not that. They're Camelia's children. She was a saint. But you can be the child of a saint and still be a bastard. The children of wretchedness, that's who they are. What can be going through their heads that they'd do this to an old man, their father? What's wrong with the world? What has broken? Nothing, I tell myself. Everything's the same. Ingratitude and rage aren't something new. There are many kinds of abandonment. There are many orphans. Young and old. Children and even the dead. I wish I could ask Camelia if she remembers. What did we do to our children that they should treat me this way? There must be something I've forgotten. Something not even they recall. Something so much a part of our blood that neither they nor I know what it is. A fear perhaps. Perhaps neither the hospital nor the home nor the union would slam the door in my face. Perhaps it's just my children's idea of fun. They find excuses. They want to do what they've done. It gives them satisfaction. It makes them laugh, they get even, they feel the itch of the worst of all evils. Gratuitous evil—because it has no price, it makes a little circus of pleasure in the gut. I'm one more orphan. The orphan of evil. The orphan of my own children, who may well merely be lovers of comfort rather than perverse. Indifferent but not exactly cruel. I can no longer do anything. Even speak. Even move. I can barely see. But the sun's coming up. The night was more generous than the day. It allowed itself to be watched. The dawn blinds me. I think about orphans. Young and old. Children and even the dead. I hear them. Their sounds reach me. The noise of feet. Some bare. Others strong, stamping the heels of their boots. Others scrape their toenails. Others are silenced by rubber soles. Others mingle with the earth. The sound of a huarache. A sound without huaraches. Chihuahua, how many Apaches, how many Indians, without huaraches. Never take a step without huaraches, my father would say. I hear the footsteps and I'm afraid. I'm going to pray again, even if I pee. Blessed be the soul and the Lord who gives it to us. Blessed be the day and the Lord who gives it to us. Sunrise. The run rises with silhouettes I watch from my chair. Posts and cables. Barbed-wire fences. Pavements. Dung heaps. Tin roofs. Cardboard houses perched on the hillsides. Television antennas scratching the ravines. Garbagemen. Infinite numbers of garbage-men. Plantations of garbage. Dogs. Don't let them come near me. And the sound of feet. Swift. Crossing the border. Abandoning the earth. Seeking the world. Earth and world, always. We have no other home. And I sit here immobile, abandoned at the line of oblivion. Which country do I belong to? Which memory? Which blood? I hear the footsteps around me. Finally I imagine everyone looking at me and, as they look, inventing me. I can no longer do anything. I depend on them, the ones who run from one border to the next. The ones I defended all my life. Successfully. Unsuccessfully. Both. They must look at me now to create me with their stares. If they stop staring, I'll become invisible. I have nothing left but them. But they, too, tell me that I do not look at them, because I don't name them. But I already told them. I can't know the names of the millions of women and men. They respond as they pass, fleeting, swift: Say the name of the last one. Call the last woman lovingly. That will be the name of everyone—a single man, a single woman, they are all men and all women. The day is reborn. Will it bring my own name among its promises? I've been talking to myself all night. Is this the perfect state of truth, of comprehension? The solitary man who speaks only to himself? The night comforted me by making me think so. By day I plead for someone to come say something to me. Anything. Help me. Insult me, as long as he named me. Mud name. Mud soul. Muddy. Camelia, my wife. Leonardo, my brother. I've forgotten the names of my children and grandchildren. I don't know the name of the last man who names all men. I don't know the name of the last woman who loves in the name of all women. Still, I do know that in this final name of the final man and in this final tenderness of the final woman lies the secret of all things. It isn't the final name. It isn't the final man. It isn't the last woman and her warmth. It's only the last being who crosses the frontier after the one who went before him but before the one who follows. The sun comes up and I look at the movement on the frontier. Everyone crosses the line where I am stopped. They run, some in fear, others in joy. But they don't begin or end. Their bodies follow or precede. Their words as well. Confused. Unintelligible. Is that what they want to tell me? That there is no beginning, no end? Is that what they're saying in not looking at me or speaking to me or paying any attention to me: Don't worry? Nothing begins, nothing ends. Is that what they're telling me? We recognize you in not acknowledging you, not noticing you, not addressing you? Do you feel exceptional, seated there, paralyzed and mute, with no labels to identify you, with a diaper and an open fly? You're our equal. We'll make you part of us. Another one like us. Our interminable origin. Our interminable destiny. Are these the words of freedom? And what freedom is that? Will they thank me for it? Will they recognize that I helped them achieve it? What freedom is that? Is it the freedom to fight for freedom? Even if it's never attained? Even if it fails? Is that the lesson of these men and women who are running, taking advantage of the first light to cross the line of oblivion? What do they forget? What do they remember? What new mixture of oblivion and remembrance awaits them on

the other side? I am between earth and world. To which did
I belong more when I was alive? To which do I belong more
now that I am dead? My life. My struggle. My conviction.
My wife. My children. My brother. My brothers and sisters
who cross the line even if they're killed or humiliated. Give
a name to the person who wanted to give them a name. Give
a word to the person who spoke in their defense. Don't abandon me as well. Don't avoid me. I'm still inevitable. Despite
everything. In that I resemble death. I am inevitable. In that
I'm also like life. I'm possible only because I'm going to die.
It would be impossible if I were mortal. My death will be
the guarantee of my life, its horizon, its possibility. Death is
already my country. What country? What memory? What
blood? The dark earth and the world that dawns commingle
in my soul to formulate these questions, mix them, solder
them to my most intimate being. To what I am, to what my
parents were or what my children will be. The feet run,
crossing the line. There is no reason to fear their sound.
What do they take, what do they bring? I don't know.
What's important is that they take and bring. That they mix.
Change. That the world doesn't stop moving. An old man,
immobile, mute, tells them so. But he's not blind. Let them
mix. Let them change. That's what I fought for. The right
to change. The glory of knowing we're alive, intelligent, energetic, givers and receivers, human containers of languages,
bloods, memories, songs, forgotten things, things avoidable
and not, of fatal angers, of hopes reborn, of injustices to be
corrected, work to be compensated, dignity to be respected,
of dark earth here and there, that world created by us and
by no one else—here or there? I don't want to hate. But I
do want to fight. Even if I'm immobile, in a mute chair,
without any identification. I want to be. My God, I want to
Be. Who will I be? Like a stream their names enter my gaze,

my eyes, my tongue, crossing all the borders of the world, breaking the crystal that separates them. They come from the sun and the moon, from the night and the day. With difficulty I raise my face to look at the face of the sun. What falls on my forehead is a drop. And then another. Harder and harder. A downpour. A harsh rain, here where it never rains. The feet hurry. The voices grow louder. The day I expected to be bright becomes cloudy. The men and women run, cover their heads with newspapers, shawls, sweaters, jackets. The rain drums on the tin roofs. The rain swells the mountains of garbage. The rain pours down the ravines, washing them clean, runs along the canyons, rinsing them, pulling along whatever it finds—a tire, a porch, a pot, a cellophane wrapper, an old sock, a rush of mudslide, a cardboard house, a television antenna. The world seems dragged along by the water, flooded, companionless, divorced from the earth . . . I think we're going to drown. I think it's the second deluge. The incessant rain washes away the line where I'm stopped. The swift feet leave tracks on the pavement as if it were sand. They approach. I hear the howling of the sirens. I hear the loud voices, shocked, beneath the rain. The swift wet footsteps. The hands that search me. The lights of the ambulances. Questioning, uncertain, spinning, wandering, groping, seeking . . . An old man, they say. An immobile old man. An old man who doesn't speak. An old man with an open fly. An old man with a urine-soaked diaper. An old man with very old, very wet clothes. An old man with sturdy shoes, the kind that leave a mark on the pavement as if it were a beach. An old man with clothing whose labels have been torn off. An old man without a wallet. An old man with no identification: no passport, no credit cards, no voter registration card, no social security card, no calendar for the new year, no green card to cross frontiers.

An old man with no plastic. An old man with a stiff neck. An old man with clear eyes open to the heavens, eyes washed by the rain. An old man with his ears open, his earlobes dripping rain. An abandoned old man. Who could have done this? Doesn't he have children, relatives? Something's funny here. Where do we take him? He's going to get pneumonia. Put him in the ambulance quickly. He's old. Let's see if we can find out who he is. Who the miserable bastards can be. An old man. A nice old man. An old man who's fighting against death. An old man by the name of Emiliano Barroso. What a pity I'll never be able to say it. How wonderful that I finally remembered it. It's me.

5

MALINTZIN OF THE MAQUILAS

For Enrique Cortázar, Pedro Garay, and Carlos Salas-Porras

Her parents gave Marina that name because of their de-sire to see the ocean. When she was baptized, they said, maybe this one will get a chance to see the ocean. In the clump of shacks in the northern desert, the young would get together with their elders, and the elders would tell how, when they were young, they wondered what the ocean was like. None of us had ever seen the ocean.

Now, as the frozen January sun rises, Marina sees only the thin waters of the Río Grande, and the sun feels that everything's so cold it would like to slip back down between the dun sheets of the desert from which it is beginning to emerge.

It's five o'clock and she has to be at the factory by seven. She's late. What made her late was making love with Rolando last night, going with him to El Paso, Texas, on the other side of the river, and returning late, alone, shivering as she crossed the international bridge to her one-room house with lavatory in Colonia Bellavista, Ciudad Juárez.

Rolando had stayed flat on his back in bed, one arm folded behind his head, the other flattening a cellular phone to his ear. He looked at Marina with weary satisfaction, and she didn't ask him to take her home. She could see how comfortable he was, so boyish, all cuddled up, and also so open, so moist and warm. Above all, she saw him ready to start working, making calls on his cellular phone since very early—the early bird catches the worm, especially if the bird's a Mexican making deals on both sides of the border.

She glanced at herself in the mirror before leaving. She was a sleepy beauty, with the thick eyelashes of a young girl. Sighing, she put on her blue down jacket, which looked bad with her miniskirt because it hung to her knees while the skirt just reached her thighs. She stuffed her work sneakers into her bag and slung it over her shoulder. Unlike the gringas, who walked to work in Keds and put on their high heels in the office, Marina always wore pointy high heels to work even if they sank into the mud from time to time. Marina wouldn't sacrifice her elegant shoes for anything: no one would ever see her in worn-out shoes looking like some Apache.

She caught the first bus on Cadmio Street, and, as she did every other morning, she tried to look beyond the dirt-colored neighborhood, the shacks that looked as though they'd popped up out of the ground. Every day, without fail, she tried to look at the vast horizon. The sky and the sun seemed her protectors; they were the beauty of the world, they belonged to everyone and cost nothing. How could ordinary people make something as beautiful as that? Everything else was ugly by comparison. The sun, the sky . . . and—so they said—the sea!

She always ended up looking toward the gullies that tumbled down toward the river, as if her eyes were pulled by the law of gravity, as if even within her soul all things were always falling down. Even at this early hour the Juárez gullies looked like anthills. Activity in the poorest neighborhoods began early, as swarms of people poured out of the shacks down by the edge of the narrow river, trying to cross. She turned away, uncertain if what she saw annoyed her, embarrassed her, aroused her sympathy, or made her feel like imitating those crossing to the other side.

Better she fix her eyes on a solitary cypress tree until she couldn't see it anymore.

Instead of the cypress, Marina saw only concrete, wall upon wall of concrete, a long avenue boxed in by concrete. The bus stopped at a field where some boys in shorts were playing soccer to keep warm, and then, shivering, it crossed the vacant lot to the next stop.

She sat down next to her friend Dinorah, who was wearing a red sweater, blue jeans, and loafers. Marina held on tight to her bag but crossed her legs so Dinorah and the other passengers could see her classy high heels with a chain instead of a leather strap across the ankle.

They made their usual small talk: How's the little one, who'd you leave him with? At first, Marina's questions irritated Dinorah and she would pretend to be distracted—looking for a piece of chewing gum in her bag or fixing her mop of short orange-colored curls. Then she realized she'd be running into Marina on the bus every day of her life and she would quickly answer, My neighbor's going to take him to a day-care center.

"There's so few of them," Marina would say.

"Of what?"

"Day-care centers."

"Around here, sister, there's not enough of anything for anything."

She wasn't about to tell Dinorah to get married, because the one time she did, Dinorah had responded angrily, Why don't you go ahead and do it first? Set an example, Miss Know-It-All. Marina wasn't about to point out that, though neither of them was married, she didn't have a child—that was the difference. Didn't the kid need a father?

"What for? Around here, men don't work. You want me to support two instead of just one?"

Marina told her that with a man at home she'd be able to defend herself better against the pests at the factory, who were always after her because they saw that she was defenseless, that no one stood up for her. Marina's comment infuriated Dinorah, and she told Marina she was sick and tired of her, God may have thrown them together on the same bus, but if Marina went on giving advice no one asked for, she'd quit talking to her. Marina should stop being such a hypocrite.

"I've got Rolando," said Marina, and Dinorah almost died laughing: All the girls have Rolando, and Rolando has all the girls. Who do you think you are, you idiot? Marina began to sob, though the tears didn't roll down her cheeks but instead welled up in her eyelashes, and Dinorah felt bad. She pulled a tissue from her pocket, hugged Marina, and wiped her eyes.

"You don't need to worry about me, honey," said Dinorah. "I know how to protect myself from the boys in the factory. And if someone tells me I've got to fuck him to get a promotion, I'll just change factories. Anyway, nobody moves up around here. We just go sideways, like crabs."

Marina asked Dinorah if she changed jobs a lot. Marina's job was her first, but she'd heard that when the girls got fed up with one place they moved on to another. Dinorah told her that after you've done the same work for nine months your sides start to hurt and your back won't let you sleep.

They had to get off to change buses.

"You're late too."

"I guess it's for the same reason you are," Dinorah said with a smile. They walked off laughing, arms around each other's waist.

The plaza, crowded with little shops and all kinds of stalls, was already bustling. Everyone was exhaling winter mist, and vendors were showing off their merchandise or hanging up their signs: Hurry, hurry, get your beans from Jean. The two women stopped to buy corn, delicious ears of it dripping melted butter and still steaming. They giggled at an advertisement: Use Macho Man for Sexual Deficiency. Dinorah asked Marina if she'd ever met a man with sexual deficiency. Marina said no, but that didn't matter as much as choosing the right man. The right man? Well, the one you really like. Dinorah said that the men with sexual deficiencies were almost always the braggarts, the ones who bothered them and tried to take advantage of them in the factories.

"Rolando's not like that. He's very macho."

"So you told me. And what else does he have?"

"A cellular phone."

"Wow." Dinorah rolled her eyes mockingly but said nothing more because the bus arrived and they got on to make the last leg of the trip to the assembly plant. A very thin but good-looking young woman, with an aquiline beauty unusual in those parts, came running up to catch the bus. She was in a Carmelite habit and sandals. As she took the seat in front of them, Dinorah asked if her little feet

weren't cold like that in winter, without stockings or anything. She blew her nose and said it was a vow that only
made sense in the frost, not in the summer—she used the
English word.

"Do you two know each other?" asked Dinorah.

"Only by sight," said Marina.

"This is Rosa Lupe. You can't recognize her when she's
in a saintly mood. But believe me, she's normally very different. Why'd you get involved with this vow business?"

"Because of my *famullo*."

She told them she'd been working in the plants for four
years but her husband—her *famullo*—still hadn't found
work. The children were the reason: who would take care
of them? Rosa Lupe looked at Dinorah, although not with
obvious malice. The *famullo* stayed home with the kids, at
least until they were grown.

"You support him?" asked Dinorah, to get back at Rosa
Lupe for her remark.

"Just ask around at the factory. Half the women working
there are the breadwinners in their families. We're what they
call heads of households. But I have a *famullo*. At least I'm
not a single mother."

To avoid a fight, Marina commented that they were coming into the nice area, and without saying another word the
three of them looked at the rows of cypresses lining both
sides of the road. They were waiting for the incredibly beautiful vision that never failed to dazzle them though they'd
seen it countless times. The television assembly plant, a mirage of glass and shining steel, like a bubble of crystalline
air. It was almost like a fantasy to work there, surrounded
by purity, by brilliance, in a factory so clean and modern,
what the managers called an industrial park.

It was one of the plants that allowed the gringos to assemble toys, textiles, motors, furniture, computers, and television sets from parts made in the United States, put together in Mexico at a tenth the labor cost, and sent back across the border to the U.S. market with a value-added tax. About such things the women knew little. Ciudad Juárez was simply the place where the jobs called them, jobs that did not exist in the desert and mountain villages, jobs that were impossible to find in Oaxaca or Chiapas or in the capital itself. Those jobs were here, and even if the salary was a tenth what it was in the United States, it was ten times more than the nothing paid everywhere else in Mexico.

At least that was what Candelaria wore herself out telling them. A woman of thirty, Candelaria was more square than fat, the same size on all four sides. She always wore traditional peasant clothing, though it was difficult to tell from which region of Mexico, as the totally sincere, serious, but smiling Candelaria mixed a little bit of everything: pigtails tied with Huichol wool, Yucatan-style smocks, Texan skirts, Tzotzil belts, huaraches with Goodrich tire soles available at any market. And since she was the lover of an antigovernment union leader, she knew what she was talking about. It was a miracle she hadn't been blackballed from all the assembly plants. But Candelaria always managed to save her skin: she was a wizard at changing jobs. Every six months she went to another factory, and each time, her boss breathed a sigh of relief because the agitator was leaving, and as far as the owners were concerned, frequent job changes meant little or no change in political consciousness: there wasn't enough time to stir anyone up. Candelaria would just shake her comical pigtails and go on raising consciousness in one place after another, every six months.

She had been working in the plants for fifteen of her thirty years and didn't want to ruin her health. She'd already

worked in a paint factory and the solvents had made her
sick—imagine, she said at the time, spending nine months
filling paint cans just to end up painted inside. That's when
she met Beltrán Herrera, a mature man—which is why Candelaria liked him—mature but with tender eyes and vigorous
hands; dark-skinned, he had graying hair and wore a moustache and glasses.

Candelaria, Bernal said to her, they wouldn't give you
water around here if you were dying of thirst. Whatever you
need you've got to earn with the sweat of your brow. They
talk about costs and profits, sure, but there's no insurance
for work-related accidents, no medical treatment, no pension, no compensation for marriage, maternity, or death.
They're doing us a big favor giving us work, thank you very
much, so keep your mouth shut. Say so much as three little
words, my dear Candelaria, "three little words," as the old
song goes, strike by coalition, strike by coalition, strike by
coalition—say it three times like a litany, Candy sweetest,
and you'll see how they turn pale, promise you raises and
bonuses, respect your opinions, urge you to switch factories.
Do it, darling. I'd rather you switched than died.

"This place is so beautiful," sighed Marina, taking care
not to let her stiletto heels puncture the green lawn marked
with the double warning NO PISE EL PASTO/KEEP OFF THE
GRASS.

"It looks like Disneyland," said Dinorah, half joking, half
serious.

"Sure, but it's full of ogres who eat innocent princesses
like you," said Candelaria with a sarcastic smile, fully aware
that her irony was lost on these three. She loved them anyway.

Everyone but Rosa Lupe put on a regulation blue smock,
and they all took their places opposite the skeletons of tele-

vision sets, each ready to do her job in order—Candelaria the chassis, Dinorah the soldering, Marina the newcomer learning to repair weldings—and Rosa Lupe checked for defects like loose wires, cracked washers and, as she worked, Rosa Lupe spoke to Candelaria. Listen, don't you think it's about time to stop treating us like jerks? And don't go into your Saint Candelaria act, okay? You're always preaching to us, always treating us like shit. Candelaria opened her eyes wide. Me? Dinorah, listen, you tell me if there's anyone more screwed than I am: I came here alone from the village, I brought my kids, then my brothers and sisters, then my dad. How's that for a load to carry? Think I make enough?

"Your union boss doesn't chip in, Candelaria?"

The square woman gave Dinorah an electric shock, a trick she knew how to do. Dinorah squealed and called the fat woman a bastard, but Candelaria just laughed and said that every one of them had a whole soap opera to tell, so maybe they should just try to get along with each other, okay? To spend their time together and not die of boredom, okay?

"Why'd you bring your dad?"

"For the memories," said Candelaria.

"Old people get in the way," said Dinorah softly.

All these women came from other places. That's why they entertained one another with stories about their backgrounds, about their families, the things that made them all different. And yet at times they were astonished at how alike they were in many things—families, villages, relatives. All of them felt torn inside. Was it better to leave all that behind and set about making a new life here on the border? Or should they feed their souls with memories, hum along with

José Alfredo Jiménez, feel the sadness of the past, agree that indifference is the death of the soul?

Sometimes they looked at one another without saying a word, all four friends, comrades—Candelaria, the one who'd worked the longest in the plants, Rosa Lupe and Dinorah, who'd come at the same time, Marina, greenest of the lot— understanding that they didn't have to use words to say these things, that they all needed love, not memories, but that even so it was impossible to separate memory from tenderness. Damned if you do, damned if you don't.

The one best at keeping track of the stories was Candelaria, and her conclusion was that all the women came from somewhere else, that none of them was from the border. She liked to ask them where they were from, but it was hard for them to talk except with Candelaria, whom they trusted and with whom they dared to link love and memory. Candelaria wanted to keep them both alive, feeling it was important they not condemn themselves to oblivion or indifference, the death of the soul. She hummed the tunes of the unforgettable José Alfredo, as the radio announcers never failed to call him.

"From the Venustiano Carranza commune."

"From deep in the heart of Chihuahua."

"No, not from the country. From a city smaller than Juárez."

"Well, from Zacatecas."

"From La Laguna."

"My dad took charge of the whole move," said Rosa Lupe, the woman with the aquiline profile who dressed like a Carmelite. "He said there were too many of us for the communal land. The land we could farm was getting smaller and smaller and drier and drier the more we divided it up among all my brothers. I was always active, very active. At the commune they put me in charge of keeping the streets clean and the walls painted white. I liked to make confetti for the fiestas, bring in the bands, organize the children's choruses. Dad said I was too clever to stay in the country. He brought me to the border himself when I was fifteen. My mother stayed behind with my little brothers and sisters. My father didn't beat around the bush. He told me that I was going to make ten times more money in a month than the whole family would make in a year on the commune. That I was very active. That it wasn't going to break me down. As long as he stayed here, I accepted things. He was like an extension of my life in the village. I didn't tell him I missed the land, my mother, my little brothers and sisters, the religious festivals, especially Candlemas—like Candelaria!—when we dress up the Christ Child, decorate the Holy Cross, and have these terrific scary fireworks. And Ash Wednesday, when the whole village wore charcoal crosses on their foreheads, Holy Week, when the Jews with their white beards and long noses and black overcoats come out to play tricks on Christians. All of it—pilgrimages, the Wise Men—I missed it all. Here I look up the dates on the calendar, I have to make an effort to remember them, but back there I didn't. The fiestas came along without having to be remembered, see? But my father set me up here in Juárez in a one-room house and told me, 'Work hard and find a man. You're the cleverest one in the family.' Then he left."

"I don't know what's better," Candelaria said immediately. "I've already told you, I'm loaded down with responsibilities. When I came to the border, I brought my kids. Then my brothers and sisters came. Finally my parents got up enough nerve. That's a big strain with a salary like mine.

Watch those jokes, Dinorah, damn you. What our men give us we deserve. What my father gives me is remembrance. As long as my father is in the house, I'll never forget. It's beautiful having things to remember."

"That's not true," said Dinorah. "Memories just hurt."

"But it's a good hurt," answered Candelaria.

"Well, I've only seen the bad hurt," Dinorah retorted.

"That's because you don't have anything to compare it with. You don't give yourself the chance to save up your good memories of the past."

"Piggy banks are for pigs," said Dinorah, incensed.

Rosa Lupe was about to say something when a supervisor came over, an extremely tall woman in her forties with eyes like marbles and lips thin and long as stringbeans. She began to scold the beautiful Carmelite with the aquiline profile. Rosa Lupe was breaking the rules—who did she think she was coming to the factory dressed like a miracle worker? Didn't she know everyone had to wear the regulation smock for hygiene and safety reasons?

"But I've made a vow, ma'am," said Rosa Lupe in a dignified tone.

"Around here there's no vow bigger than mine," said the supervisor. "Come on, take off that getup and put on your smock."

"Okay. I'll change in the bathroom."

"No, dear lady, you aren't going to hold up production with your saintly act. You can change right here."

"But I don't have anything on underneath."

"Let's see," said the supervisor. She grabbed Rosa Lupe by the shoulders and pulled the habit down to her waist. There were Rosa Lupe's splendid breasts. The woman with eyes like marbles, unable to contain herself, seized them and fastened her stringbean lips on the beautiful Carmelite's stiffened nipples. Rosa Lupe was so shocked she froze, but Candelaria grasped the supervisor by her permanent, cursing her and pulling her off, while Dinorah gave the pig a kick in the ass and Marina ran over to cover Rosa Lupe with her hands, feeling how hard her friend's heart was pounding, how her own nipples had stiffened involuntarily.

Another supervisor came over to separate the women, settle things down, and laugh at his colleague. Don't start taking my girlfriends away from me, Esmeralda, he said to the disheveled supervisor who was as inflamed as a fried tomato, Leave these cuties to me and go find yourself a man.

"Don't make fun of me, Herminio, you'll be sorry," said the wretched Esmeralda, retreating with one hand on her forehead and the other on her belly.

"Don't try poaching on my territory."

"Going to report me?"

"No, I'm just going to screw you up."

"Okay, girls, clear out," said Herminio the supervisor, smiling. He was hairless as a sugar cube and exactly the same color. "I'm moving up your break. Go on, go have a soda and remember what a nice guy I am."

"Going to make us pay for the favor?" asked Dinorah.

"You all come around on your own." Herminio smiled lasciviously now.

They bought some Pepsis and sat for a while opposite the factory's beautiful lawn—KEEP OFF THE GRASS—waiting for Rosa Lupe, who reappeared with Herminio. The supervisor looked very satisfied. The worker was wearing her blue smock.

"He looks like the cat who ate the canary," said Candelaria when Herminio was gone.

"I let him watch me change. I'd just as soon you knew. I did it to thank him. I'd rather be the one who calls the shots. He promised he wouldn't bother any of us, that he'd protect us from that bitch Esmeralda."

"Well, it didn't take much to—" Dinorah started to say, but Candelaria shut her up with a glance. The others lowered their eyes, never imagining that from the high administrative tower sheathed in opaque glass those inside could see them without themselves being seen. The Mexican owner of the business, Don Leonardo Barroso, was observing them as he recited for the benefit of his U.S. investors the line about their being blessed among women because the assembly plants employed eight of them for every man. The plants liberated women from farming, prostitution, even from machismo itself—Don Leonardo smiled broadly—because working women soon became the breadwinners in the family. Female heads of households acquired a dignity and strength that set them free, made them independent, made them modern women. And that, too, was democracy—didn't his partners from Texas agree?

Besides—Don Leonardo was used to giving these periodic pep talks to calm the Yankees and soothe their consciences— these women, like the ones you see down there sitting together by the grass drinking sodas, were becoming part of a dynamic economic growth instead of living a depressed life in the agrarian stagnation of Mexico. In 1965, under Gustavo Díaz Ordaz, there were no plants on the border, zero. Then in 1972, under President Echeverría, there were 10,000; in 1982, under López Portillo, 35,000; in 1988, under De la Madrid, 120,000; and now, in 1994, under Salinas, 135,000. And the plants generated 200,000 jobs in related fields.

"The progress of the nation can be measured by the progress of the assembly plants," exclaimed a satisfied Mr. Barroso.

"There must be some problems," said a Yankee drier than a corncob pipe. "There are always problems, Mr. Barroso."

"Call me Len, Mr. Murchinson."

"And I'm Ted."

"Labor problems? Unions aren't allowed."

"Problems with worker loyalty, Len. I've always tried to maintain the loyalty of my workers. Here the women last six or seven months and then move to another factory."

"Sure, they all want to work with the Europeans because they treat them better. They fire or punish abusive supervisors, feed them fancy lunches, and God knows what else. Maybe they even send them on vacation to see the tulips in Holland . . . You do that and earnings will plummet, Ted."

"We don't do things that way in Michigan. The workers leave, the cost for services—water, housing—go up. Maybe those Dutch have the right idea."

"We all change jobs," chimed in Barroso merrily. "Even you. If we enforce work-safety rules, they move on. If we're strict about applying the Federal Labor Law, they move on. If there's a boom in the defense industry, they move on. You talk to me about job rotation? That's the law of labor. If the Europeans prefer quality of life to profits, that's their decision. Let the European Community subsidize them."

"You still haven't answered my question, Len. What about the loyalty factor?"

"Anyone who wants to hold onto a loyal labor force should do what I do. I offer bonuses to workers so they'll stay. But the demand for labor is huge, the girls get bored, they don't move up, so they move sideways, and that way they fool themselves into thinking they're better off for changing. That does generate some costs, Ted, you're right, but it avoids other costs. Nothing's perfect. The plant isn't a zero-sum situation. It's a sum-sum one. We all end up making money."

They laughed a little, and a man with graying long hair pulled back in a ponytail came in to serve coffee.

"No sugar for me, Villarreal," said Don Leonardo to the servant.

"Look here, Ted," Barroso went on. "You're new at this game, but your partners in the States must have told you what the real business is here."

"Running a national business that sells to one guaranteed buyer doesn't seem like a bad idea to me. We don't have that in the States."

Barroso asked Murchinson to look outside, beyond the little group of workers drinking Pepsis, to look at the horizon. Yankee businessmen have always been men of vision, he said, not provincial chile counters the way they are in Mexico. It's a huge horizon you see from here, right? Texas is the size of France; Mexico, which looks so small next to the U.S. of A., is six times larger than Spain—all that space, all that horizon, what inspiration! Barroso almost sighed.

"Ted, the real business here isn't the plants. It's land speculation. The location of the plants. The subdivisions. The industrial park. Did you see my house over in Campazas? People laugh at it. They call it Disneyland. But I'm the one laughing. I bought all those lots for five centavos per square meter. Now they're worth a thousand dollars per square meter. That's where the money is. I'm giving you good advice. Take advantage of it."

"I'm all ears, Len."

"The girls have to travel for more than an hour, on two

buses, to get here. What we should do is set up another center due west of here. Which means we should be buying land in Bellavista. It's a dump. Shitty shacks. In five years, it'll be worth a thousand times more."

Ted Murchinson was in favor of supplying money, with Leonardo Barroso as the front man—the Mexican constitution prohibits gringos from owning property on the border. There was talk about trusts, stocks, and percentages while Villarreal served the coffee, watered-down the way the gringos like it.

"What my husband wants is for me to leave the plant and work with him in a business. That way we'd see each other more and take turns with the kid. It's the only brave idea he's ever suggested to me, but I know that deep down he's just as big a coward as I am. The plant is a sure thing, but as long as I work here, he's tied to the house."

Something Rosa Lupe said upset Dinorah terribly, to the point that she became violently sick and asked to go to the bathroom. Wanting to avoid any new conflict, the supervisor, Esmeralda, did not object. Sometimes she made vulgar comments when the women asked.

"What's with her?" said Candelaria. Instantly she was sorry she'd opened her mouth. It was an unwritten law among them not to probe inside one another. What was going on outside could be seen and therefore discussed, especially in a joking spirit. But the soul, what songs called the soul . . .

Candelaria sang, and Marina and Rosa Lupe joined in:

Your ways drove me mad,
You're so selfish, so solitary,
A jewel in the night,
While I'm so ordinary . . .

They laughed, then turned sad, and Marina thought about
Rolando, wondering what he was up to in the streets of Juárez
and El Paso, a man with one foot on that side and the other on
this, a man connected to both places by his cellular phone.

"Don't call me at my place at night. It's better to call me
in the car. Call my cellular phone," he told Marina at the
beginning. But when she asked for the number, Rolando
wouldn't give it to her. "They've got a tap on my cellular,"
he explained. "If they pick up one of your calls, I might get
you in trouble."

"So how will we see each other?"

"You know. Every Thursday night at the courts on the
other side . . ."

But what about Mondays, Tuesdays, and Wednesdays?
We all work, Rolando said, life's tough, it's not a free ride.
A night of love, can't you see? Some people don't even have
that . . . And Saturdays and Sundays? My family, Rolando
would say, weekends are for my family.

"But I don't have one, Rolando. I'm all alone."

"And Fridays?" he shot back with the speed of light. Rolando was fast, no one could take that away from him, and
he knew that Marina would get flustered as soon as he mentioned Friday.

"No. Fridays I go out with the girls. It's our day to be
together."

Rolando didn't have to say another word, and Marina
would anxiously wait for Thursday so she could cross the
international bridge, show her green card, take a bus that
left her three blocks from the motel, stop at the soda fountain for an ice-cream soda with a cherry on top (the kind
they knew how to make only on the gringo side), and, fortified in her body, sleepy in her soul, fall into the arms of
Rolando, her Rolando . . .

"Your Rolando? Yours? Every woman's Rolando."

The jokes the girls made echoed in her ears as she braided the black, blue, yellow, and red wires, an interior flag that announced the nationality of each television set. Made in Mexico—there's something to be proud of. When would they put a label on the sets that said "Made by Marina, Marina Alva Martínez, Marina of the Assembly Plants"? But she didn't have that pride in her work, that fleeting feeling she was doing something worthwhile, not useless, something that erased the jealousy Rolando made her feel, Rolando and his conquests. All the girls insinuated it, sometimes they said it: every woman's Rolando. Well, if that was the way it was, at least she got her little piece of the action from a real star, well-dressed, with suits that were silvery like an airplane and shone even at night, nicely cut black hair (no sideburns), not like a hippy's, a perfectly combed little moustache, an even olive-colored complexion, dreamy eyes. And his cellular phone stuck to his ear—everyone had seen him, in fancy restaurants, outside famous shops, on the bridge itself, with his phone to his ear, taking care of *biznez*, connecting, making deals, conquering the world. Rolando, with his Hermès tie and his jet-plane-colored suit, arranging the world, how could he afford to give more than one night a week to Marina, the new arrival, the simplest, the humblest? He, someone so lusted after, the main man?

"Come here," he said the third time they met in the motel, when she burst into tears and made a jealous scene. "Come here and sit in front of this mirror."

All she saw was that the tears were gathering in her thick eyelashes, the eyelashes still of a little girl.

"What do you see in the mirror?" asked Rolando, standing behind her, bending toward her face, caressing her bare shoulders with those smooth coffee-colored hands covered with rings.

"Me. I see myself, Rolando. What are you talking about?"

"That's right, look at yourself, Marina. Look at that unbelievably beautiful girl with thick eyelashes and dark little eyes, look at the beauty of those lips, that perfect little nose, those divine dimples. Look at all that, Marina, look at that lovely girl, and then look at me when I ask myself, How can a girl that pretty be jealous, how can she think Rolando could like any other woman? Maybe she can't see herself in the mirror, maybe she doesn't realize how lovable she is. Doesn't Marina have any self-confidence? Rolando Rozas will have to educate her."

Then her tears flowed, tears of sorrow and happiness, and she threw her arms around Rolando's neck, asking him to forgive her.

Today was Friday, but it was different. As they were leaving the assembly plant, Villarreal, the managers' waiter, told Candelaria something that excited her, something that completely unnerved her—a woman usually so self-possessed. Rosa Lupe, though she pretended to be composed, was in a state of turmoil. She'd been sullied both by Esmeralda, who'd humiliated her, and by Herminio, who'd protected her—which of them was worse, the bestial old woman or the sex-crazed young man? Dinorah, too, was burdened, and Marina tried to recall all the day's conversations to figure out what had upset Dinorah so much. Dinorah was a good woman, her cynicism was all pose, she was just defending herself against a life that seemed unfair to her, insane—usually she said it but now she was just insinuating it . . . Marina saw how sad they all looked, how preoccupied, and decided to do something unusual, something forbidden, something that would make all of them feel happy, different, free, who knows . . .

She took off her patent-leather stilettos, tossed them aside, and ran onto the grass barefoot, dancing over the grass, laughing, mocking the warning NO PISE EL PASTO/KEEP OFF THE GRASS, feeling a marvelous physical emotion. The lawn was so cool, so moist and well-kept, it tickled the soles of her feet; running over it barefoot was like bathing in one of those enchanted forests in the movies, where the pure maiden is surprised by the prince in shining armor, everything is shining, the water, the forest, the sword. Her bare feet, the freedom of her body, the freedom of that other thing—what is it called?—the soul. What the songs sing about—the body free, the soul free . . .

KEEP OFF THE GRASS

The women all laughed, made wisecracks, cheered, warned her, Don't be such a nut, Marina, get out of there, they'll fine you, fire you . . .

No, said Don Leonardo Barroso, laughing from behind his opaque windows. Just look, Ted, he said to the gringo who was dry as a corncob pipe. Look at the joy, the freedom of those girls, the satisfaction they take in having done their jobs. What do you think? But Murchinson looked at him skeptically, as if to say, How many times have you staged this little act?

The four women, Dinorah and Rosa Lupe, Marina and Candelaria, sat at their usual table right next to the discotheque's dance floor. The manager knew them and reserved the table for them every Friday. It was Candelaria's doing. The others knew it. Fridays it was extremely difficult to get a table at the Malibú, it was the great day of freedom, the death of the workweek, the resurrection of hope and hope's companion, joy.

"Malibú? Maquilú! Maquilá!" said the MC—in a blue tux with a ruffled shirt and fluorescent tie—to the wave of women filling the stands around the dance floor, over a thousand working women all crowded in together. It's the lights, just the lights, said Dinorah, the wet blanket. Without the lights this is a miserable corral, but the lights make it all nice and pretty. But Marina felt as if she were on a beach, yes, a marvelous beach at night, where the beams of light—blue, orange, pink—caressed her, especially the white, silvery light, which was like the moon touching her and tanning her at the same time, turning all to silver, not a suntan for others to envy (when would she ever go to a beach?) but a moon tan.

No one paid attention to sour Dinorah, and they all got up to dance with themselves, without men. Rock and roll lent itself to that—you didn't have to put an arm around anyone's waist or dance cheek-to-cheek. Rock was as pure as going to church: Sundays were for Mass, Fridays for the disco—the soul and the body were purified in the two temples. How well they all got along, what wild ideas they had, arms here, feet there, knees bent, hair flying, breasts bouncing, asses shaking freely, and most of all the faces, the expressions—ecstasy, mockery, seduction, shock, threat, jealousy, tenderness, passion, abandon, showing off, clowning around, imitating celebrities. All of it was allowed on the Malibú dance floor, all the lost emotions, the forbidden moves, the forgotten sensations, everything had its place here, justification, pleasure—pleasure above all—though the best thing was missing.

Sweaty, they returned to their seats—Candelaria in her

multiethnic outfit, Marina tricked out in her miniskirt, a sequined blouse, and her stilettos, Dinorah on display in an attractive low-cut dress of red satin, Rosa Lupe wearing her Carmelite robe, carrying out her vow. But here fantasy was allowed, and it was somehow soothing to see someone dressed like that, all coffee-colored and draped in a scapular.

Then the Chippendales paraded onto the runway, gringos brought over from Texas. Bare-chested, they wore bow ties, ankle-high boots, and jocks whose straps slipped between their buttocks and whose pouches barely supported the weight of their sexes while revealing the forms and challenging the girls: Arouse me with your eyes. The boys were identical yet varied, each carrying his sack of gold, as Candelaria said laughing, but each different in certain details: this one with his pubis shaved, that one with a diamond in his navel, another with a tattoo of the two crossed flags—the stars and stripes, the eagle and the serpent—on his shoulder, one boy, if you looked lower down, with spurs on his boots. All of them moving to a delightful, manly, exciting beat while the girls stuck money in their jocks—Rosa Lupe, all of them—blond but tan, oiled so they'd shine more, their faces made up, all gringos, desirable little gringos, adorable, for me, for you. The girls elbow one another. In my bed, just imagine. In yours. If he'd only take me, I'm ready. If he'd only kidnap me, I'm kidnappable. A Chippendale squatted down and pulled the rope that bound Rosa Lupe's penitential robe, and all the girls laughed. He began to play with the rope as Rosa Lupe said, This is my day, this makes the third time someone's tried to strip me, but the boy, tanned, oiled, made up, with no hair in his armpits, played with the rope as if it were a snake and he a snake charmer, raising the rope, giving it an erection. The other girls elbowed Rosa Lupe, asking her if she'd rehearsed it all with this hunk, and she swore, laughing till the tears rolled down her face, that no, that was the good part, it was all a surprise. But the girls howled, begging the boy to toss them the rope, the rope, the rope, and he ran it between his legs and stuck it under the diamond in his navel as if it were an umbilical cord, driving the girls crazy, all of them shouting for him to give them the rope, to tie himself to them, to be a son by the rope, a lover by the rope, a slave, a master—they tied to him, he tied to them—until the Chippendale slid the end of the rope into Dinorah's lap as she sat there next to the runway, and she yanked it so hard she almost pulled the boy down. Hey! he shouted, and she shouted wordlessly, howled, tugging on the rope, pulling herself forward, elbowing her way through the crowd, the astonishment, the comments . . .

The girlfriends looked at one another, astounded but not wanting to show it, wanting instead to show they approved of Dinorah. To vast applause, their jocks stuffed with money, the Chippendales took a break, losing, one after another, their assembly-line smiles, each one returning, as he stepped off the runway, to his everyday face. A parade of difference: one bored, one contemptuous, this one satisfied, as if everything he did had been admirable and should have earned him an Oscar, that one shooting murderous looks around the corral full of Mexican cows, as if, perhaps, he wished it were another corral, full of Mexican bulls. Frustrated ambition, ruin, fatigue, indifference, cruelty. Evil faces, said Marina without meaning to. Those boys wouldn't know how to love me, they're not like my Rolando, whatever his faults may be.

But now came the most beautiful part.

They began to play Mendelssohn's wedding march, and the first model appeared on the runway, her face covered by a veil of tulle, her hands clutching a bouquet of forget-menots, a crown of orange blossoms on her head, her skirt puffed out like that of a queen, like a cloud. The girls let out a collective exclamation, a sigh really, and none of them had any doubt about the person whose face was hidden by the veil: she was one of them, dark-skinned, a Mexican woman—they would have been offended if a gringa had come out in a bridal gown. The boys had to be gringos, but the brides had to be Mexican . . . Once they did bring out a little blond bride with blue eyes, but in the riot that ensued, the place almost burned down. Now they knew. The parade of bridal gowns featured Mexican girls, it was meant for Mexican girls: five brides in a row, modest and virginal, then one in a mock bridal outfit, a taffeta miniskirt, and at the end a naked bride, wearing only a veil, the flowers in her hands, and high heels, ready for the nuptial bed, ready to give herself. Everyone laughed and shouted, and at the end a little man dressed as a priest appeared and blessed them all, filling them with emotion, with gratitude, with the desire to come back the next Friday to see how many promises had been kept. But there at the exit were Villarreal—Don Leonardo Barroso's man, the boss's servant—and Beltrán Herrera—Candelaria's lover, the union leader, a serene, dark-skinned, graying man with tender eyes, now more tender than ever behind his glasses. His moustache was wet, and he took Candelaria by the arm to whisper something in her ear. Candelaria covered her mouth to keep from screaming or weeping, but she was a solid woman, maternal to the core, intelligent, strong, and discreet. She only told Marina and Rosa Lupe, "Something terrible's happened."

"To whom? Where?"

"To Dinorah. Come on, she's going home as fast as she can."

They hurried into Herrera's car and Villarreal repeated

the story he'd heard in Don Leonardo Barroso's office, that they were going to tear down Colonia Bellavista to build factories, were going to buy the lots for nothing and sell them for millions. What were the workers going to do? They had enough weapons to prevent an outright looting, to get some notice, to demand that they, too, reap some benefits.

"But the houses aren't even our own," said Candelaria.

"We could organize like renters and throw a monkey wrench into the works," Beltrán Herrera argued.

"Not even the lots are ours, Beltrán."

"But we've got rights. We can refuse to move out until they pay us something comparable to what they're going to make on this."

"What they're going to do is fire all of us women from the plants . . ."

"Enough is enough," said Rosa Lupe, though she didn't really understand what was going on and was speaking just so she wouldn't seem completely passive and so someone would clarify the anxious question in Marina's eyes: What happened to Dinorah?

"We appreciate your loyalty," Herrera said, squeezing Villarreal's shoulder. Villarreal was at the wheel, his ponytail blowing behind him. "Let's hope it doesn't get you into big trouble."

"This isn't the first time I've passed you information, Beltrán," said the waiter.

"No, but this is something big. We're going to organize once and for all, spread the word."

"The girls hardly ever join up." Villarreal shook his head. "Now, if they were men . . ."

"What about me?" said Candelaria in a loud voice. "Don't be so macho, Villarreal."

Herrera sighed and hugged Candelaria as he looked at

the nighttime landscape, the brilliant lights on the American side, the absence of streetlights on the Mexican side. Forests, textiles, mines, he said, fruit, everything disappeared in favor of the factories, all the wealth of Chihuahua, forgotten.

"Wealth that didn't give us enough to eat or a fifth the number of jobs we have now," declared Candelaria. "So thanks for your wealth but no thanks!"

"You think the girls will join up?"

Herrera laid his gray head next to Candelaria's black, shiny one.

"I do." Candelaria hung her head. "This time they'll join up as soon as they hear."

"The house is never clean," Dinorah was saying from the hard bench in her adobe shack. "I don't have the time. Just a few hours' sleep."

The neighbors had gathered outside, but some went in to console Dinorah. The oldest women were talking about holding a beautiful wake for the child, his flowers, his little white box, the way they did in the old days back in the villages: Candelaria brought candles but could only find a couple of Coca-Cola bottles to use as candlesticks.

The old men came too, the whole neighborhood gathered, and Candelaria's father, standing in the doorway, wondered out loud if they were right in coming to work in Juárez, where a woman had to leave a child alone, tied like an animal to a table leg. The poor innocent kid, how could he not hurt himself? The old people pointed out that such a thing couldn't happen in the country—families there always had someone to look after the kids, you didn't have to tie them up, ropes were for dogs and hogs.

"My father used to tell me," answered Candelaria's grandfather, "that we should stay peacefully in our homes, in one place. He would stand just the way I am now, half in and half out, and say, 'Outside this door, the world ends.' "

He said he was very old and didn't want to see anything more.

Marina had no idea how to comfort Dinorah. Crying, she listened to Candelaria's grandfather and felt thankful that in her house there were no memories. She was on her own and it was better to be alone in this life than to put up with the grief suffered by those who had children, like poor Dinorah, her hair a mess, her makeup smeared, her red dress wrinkled and sliding up her thighs, her knees together, her legs splayed, she who was normally so fastidious and co-quettish.

Then Marina, seeing the terrible scene of death and weeping and memories, thought it wasn't true, she wasn't alone, she had Rolando, even if she shared him with other women. Rolando would do her the favor of taking her to the sea, somewhere, to San Diego in California or Corpus Christi in Texas or even Guaymas in Sonora, he owed it to her, she asked for nothing but to go with Rolando to see the ocean for the first time. After that he could leave her, tell her she was a pain, but he should do her that one small favor . . .

She left Dinorah's shack and heard the grandfather talking about a fiesta for the strangled child. To raise everyone's spirits, he had some liquor brought in, saying, "The good thing about these big jugs is they look full until they're empty."

Marina dug around in her handbag until she found the number of Rolando's cellular phone. What did it matter to her if she got into trouble? This was a life-or-death matter. He had to know that she depended on him for one thing only, to take her to see the ocean, not to say, like Cande-laria's grandfather, that there was nothing more he wanted to see. She dialed the number, but it was busy at first, then went dead. That made her think he had heard her but hadn't answered so he wouldn't get her into trouble. Would he hear her when she said, Take me to the ocean, honey, I don't want to die like Dinorah's little kid without seeing the ocean—do me that little favor even if afterward we stop seeing each other and we break up.

The silence of the telephone disappointed her but it got her stirred up too. Rolando had no business playing around with her. She was making a commitment—why couldn't he commit himself a little too? She was giving him an out, telling him they could put all the love they felt for each other into one weekend at the beach and then never see each other again if he wanted. But what I won't stand for anymore is a man's picking me up like something he's found thrown out on the street and takes in from pity. I'm never going to allow that again, Rolando. You taught me about life. I didn't know how much you'd taught me until Dinorah's little boy died and Candelaria's grandfather was there, dry and old, uprooted, but as if he'd never die, and I only want to live, really live, this moment, when I've saved myself from dying young and don't want to live to be old. I'm asking you to raise me up to where you are, Rolando; let's go up together. I'm giving you this chance, sweetheart. I know deep inside that with me you're rising and you're going to take me where it's high and beautiful if you want, Rolando, and if you don't, we're both going to be ruined, you're going to bring us down so we won't even matter to ourselves.

But Rolando didn't answer his phone. It was 11:00 p.m. and Marina made her decision.

This time she didn't stop for an ice-cream soda at the soda fountain; she crossed the bridge, took the bus, and walked the three blocks to the motel. The people at the desk recognized her but were surprised she was there on a Friday.

"Aren't we free to change our plans if we want?"

"I guess so," said the receptionist with mixed irony and resignation as he handed her a key.

The place smelled of disinfectant: the halls, the stairs, even the ice and soda machines smelled of something that kills bugs, cleans bathrooms, fumigates cushions. She stopped outside the door of the room she shared with Rolando on Thursdays, wondering if she should knock or put the key in the lock. She was impatient. She inserted the key, opened the door, walked in, and heard the agonized voice of Rolando, the high voice of the gringa. She turned on the light and stood there staring at them naked in the bed.

"You've had a good look, now get out," said her Don Juan.

"I'm sorry. I kept calling you on the cellular phone. Something happened that . . ."

She saw the phone on the dresser and pointed at it. The gringa looked at both of them and burst out laughing.

"Rolando, did you fool this poor girl?" she said through her giggles as she picked up the phone. "At least you could tell the truth to your sweethearts. It's okay that you go into banks and office buildings with this thing in your ear or that you talk into it in restaurants and fool half the world, but why fool your girlfriends? Just look at the confusion you cause, honey," said the gringa as she stood up and started getting dressed.

"Baby, don't leave now . . . Just when we were getting along so nicely . . . This kid isn't anyone . . ."

"You can't let an opportunity go by, can you?" The

gringa wiggled into her pantyhose. "Don't worry, I'll come back. It's not so important that I'd break up with you."

Baby picked up the cellular phone, opened up the back, and showed Marina. "Look. No batteries. It's never had batteries. It's just to trick people, like that song: 'Call me on my cell phone, I look so loose, it makes me look like someone, even with no juice . . .' "

She tossed it onto the bed and walked out—laughing.

Marina crossed the international bridge back to Ciudad Juárez. Her feet were tired, so she took off her high, pointy shoes. The pavement still held the cold tremor of the day. But the sensation in her feet wasn't the same as when she'd danced freely over the forbidden grass of Don Leonardo Barroso's assembly plant.

"This city is a disaster built on chaos," said Barroso to his daughter-in-law, Michelina, as they passed Marina, she on her way back to Juárez, they on their way to a hotel in El Paso. Michelina laughed and kissed the businessman's ear.

6

LAS AMIGAS

For my sister Berta

"Tell them I'm not here! Tell them I don't want to see them! Tell them I don't want to see anyone!"

One day no one came to visit Miss Amy Dunbar. Even the servants, who never lasted long in the old lady's service, stopped coming to work. Rumors circulated about Miss Dunbar's difficult nature, her racism, her insults.

"There's always someone whose need for work is stronger than their pride."

It wasn't so. The whole black race, according to Miss Amy, refused to work for her. The last maid, a fifteen-year-old girl named Bathsheba, spent her month in Miss Dunbar's house weeping. Each time she answered the door, the rarer and rarer visitors first saw a girl bathed in tears, then invariably heard behind her the broken but still acid voice of the crone. "Tell them I'm not in! Tell them I'm not interested in seeing them!"

Miss Amy Dunbar's nephews knew the old lady would

never leave her house in the Chicago suburbs. She said that one migration—leaving the family home in New Orleans and coming north to live with her husband—was enough for a lifetime. Dead was the only way she would leave her stone house facing Lake Michigan and surrounded by forest.

"It won't be long now," she told the nephew responsible for paying bills, attending to legal matters, and looking after other things great and small that completely escaped the attention of the little old woman.

What she did not fail to notice was her relative's tiny sigh of relief as he imagined her dead.

She took no offense. "The problem is that I'm used to living," she invariably responded. "It's become a habit," she would say with a laugh, showing those horse teeth that with age protrude farther and farther in Anglo-Saxon women, although she was only half Anglo-Saxon, the daughter of a Yankee businessman who set himself up in Louisiana to show the languid Southerners how to do business, and a delicate lady of distantly French origin, Lucy Ney. Miss Amy said she was related to Bonaparte's marshal Ney. Her full name was Amelia Ney Dunbar. Like all the other wellborn ladies of the Delta city, she was called Miss, Miss Amy, with the right to be addressed by both the title of matrimonial maturity and that of a double childhood; they were girls at fifteen and girls again at eighty.

"I'm not suggesting you go to a senior citizens' residence," explained her nephew, a lawyer determined to deck himself out with all the clothes and accoutrements he imagined to be his profession's height of elegance: blue shirts with white collars, red ties, Brooks Brothers suits, oxfords, never loafers on workdays, God forbid! "But if you're going to stay in this big old house, you'll need domestic help." Miss Amy was about to say something nasty, but she bit her tongue. She even showed the whitish tip of that organ. "I hope you make an effort to hold onto your servants, Aunt Amy. The house is huge."

"It's that they've all left."

"You'd need at least four people in service here just to take care of you the way it was in the old days."

"Those were the young days. *These* are the old days, Archibald. And it wasn't the staff who left. It was the family. They left me alone."

"Of course, Aunt Amy. You're right."

"As always."

Archibald nodded.

"We've found a Mexican lady willing to work for you."

"Mexicans are supposed to be lazy."

"That's not true. It's a stereotype."

"I forbid you to touch my clichés, young man. They're the shield of my prejudices. And prejudices, as the word itself indicates, are necessary for making judgments. Good judgment, Archibald, good judgment is prejudgment. My convictions are clear, deep rooted, and unshakable. At this point in my life, no one's going to change them." She allowed herself a deep, slightly lugubrious breath. "Mexicans are lazy."

"Try her out. These people are eager to serve and accustomed to obeying."

"You've got your own prejudices, see?" Miss Amy laughed a little as she arranged her hair, which was so white and so old that it was turning yellow, like papers exposed to light for a long time. Like a newspaper, said her nephew Archibald. All of her has become like an old newspaper, yellowed, wrinkled, and full of news no longer interesting to anyone.

Archibald went to the Mexican section of Chicago frequently because his firm defended a lot of cases involving trade, naturalization, people without green cards—a thousand matters having to do with immigration and labor from south of the border. He also went because at the age of forty-two he was still a bachelor, convinced that before embarking on marriage he had to drink the cup of life to the dregs, with no ties, no family, no children, no wife. Chicago was a city where many cultures mixed, so Miss Amy Dunbar's only nephew chose his girlfriends according to ethnic zones. He'd already gone through the Ukrainian, Polish, Chinese, Hungarian, and Lithuanian sectors. Now the happy conjunction of business and amatory curiosity brought him to Pilsen, the Mexican neighborhood with the Czechoslovakian name of a beer-producing city in Bohemia. The Czechs had left and the Mexicans were taking over little by little, filling the neighborhood with markets, luncheonettes, music, colors, cultural centers, and, of course, beer as good as Pilsen's.

Many people came to work as meatpackers, some legal, others not, but all respected for their dexterity in cutting and packing the meat. Miss Amy's nephew, the lawyer, started going out with one of the girls in a huge family of workers, almost all of whom came from the Mexican state of Guerrero and all of whom were linked by blood, affection, and solidarity, and occasionally by name.

They were extremely helpful to one another. Like a great family, they organized parties and, like all other families, they fought. One night, there was trouble and the result was two deaths. The police didn't waste time. There were four killers, one of them named Pérez, so they rounded up four Pérezes and charged them. As they barely spoke English, they couldn't explain themselves or understand the charges, but one of them, visited in jail by Archibald, claimed that the charges were unfair, based on false testimony intended to

protect the real murderers. The idea was to sentence the sus-
pects as soon as possible and close the case; they didn't know
how to defend themselves. Archibald took them on, and
that's how he met the wife of the defendant he'd visited in
jail.

Her name was Josefina and they'd just been married—
about time, too, since they were both forty-one. Josefina
spoke English because she was the daughter of an iron-
worker named Fortunato Ayala, who'd fathered her and
then abandoned her in Chicago. But she'd been in Mexico
when everything happened so she hadn't been able to help
her husband.

"He could learn English in jail," suggested Archibald.

"He could," said Josefina without really agreeing. "He
wants to study English and become a lawyer. Can you make
him a lawyer?"

"Sure, I can give him classes. And what about you, Josefina?"

"I have to get a job so I can pay you for the lawyer
classes."

"No need for that."

"Well, I have the need. It's my fault Luis María is in jail.
I should have been with him when everything happened. At
least I speak English."

"I'll see what I can do. In any case, we're going to fight
to save your husband. Meanwhile, he's got the right to study,
to keep himself busy, while he's in jail. I'll look after that.
But tell me why Mexicans rat on other Mexicans."

"The ones who come first don't like the ones who come
later. Sometimes we're unfair among ourselves. It isn't
enough that others treat us badly."

"I thought you were like one big family."

"The worst things happen in families, sir."

In the beginning, Miss Amy wouldn't even look at Josefina. The first time she saw her confirmed all her suspicions. Josefina was an Indian. Miss Amy couldn't understand why people who were in no way different from the Iroquois insisted on calling themselves "Latinos" or "Hispanics." Josefina did have one virtue. She was silent. She entered and left the old lady's bedroom like a ghost, as if she didn't have feet. The rustle of the maid's skirts and aprons could be confused with that of the curtains when the breeze blew off the lake. Autumn was coming, and soon Miss Amy would be closing the windows. She liked the summer, the heat, the memory of her hometown, so French . . .

"No, Aunt Amy," said the nephew when he wanted to argue with her, "the architecture of New Orleans is completely Spanish, not French. The Spaniards were here for almost a century and gave the city its shape. The French part is a varnish for tourists."

"*Taisez-vous*," she would say to him indignantly, suspecting that this time Archibald was involved with some Latina or Hispanic or whatever these Comanches who had come too far north were called.

Josefina knew the old lady's routine—Archibald explained it in detail—and opened the bedroom curtains at 8:00 a.m., had breakfast ready on a small table, and came back at noon to make the bed. The old lady insisted on getting dressed by herself. Josefina went off to cook and Miss Amy came down to eat a Spartan solitary lunch of lettuce, radishes, and cottage cheese. In the afternoon she sat in front of the television set in the living room and gave free rein to her perverse energy, commenting on everything she saw with sarcasm, insults, and disdain for blacks, Jews, Italians, Mexicans. She delivered it all out loud, whether anyone heard or not, but she alternated these disagreeable comments that paralleled the picture on the television with sudden, unexpected orders to Josefina, as to Bathsheba and the others before her. My plaid blanket for my knees. The Friday tea should be Lapsang souchong, not Earl Grey. How many times do I have to . . . See here, who told you to move my glass marbles? Who else could have moved them but you, dummy? You're useless, lazy, like all the black women I've ever known. Where is the photograph of my husband that was on the night table last night? Who put it in that drawer? I didn't do it, and there's no other "person" here but you, absentminded, useless. Do something to earn your pay. Have you ever worked hard a single day in your life? What am I saying? No black has ever done anything but live off the work of whites.

Out of the corner of her eye, she spied on the new Mexican maid. Would she say the same things to her that she did to the fragile and weepy Bathsheba, or would she have to invent a new repertoire of insults to wound Josefina? Would she hide the photo of her husband in a drawer again so she could accuse Josefina of moving it? She spied on her. She licked her chops. She prepared her offensive. Let's see how long she lasts, this fat solid woman with a delicate face and fine features that seem more Arabian than Indian, an ash-colored woman with liquid, very black eyes and very yellow corneas.

For her part, Josefina decided three things. The first, to be thankful for having a job and bless every dollar that came in for the defense of her husband, Luis María. The second, to carry out to the letter the instructions of the lawyer, Don Archibaldo, as to his aunt's care. And the third, to risk making her own life inside the big house facing the lake. This was the most dangerous decision, and the one Josefina recognized she could not avoid if she intended to endure. Flowers, for instance. The house needed flowers. To her cramped maid's room, she brought the violets and pansies she always kept on her dresser, along with the lamp and the religious pictures that were her most important companions after Luis María.

For Josefina, there was an intensely mysterious but real relationship between the life of images and the life of flowers. Who could deny that flowers, though they don't speak, still live, breathe, and one day wither and die? Well, the images of Our Lord on the cross, the Sacred Heart, the Virgin of Guadalupe were like flowers: even if they didn't speak, they lived, breathed. Unlike the flowers, they never withered. The life of flowers, the life of images. For Josefina, they were two inseparable things, and in the name of her faith she gave to flowers the tactile, perfumed, sensual life she would have liked to give to the religious pictures as well.

"This house smells musty," Miss Amy exclaimed one night as she ate dinner. "It smells like a storage closet, as if there's no air, musty. I want to smell something nice," she said to Josefina in an insulting tone, sniffing for a kitchen odor as the maid laid the plates and served her vegetable soup, staring at Josefina's armpits for a telltale stain, an offensive whiff. But the maid was clean. Every night, Miss Amy heard the water running for Josefina's punctual bath before bed; if anything, she felt more like accusing Josefina of wasting water, but she was afraid Josefina would laugh at her, pointing toward the immense lake, like an inland sea.

Josefina placed a bouquet of tuberoses in the living room, a room it had never occurred to Miss Amy to decorate with flowers. When the old lady came in to watch her evening television after dinner, she first sniffed the air like an animal surprised by an enemy presence. Then she fixed her gaze on the tuberoses; finally she exclaimed with concentrated rage: "Who's filling my house with flowers for the dead?"

"No, these are fresh flowers, they're alive," Josefina managed to say.

"Where did you get them?" growled Miss Amy. "I bet you stole them! You can't touch other people's gardens around here! Around here we have something called private property, *capisce*?"

"I bought them," Josefina said simply.

"You bought them?" repeated Miss Amy, for once in her life bereft of arguments or words.

"Yes." Josefina smiled. "To brighten up the house. You said it smelled musty, closed up."

"And now it smells like the dead! What kind of joke is this?" Miss Amy shouted, thinking about the photograph of her husband hidden in the drawer, the misplaced glass marbles: she, not the maids, was responsible for those things, she offended herself to offend the maids—no maid must take the initiative. "Remove your flowers immediately."

"Certainly, ma'am."

"And tell me, how did you pay for them?"

"With my own money, ma'am."

"You spend your salary on flowers?"

"They're for you. For the house."

"But the house belongs to me, not you. Who do you think you are? Are you sure you didn't steal them? The police aren't going to come to find out where you robbed the flowers?"

"No. I have a receipt from the florist, ma'am."

Josefina left the room, though behind her lingered the scent of mint and coriander that she caused to emanate from the kitchen, having taken to heart her mistress's complaint that the house smelled like a storage closet. Miss Amy, uncertain as to how she should attack her new employee, imagined for a moment lowering herself to the indignity of spying, something she'd never done with her other servants, convinced it would mean giving them a weapon against her. It was her greatest temptation, she admitted it to herself, to enter the maid's room secretly and poke around in her possessions, perhaps discover a secret. Of course, that would mean showing her hand, losing her authority, the authority of prejudice, lack of proof, irrationality. Others had to come and tell her things, that the room was a pigsty, that the plumber had to come unplug the toilet, which was blocked up with filth—what could you expect from a black, a Mexican?

Lacking the pretext of the plumber, she had made use of her nephew Archibald. "My nephew informs me you never make your own bed."

"He can make my bed when he gets in it to screw me," said a sharp-tongued young black woman who left without saying good-bye.

Miss Amy wanted to lure Josefina into her own territory—the living room, the dining room, the bedroom—force her to reveal herself there, to make a big mistake there, to see herself there, in the bedroom after breakfast, in the ornate hand mirror that Miss Amy suddenly turned so as to banish her own reflection and force Josefina to look at herself. "You'd like to be white, wouldn't you?" asked Miss Amy abruptly.

"There are lots of *güeritos* in Mexico," said Josefina impassively, without lowering her eyes.

"Lots of what?"

"Blond people, ma'am. Just as there are lots of blacks here. We're all God's children," she concluded plainly and truthfully but without sounding impolite.

"Know something? I'm convinced Jesus loves me," said Miss Amy, pulling the covers up to her chin, as if she wanted to deny her own body and be like one of those cherubs who are all face and wings.

"Because you're a good person, ma'am."

"No, stupid, because he made me white. That's proof God loves me."

"As you say, ma'am."

Wouldn't this Mexican woman ever answer back? Would she ever get mad? Would she ever retaliate? Did she think she'd beat Miss Amy that way, by never getting mad?

She expected everything except that Josefina would retaliate that very night after dinner as Miss Amy watched a news program to prove to herself that the world was hopeless.

"I put your husband's picture in the drawer, the way you like to do it," said Josefina. Miss Amy sat there open-mouthed, indifferent to Dan Rather's commentary on the situation of the universe.

"What does she have in her bedroom?" she asked her nephew Archibald the next day. "How has she decorated it?"

"The way all Mexican women do. Pictures of saints, images of Christ and the Virgin, an old ex-voto giving thanks, and God knows what else."

"Idolatry. Sacrilegious papism."

"That's the way it is, and nothing can change it," said Archibald, trying to pass along a little resignation to Miss Amy.

"Don't you find it disgusting?"

"To her, our empty, undecorated, Puritan churches seem disgusting," said Archibald, inwardly savoring the excitement of sleeping with a Mexican girl in Pilsen who covered the image of the Virgin with a handkerchief so the Virgin wouldn't see them screw. But she left the candles burning—the girl's delicious cinnamon body shone . . . It was useless to ask tolerance of Miss Amy.

"By the way, where is Uncle's photo, Aunt Amy?" Archibald asked with some sarcasm. But the lady pretended not to hear, as she knew that the next day she wouldn't be able to tell Archibald that the maid had put the photo away.

"What do you think of my husband?" she asked Josefina as she took the photo out of the drawer to put it on the night table.

"Very handsome, ma'am, very distinguished."

"You're lying, you hypocrite. Take a good look. He was at Normandy. Look at the scar crossing his face like a bolt of lightning splitting a stormy sky."

"Don't you have pictures of him before he was wounded, ma'am?"

"Do you have any pictures of Christ on the cross without wounds, blood, just nailed, dead, crowned with thorns?"

"Yes, of course. I have pictures of the Sacred Heart and the Christ Child, very beautiful ones. Would you like to see them?"

"Bring them to me some day." Miss Amy smiled mockingly.

"Only if you promise to show me your husband when he was young and handsome." Josefina smiled tenderly.

"Impertinent," Miss Amy managed to mutter when the maid left with the tea tray.

The Mexican made a mistake—Miss Amy almost cackled with pleasure when she saw Archibald again—the idolater made a mistake. The day after the conversation about Christ and the wounded husband, Josefina brought the old lady her breakfast as usual, placed the bed tray over her lap, and instead of leaving as she usually did, rearranged the pillows for her and touched her head, stroking the old lady's forehead.

"Don't touch me!" shouted Miss Amy, hysterical. "Don't you ever dare touch me!" she shouted again, upsetting the bed tray, spilling tea on the sheets, knocking the croissants and jam over the bedclothes.

"Don't judge her harshly, Aunt Amy. Josefina has her sorrows, just as you do. It's possible she wants to share them."

"Sorrows, me?" Miss Amy raised her eyebrows all the way to where her hair, arranged that afternoon to give her a youthful, renewed look, began. A white inverted question mark adorned her forehead, like this: ¿

"You know very well what I'm talking about. I could have been your son, Aunt Amy. It was an accident that instead I ended up being your nephew."

"You have no right to say such things, Archibald." Miss Amy's voice was muffled, as if she were speaking through a handkerchief. "Don't say that ever again, or I won't allow you back in my house."

"Josefina has her sorrows too. That's why she stroked you yesterday morning."

Did Archibald achieve his goal? Miss Amy divined her nephew's Machiavellian plot, and she knew that Niccolò Machiavelli was the Devil himself. Wasn't the Devil called Old Nick in English legend? This Miss Amy knew because as a teenager she'd had a part in Marlowe's *Jew of Malta*, and the first person who speaks is Machiavelli, transformed into the Devil, Old Nick.

She sat with the window open to the park. Josefina came in with her tea, but Miss Amy didn't turn to look at her. It was almost autumn, the most beautiful season on that lake, with its prolonged winters, daggerlike winds, brief spring-times, insolently coquettish, and summers when not a leaf stirred and the humidity hovered as high as the fiery red in the thermometers.

Miss Amy thought that her garden, however familiar to her, was a forgotten garden. An avenue of cedars led to its entrance and to the view of the lake, which was beginning to turn rough. This was the beauty of autumn, always nostalgically mixed, in Miss Dunbar's eyes, with the punctual appearance of the maple buds in spring. Nevertheless, her garden was now a lost garden, and this afternoon—without consciously planning to, almost without realizing what she was saying, convinced she always talked that way to herself but enunciating the words clearly, not for her maid, who just happened to be standing behind her holding a tea tray, but as if she were saying something she had said before or would have said in any case—she remarked that in New Orleans her mother would appear on the balcony on special occasions wearing all her jewels so everyone could admire her as they walked by.

"It's the same in Juchitán."

"Hoochy what?"

"Juchitán is the name of our village, in Tehuantepec. My mother would go out to show off her jewelry on feast days."

"Jewelry? Your mother?" said Miss Amy, more and more confused. What was this maid talking about? Who did she think she was? Did she have delusions of grandeur?

"That's right. It goes from mother to daughter, ma'am, and no one dares sell them. The stones come from far away. They're sacred."

"Are you telling me that you could live like a grand lady in your hoochy town and instead you're here cleaning my bathrooms?" said Miss Amy with renewed ferocity.

"No, I would use them to pay lawyers. But as I was saying, in Juchitec families jewels are sacred, for fiesta days, and pass from mother to daughter. It's very beautiful."

"So they must wear them all the time, because by all accounts it's a perpetual feast day all year round—this saint, that martyr . . . Why are there so many saints in Mexico?"

"Why are there so many millionaires in the United States? God has his own plan for distributing things, ma'am."

"Did you say you have to pay lawyers? Don't tell me my idiot nephew is helping you!"

"Mr. Archibaldo is very generous."

"Generous? With my money? He's got nothing beyond what he'll inherit from me. Charity may begin at home, but his home isn't mine."

"No, he doesn't give us money, ma'am. Not at all. He's teaching my husband law so he can become a lawyer and defend himself and his friends."

"Where is your husband? What does he have to defend himself against?"

"He's in jail, ma'am. He was unjustly accused—"

"That's what they all say," said Miss Amy, grimacing sarcastically.

"No, it's true. In jail, the prisoners can learn things. My husband decided to study law to defend himself and his friends. He doesn't want Don Archibaldo to defend him. He wants to defend himself. That's his pride, ma'am. All Don Archibaldo does is give him classes."

"Free?" The old woman made a fierce, unconscious grimace.

"No. That's why I'm working here. I pay with my salary."

"Which is to say, I pay. That's a good one."

"Don't get mad, ma'am, please. Don't get upset. I'm not

very clever, I don't know how to conceal things. I'm not lying to you. Excuse me."

She walked away, and Miss Amy sat there wondering how her maid Josefina's sorrow could in any way resemble her own—evoked with such lack of delicacy by her nephew a few days before. What did a criminal case involving Mexican immigrants have to do with a case of lost love, a missed opportunity?

"How is Josefina working out?" Archibald asked the next time they saw each other.

"At least she's punctual."

"See? Not all stereotypes are accurate."

"Is her room a mess with all those idols and saints?"

"No, it's neat as a pin."

When Josefina served tea that afternoon, Miss Amy smiled at her and said that soon autumn would really begin and then the cold. Didn't Josefina want to take advantage of the last days of summer to give a party?

"Just to show you my heart's in the right place, Josefina. You told me a few days ago that there are lots of parties—fiestas—in your country. Isn't there something coming up you'd like to celebrate?"

"The only thing I want to celebrate is my husband's being declared innocent."

"But that might take a while. No, I'm offering you a chance to throw a party for your friends in the back part of the garden, by the grape arbor."

"If you think it's a good idea . . ."

"Yes, Josefina, I've already said this house smells shut-up. I know you all are very spirited people. Invite a small group. I'll come out to say hello, of course."

On the day of the party, Miss Amy first spied from the dressing room on the second floor. Josefina, with her mistress's permission, had set up a long table under the arbor. The house filled with unusual smells, and now Miss Amy watched a parade of clay platters piled with mysterious foods all mixed together and drowned in thick sauces, little baskets of tortillas, pitchers holding magenta- and amber-colored liquids.

As the guests began to arrive, she watched them closely from her hiding place. Some were dressed in everyday clothes—that was clear—but others, especially the women, had put on their best outfits for this special occasion. There were short jackets and T-shirts, but coats and ties as well. Some women wore pants while others wore satin dresses. There were children. Lots of people.

Other people. Miss Amy tried to use her intelligence to penetrate those black eyes, the dark complexions and wide smiles of her maid's friends, the Mexicans. They were impenetrable. She felt she was staring at a wall of cactus, prickly, as if each one of those beings were really a porcupine. They wounded Miss Amy's gaze just as they would have wounded her hands if she'd touched them. They were people who cut her flesh, like a sphere one could imagine made of razor blades. There was no way to take hold of them. They were other, alien; they confirmed the old lady's revulsion, her prejudice.

Now what were they doing? Were they hanging a pot from the arbor, then giving a child a stick, blindfolding him, and watching while he swung blindly until he hit the pot and it fell in pieces and the other children rushed to pick up candies and peanuts? What? Had someone dared to bring a portable phonograph to play raucous music, guitars and trumpets, wolf howls? Were they going to dance in her garden, hug each other in that filthy way; were they going to touch, laughing uproariously, arms around one another's waists, caressing one another's backs, about to laugh, cry, or something worse?

As she had promised, she appeared in the garden. She had her cane in her hand. She went straight to the second piñata and smashed it. Next, she struck the record player. To all, she shouted, Out of my house. What do you think this is? This isn't a cheap bar, this is no bordello. Get out of here and take your blaring music and your indigestible food somewhere else. Don't abuse my hospitality, this is my house, here we do things differently, we don't keep hogs in the kitchen around here.

The guests all looked at Josefina. First she trembled, then she became calm, almost rigid.

"The mistress is right. This is her house. Thank you for coming. Thank you for wishing my husband good luck."

They all left, some staring at Miss Amy angrily, others disdainfully, still others fearfully—but all with the feeling we call shame for others.

Only Josefina remained, standing tall, unchanged.

"Thank you for lending us your garden, ma'am. The party was very nice."

"It was an abuse," Miss Amy said through clenched teeth, disconcerted. "Too many people, too much noise, too much of everything."

With a swing of her cane, she swept the platters from the table. The unaccustomed effort overwhelmed her. She lost her breath.

"You're right, ma'am. Summer is coming to an end. Don't get a chill now. Come back to the house and let me make you your afternoon tea."

"You did it on purpose," said a visibly annoyed Archibald as he nervously fingered the knot of his Brooks Brothers tie. "You suggested she give the party only to humiliate her in front of her friends."

"It was an abuse. She went too far."

"What do you want, for her to leave you like all the others? Do you want me to have you put away in an asylum?"

"You'd lose your inheritance."

"But not my mind. You could drive anyone insane, Aunt Amy. How smart my father was not to marry you."

"What are you saying, you ingrate?"

"I'm saying that you did this to humiliate Josefina and make her leave."

"No, you said something else. But Josefina won't leave. She needs the money to get her husband out of jail."

"Not anymore. The court turned down the appeal. Josefina's husband will stay in jail."

"What will she do?"

"Why don't you ask her?"

"I don't want to talk to her. I don't want to talk to you either. You come to my house to insult me, to remind me of things I want to forget. You're risking your inheritance."

"Listen to me now, Aunt Amy. I renounce my inheritance."

"You're cutting off your nose to spite your face. Don't be a fool, Archibald."

"No, really. I'll renounce it unless you listen to me and hear the truth."

"Your father was a coward. He wouldn't take the final step. He didn't ask me at the right moment. He humiliated me. He made me wait too long. I had no choice but to marry your uncle."

"It's that you never showed my father affection."

"And he expected it?"

"Yes. He told me so, several times. If Amy had showed she loved me, I'd have taken the final step."

"Why? Why didn't he do it?" The voice and spirit of the old lady broke. "Why didn't he show he loved me?"

"Because he was convinced you never loved anyone. He needed you to give him proof of your affection."

"Are you telling me my life has been nothing but a huge misunderstanding?"

"No. There was no misunderstanding. My father convinced himself he'd done the right thing not asking you to marry him, Aunt Amelia. He told me that time had borne him out. You've never loved anyone."

That afternoon when Josefina served tea Miss Amy, without meeting her maid's gaze, said she was very sorry for what had happened. Josefina took the unfamiliar words calmly. "Don't worry, ma'am. You are the owner of the house. What else is there to say?"

"No, I'm not talking about that. I mean about your husband."

"Well, it's not the first time there's been a miscarriage of justice."

"What are you going to do?"

"What, ma'am? Don't you know?"

"No, Josefina, tell me."

Then Josefina did raise her eyes to look directly into the faded eyes of Miss Amelia Dunbar, dazzling the old lady as if her eyes were two candles. She told her mistress that she was going to continue fighting, that when she chose Luis María it was forever and for everything, the good and the bad. She knew that was what they said in the marriage ceremony, but in her case it was the truth. Time passed, the bitterness was greater than the joy, but for that reason love itself got greater and greater, more certain. Luis María could spend his life in jail without doubting for a single moment that she loved him, not only the way she would if they were living together as they had at the beginning but much more, more and more, ma'am, do you understand me? Without pain, without malice, without pointless games, without pride, without arrogance, each of us given to the other.

"Will you allow me to confess something to you, Miss Amelia, without your getting angry with me? My husband has strong hands, fine, beautiful hands. He was born to carve meat. He has a marvelous touch. He always hits the mark. His hands are dark and strong, and I can't live without them."

That night, Miss Amy asked Josefina to help her undress and put on her nightgown. She was going to wear the woolen nightgown. The autumn air was beginning to make its presence felt. The maid helped her get into bed. She tucked her in as if she were a child. She arranged the pillows and was about to leave, wishing her good night, when Miss Amelia Ney Dunbar's two tense, old hands took the strong, fleshy hands of Josefina. Miss Amy brought her maid's hands to her lips, kissed them, and Josefina embraced the almost transparent body of Miss Amy, an embrace that while never repeated would last an eternity.

7

THE CRYSTAL FRONTIER

For Jorge Bustamante

1

Don Leonardo Barroso was in the first-class section of Delta's nonstop flight from Mexico City to New York. With him was an incredibly beautiful woman with a mane of long black shiny hair. The hair was like a frame for the striking cleft in her chin, her face's star. Don Leonardo, in his fifties, felt proud of his female companion. Seated by the window, she was imagining herself in the irregularity, the variety, the beauty, and the distance of the landscape and the sky. Her lovers had always told her she had cloudlike eyelids and a slight storm in the shadows under her eyes. Mexican boyfriends speak in serenades.

Michelina was looking at much the same sight from the sky, recalling the periods in her adolescence when her boyfriends serenaded her and wrote her syrupy letters. Cloudlike eyelids, slight storm in the shadows under her eyes. She sighed. You can't be sixteen forever. Why, then, did this unwanted nostalgia suddenly return—for her youth, for when she went to dances and was wooed by all the rich boys in Mexico City?

Don Leonardo preferred sitting on the aisle. The idea of being stuck in an aluminum pencil at 30,000 feet, with no visible support, still made him nervous, even if he was used to it. By the same token, he was enormously satisfied that the trip was the product of his own doing.

As soon as the North American Free Trade Agreement had gone into effect, Don Leonardo had begun lobbying intensively to have the migration of Mexican workers to the United States classified as "services," even as "foreign trade." The dynamic promotor and businessman explained, in Washington and Mexico City, that Mexico's principal export was not agricultural or industrial products, not assembly-line products, not even capital to pay the external debt (the eternal debt) but labor. Mexico was exporting more labor than cement or tomatoes. He had a plan to keep labor from becoming a conflict. Very simple: simply avoid the frontier. Prevent illegality.

"They'll still come," he explained to Secretary of Labor Robert Reich, "and they'll keep on coming because you need them. Even if there were too many jobs in Mexico, you'd still need Mexican workers."

"Legal workers," said the secretary. "Legals yes, illegals no."

"You can't believe in the free market and then suddenly close the doors to the flow of labor. It's like closing off investments. What happened to the magic of the marketplace?"

"We have an obligation to protect our borders," Reich went on. "It's a political problem. The Republicans are exploiting the growing anti-immigrant sentiment."

"You can't militarize the border," said Don Leonardo, scratching his chin irritably, seeking the same cleft that was the beauty of his daughter-in-law. "It's too long, too much of a desert, too porous. You can't be lax when you need workers and tough when you don't."

"I'm in favor of everything that contributes to the U.S. economy," said Reich. "That's the only way we can contribute to the world economy—and vice versa. So what do you propose?"

What Don Leonardo proposed was already a reality, and it—or rather he—was traveling in tourist class. His name was Lisandro Chávez, and he was trying to look out the window, but the man sitting to his right, staring at the clouds intently, as if recovering a lost homeland, blocked his view. The brim of the man's lacquered straw hat covered the window. To Lisandro's left, another laborer slept with his hat pulled down over the bridge of his nose. Only Lisandro traveled hatless, and he ran his hand through his soft black curly hair, then stroked his thick, well-trimmed moustache and rubbed his heavy, oily eyelids.

Boarding the jet, he had immediately recognized the famous businessman Leonardo Barroso in first class. Lisandro's heart skipped a beat. He also recognized, next to Barroso, a girl he knew when he was young and went to parties and dances in posh parts of Mexico City—Las Lomas, Pedregal, and Polanco. It was Michelina Laborde, the girl everyone wanted to dance with. In reality, what they wanted was to take advantage of her a bit.

"She's got a good name but she doesn't have a cent," the other boys said. "Watch it. Don't marry her. No dowry."

Lisandro danced with her once and now no longer re-called if he actually told her or simply thought that the two of them were poor, that they had that in common, that she was invited to these parties because her family had class and he because he went to the same school as the rich kids. But there was more that made them alike than made them dif-ferent, didn't she think?

He couldn't remember what Michelina's answer was, couldn't even remember if he actually said those things to her or simply thought them. Then other boys danced with her, and he never saw her again. Until today.

He didn't dare say hello. How would she remember him? What would he say to her? Remember how we met at a party at Chubby Casillas's eleven years ago and danced together? She didn't even look at him. Don Leonardo did. He looked up from reading an article in *Fortune* that gave figures for the richest men in Mexico but, luckily, once again omitted his name. Neither he nor the rich politicians ever appeared— the politicians because none of their businesses had their names on them: they hid behind the seven veils of multiple partnerships, borrowed names, foundations . . . Don Leo-nardo imitated them. It was difficult to attribute to him the wealth he actually possessed.

He looked up because he saw or sensed someone differ-ent. When the workers contracted as "services" had begun boarding the plane, Don Leonardo had at first congratulated himself on the success of his lobbying, then had admitted that it made him angry to see so many dark-skinned men in lacquered straw hats parade through first class. He had therefore stopped looking at them. Other planes had two entrances, one forward, the other at the rear. It was slightly irritating to pay for first class and have to put up with a parade of badly dressed, badly washed people.

Something made him look, and it was the passing of Lisandro Chávez, who wasn't wearing a hat, who seemed to be of another class, who had a different profile, and who came prepared for the cold of a New York December. The others wore light clothing. They hadn't been told that it's cold in New York. Lisandro was wearing a red-and-black-checked wool jacket that zipped up to the neck. Don Leonardo went on reading *Fortune*. Michelina Laborde de Barroso slowly sipped her mimosa.

Lisandro Chávez decided to keep his eyes shut for the rest of the trip. He asked to not be served any food and to be allowed to sleep. The stewardess gave him a puzzled look. Only people in first class made those kinds of requests. She tried friendliness: Our rice pilaf is excellent. In reality, an insistent question, like a steel mosquito, was drilling its way through Lisandro's forehead: What am I doing here? I shouldn't be doing this. I'm not the man.

The "I" who wasn't there had had other ambitions, and even when he was in high school his family had encouraged them. His father's soda factory was prospering and a hot country like Mexico would always consume soft drinks. The more soft drinks, the easier it was to send Lisandro to private schools, take on a mortgage for the house in Colonia Cuauhtémoc, make the monthly payments on the Chevrolet, maintain the fleet of delivery trucks, and go to Houston once a year, even if just for a couple of days, stroll through the malls, say they'd gone for their annual medical exams . . . Lisandro was likable, he went to parties, read García Márquez; with luck, he'd stop taking the bus to school next year, he'd have his own Volkswagen.

He didn't want to look down for fear of discovering something horrible that could be seen only from the air. There was no homeland anymore, no such thing as Mexico;

the country was a fiction or, rather, a dream maintained by a handful of madmen who at one time believed in the existence of Mexico . . . A family like his was not going to be able to withstand twenty years of crisis, debt, bankruptcy, hopes raised only to fall again with a crash, every six years, more and more poverty, unemployment. His father could no longer come up with the dollars to pay his debts and maintain the factory; the soft-drink business became concentrated and consolidated in a couple of monopolies; the independent labels, the small outfits, had to sell out and leave the market. What kind of work will I do now? his father asked himself as he walked like a ghost through the apartment in the Narvarte district when it was no longer possible to pay the mortgage on the Cuauhtémoc house, when it was no longer possible to make the payments on the Chevrolet, when Lisandro's mother had to put a sign in the window SEWING DONE HERE, when what was left of the savings evaporated first in the inflation of 1985 and then in the devaluation of 1995. The accumulated unpayable debts meant the end of private schools, the end of any illusions about having his own car. Your uncle Roberto has a good voice and earns a few pesos singing and playing the guitar on the corner, but we haven't fallen that low yet, Lisandro, we don't yet have to stand outside the cathedral offering our services, tools in hand and a sign saying PLUMBER CARPENTER ELECTRICIAN BRICKLAYER, we haven't yet fallen as low as the children of our former servants, who have to quit school, walk the streets, dress up as clowns and paint their faces white and toss balls in the air at the corner of Insurgentes and Reforma. Remember Rosita's son, the one you played with, the one who was born here in the house? Well, I mean in the house we had before, on Río Nazas. Well, he's dead. I think his name was Lisandro, like you, of course—they named him that so we would be his godparents. He had to leave his house when he was seventeen and become a fire-eater on street corners; he painted two black tears on his face and ate fire for a year, taking a mouthful of gasoline and sticking a burning wick down his throat until it destroyed his brain, Lisandro, his brain just melted, became like dough, and remember, he was the oldest son, the hope. Now the little ones sell Kleenex, chewing gum—Rosita, our maid—Remember her?—told me. She's desperate, struggling to keep the little ones from starting to sniff glue to get high after working in the streets with bands of homeless kids as numerous as stray dogs, and just as hungry, and forgotten. Lisandro, what's a mother going to tell you whose kids walk the streets to keep her alive, to bring something home? Lisandro, look at your city sinking into the oblivion of what it once was but most of all into the oblivion of what it wanted to be. I have no right to anything, Lisandro Chávez said to himself one day, I have to join the sacrifice of all, join the sacrificed nation, ill-governed, corrupt, uncaring. I have to forget my illusions, make money, help my parents, do what humiliates me least, an honest job, a job that will save me from having contempt for my parents, anger toward my country, shame for myself but that will also save me from the mockery of my friends. He spent years trying to tie together loose ends, to forget the illusions of the past, stripping away ambition for the future, inoculating himself with fatalism, defending himself against resentment, proudly humiliated in his tenacious will to get ahead despite everything. For Lisandro Chávez, twenty-six years old, illusions lost, there was now a new opportunity, to go to New York as a service worker, ignorant that Don Leonardo Barroso had said:

"Why are they all so dark, so obviously lower class?"

"It's the majority, Don Leonardo. The only thing the country can produce."

"Well, let's see if you can find me one who looks like a better sort, whiter—I'll take him. What kind of impression are we going to make, partner?"

And now, as Lisandro passed through first class, Don Leonardo looked at him without imagining that he was one of the contracted workers but wishing instead that all of them were like this working fellow with a decent face and sharp features (although with a big moustache like that of a prosperous member of a mariachi band) and—heavens!— skin lighter than Leonardo Barroso's own. Different, the millionaire noticed, a different boy, don't you think, Miche? But his daughter-in-law and lover had fallen asleep.

<u>2</u>

When they landed at JFK, in the middle of a snowstorm, Barroso wanted to leave the plane as soon as possible, but Michelina was curled up next to the window, covered with a blanket, her head resting on a pillow. She wanted to wait. Let everyone else leave, she asked Don Leonardo.

He wanted to get out and say hello to the agents responsible for recruiting the Mexican workers contracted to clean various buildings in Manhattan over the weekend, when the offices would be empty. The service contract made everything explicit: the workers would come from Mexico to New York on Friday night to work on Saturday and Sunday, returning to Mexico City on Sunday night.

"Everything included, even the airfare—it's cheaper than hiring workers here in Manhattan. We save between 25 and 30 percent," his gringo partners explained.

But they'd forgotten to tell the Mexicans it was cold,

which was why Don Leonardo, surprised by his own humane spirit, wanted to get out first to warn the agents that these boys needed jackets, blankets, something.

They began to parade by, and the fact was there was a bit of everything. Don Leonardo's sense of humanitarian, and now national, pride doubled. The country was so beaten down, especially after having believed that it wasn't; we dreamed we were in the first world and woke to find ourselves back in the third. It's time to work more for Mexico, not to be discouraged, to find new solutions. Like this one. There was a bit of everything, not only the boy with the big moustache wearing the checked jacket but others, too, whom the investor hadn't noticed because the stereotype of the wetback, the peasant with a lacquered hat and skimpy beard, had consumed them all. Now he began to distinguish them, to individualize them, to restore their personalities to them, possessing as he did forty years' experience dealing with workers, supervisors, professional types, bureaucrats, all at his service, always at his service, never anyone above him: that was the motto of his independence, no one, not even the president of the republic, above Leonardo Barroso, or as he put it to his U.S. partners:

"I'm my own man. I'm just like you, a self-made man. I don't owe nobody nothing."

He'd never take that privilege away from anyone. Besides the moustachioed, handsome boy, Barroso tried to differentiate the young men from the provinces, who dressed in a certain way and appeared more backward but also more attractive and somewhat grayer than the young men from Mexico City, the *chilangos*. Even among them he began to distinguish from the herd those who two or three years earlier, during the euphoria of the Salinas de Gortari period, could be seen eating at a Denny's, taking vacations in Puerto

Vallarta, or going to the multiplex cinemas in Ciudad Satélite.

He picked them out because they were the saddest, though the least resigned as well, those like Lisandro Chávez who asked themselves, What am I doing here? I don't belong here. Yes, yes, you belong here, Barroso would have answered, you belong here so thoroughly that in Mexico, even if you dragged yourself on your knees to the Basilica of Guadalupe to visit the Virgin, you couldn't, even with a miracle, earn a hundred dollars for two days' work, four hundred a month, three thousand pesos—not even the Virgin would give you that.

He looked at them as if they were his—his pride, his sons, his idea.

Michelina kept her eyes closed. She didn't want to see the parade of workers. They were young. They were dead ducks. But she was getting tired of traveling with Leonardo. At first she had liked it, it gave her cachet, and although it cost her the ostracization of some and left others resigned, her own family understood and were not in the least disgusted, finally, with the comforts Don Leonardo offered them—especially in these times of crisis, what would become of them without Michelina?

What would become of grandmother Doña Zarina who was over ninety and still collecting curios in cardboard boxes, convinced Porfirio Díaz was still president? What would become of her father, the career diplomat who knew all the genealogies of the wines of Burgundy and the châteaus of the Loire? What would become of her mother, who needed the comforts and money to do the only thing she really liked: to be left alone, to just sit quietly, not doing a thing, with her mouth shut, not even eat because she was ashamed to do it in public? What would become of her brothers, who relied on Leonardo Barroso's generosity—this little job here, that concession there, this little contract, that agency . . . ? But now she was tired. She didn't want to open her eyes. She didn't want to discover those of any young man. Her obligation was to Leonardo. She especially didn't want to think about her husband, Leonardo's son, who didn't miss her, who was happy isolated on the ranch, who didn't blame her for anything, for going off with his dad . . .

Michelina began to fear the eyes of any other man.

The men were given blankets, which they used in atavistic style as serapes. Then they were loaded onto buses. All it took was feeling the cold between the terminal exit and the bus for them to be thankful for the providential jacket, the occasional scarf, the heat of other bodies. They sought one another out, sorted one another out, looked for a comrade who might be like himself, might think the same way, share the same territory. With the peasants, with the villagers, there was always a verbal bridge, but its nature was a species of ancient formality, forms of courtesy that couldn't manage to conceal a hierarchy, although inevitably there are wise-guys who treat the more humble as inferiors, speaking familiarly to them, giving them orders, scolding them. Here, now, that was impossible. They were all beaten down, and being screwed rendered them equal.

An anguished reserve imposed itself on those who did not have rural faces or clothes, a resolve not to admit they were there, that things were going so badly in Mexico, at home, that they had no other recourse but to give in to the three thousand pesos per month for two days a week's work in New York, an alien city, totally strange, where it wasn't necessary to be friendly, to risk confession, mockery, and incomprehension in dealing with one's compatriots.

For that reason, a silence as cold as the air ran from row

to row in the bus where ninety-three Mexican workers were squeezing in, and Lisandro Chávez imagined that in reality all of them, even if they had things to tell one another, were silenced by the snow, by the silence snow imposes, by that silent rain of white stars that fall without making noise, dissolving on whatever they touch, turning back into water, which has no color. What was the city like beneath its long veil of snow? Lisandro could barely make out the urban profiles of Manhattan, known to him from movies, the phantoms of the city, the foggy, snow-covered faces of skyscrapers and bridges, of shops and docks . . .

Tired, the men entered the gymnasium quickly, tossed their bags onto the rickety army-surplus beds Barroso had picked up in an army-navy store, and made for a buffet set up around the corner; the bathrooms were in back. Some of the men began to get familiar, poking one another in the belly, calling one another Bro, Bud and *mano*. Two or three even sang, out of tune, "The Ship of Gold," but the others quieted down, wanting to sleep—the day had begun at five. *I'm on my way to the port where the ship of gold is waiting to carry me away.*

On Saturday morning at six, it was most certainly possible to feel, smell, touch, but not yet see the city. The fog, laden with ice, made it invisible, but the smell of Manhattan entered Lisandro Chávez through his nose and mouth like a steel dagger: it was smoke, acrid, acid smoke from sewers and subways, from enormous twelve-wheel trailers with exhaust pipes and grills at the level of the hard, shiny streets, like patent-leather floors. And on every street, metal mouths opened to eat boxes and more boxes of fruits, vegetables, cans, beers, sodas that reminded him of his dad, suddenly a foreigner in his own Mexico City, just as his son was in New York City, both asking themselves, What are we doing here?

Were we perhaps born to do this? Wasn't our destiny different? What happened?

"Good, upstanding citizens, Lisandro. Don't let anyone tell you otherwise. We've always been good, upstanding citizens. We did everything properly. We never broke a rule. Why did things go so wrong? Because we were good, upstanding citizens? Why do things always go so wrong? Why doesn't this story ever turn out well, son?"

In New York, he thought of his father lost in an apartment in Narvarte as if he were walking across a desert with no shelter, no water, no map, transforming his apartment into the desert of his confusion, caught up in a whirlpool of unforeseen, inexplicable events, as if the whole country had gone wild, jumped its tracks, run away from itself, escaping with shouts and bullets from the prison of order, foresight, institutions. Where was he now? What was he? Of what use was he? Lisandro saw corpses, murdered men, dishonest government officials, endless, incomprehensible intrigues, life-and-death struggles over power, money, women, queers . . . Death, misery, tragedy. His father had fallen into this inexplicable vertigo, giving up in the face of chaos, incapable of standing up to fight, to work. Depending on his son, just as Lisandro the child had depended on him. How much did Lisandro's mother earn sewing torn clothing, eternally knitting a sweater or shawl?

If only a curtain of snow would fall on Mexico City, covering it, hiding its rancor, its answerless questions, the sense of collective fraud. To look at Mexico's burning dust, the mask of an indefatigable sun, resigning oneself to the loss of the city, was not the same as to admire the crown of snow that ornamented the gray buildings and black streets of New York. New York: building itself up out of its own disintegration, its inevitable destiny as the city for everyone, energetic, tireless, brutal, murderous city of the entire world, where we all recognize ourselves and see our worst and our best.

This was the building. Lisandro Chávez refused to stare like a hick all the way up the forty floors. He only wondered how they were going to wash the windows in the middle of a snowstorm that at times managed to dissolve the very profile of the building, as if the skyscraper, too, were made of ice. It was an illusion. As the day cleared up a bit, a building completely made of glass became visible, with nothing in it that wasn't transparent: an immense music box made of mirrors, unified by its own chrome-covered, nickel-plated glass, a palace like a crystal deck of cards, a toy of quicksilver labyrinths.

They were here to clean the inside, it was explained to them, gathered together in the interior atrium, which was like a patio of gray light whose six sides rose like sheer blind cliffs, six walls of pure glass. Even the two elevators were glass. Six times forty floors, two hundred forty interior facades for offices that lived their simultaneously secret and transparent life around a shared agnostic atrium, a cube excavated in the heart of the toy palace, the dream of a child building a castle on the beach, except that instead of sand he was given glass.

The scaffolding was waiting to lift them to the different floors, adjusting to the surface at each level as the building became narrower, like a pyramid, at the top. As if in a Teotihuacán made of glass, the workers began to rise to the tenth, twentieth, thirtieth floor to clean the glass and descend, in ranks of ten, armed with manual cleaning devices and tanks of a special glass cleanser on their backs, like the oxygen tanks worn by underwater explorers. Lisandro ascended to the crystal sky but he felt submerged, descending to a strange sea of glass in an unknown, upside-down world.

"Is that stuff safe?" Leonardo Barroso asked.

"Very safe. It's biodegradable. Once it's used, it decomposes into innocuous elements," his Yankee partners answered.

"It sure better. I put a clause in the contract making you responsible for work-related illnesses. You could die of cancer here just by breathing."

"Come on, Don Leonardo," laughed the Yankees. "You're tougher than we are."

"Welcome a tough Mexican," concluded the businessman.

"You're one tough hombre!" cheered the gringos.

<u>3</u>

She walked with a feeling of thankfulness from her apartment on East 67th Street to the building on Park Avenue. She had spent Friday night in seclusion, giving orders to the doorman to let no one up, especially not her ex-husband, whose insistent voice she listened to all night on the answering machine as it begged to see her. Listen, sweetheart, let me talk to you, we were very hasty, we should have thought things through more, waited until our wounds healed. You know I don't want to hurt you, but life sometimes gets complicated, and I always knew, even in the worst moments, that I had you, I could come back to you, you would understand, you would forgive me, because if the situation had been the other way around, I would have forgiven . . .

"No!" the desperate woman shouted at the telephone, at the voice of her ex-husband, invisible to her. "No! You would have gotten even as cruelly as you could. In your usual selfish way, you'd have enslaved me with your forgiveness."

She spent a fearful night pacing back and forth in the small apartment, nicely appointed, even lavish in many details—pacing back and forth between the picture window, whose wool drapes she'd opened to give herself over completely to the sumptuous snow scene, while the distorting eye of the Cyclops at the door protects people from eternal observation, the city's perpetual threat. The crystal hole in the door that allows the hall to be seen, allows one to see without being seen but to see a distorted, submarine world, as if through the blind eye of a tired shark that can't allow itself the luxury of rest lest it drown, sink to the bottom of the sea. Sharks have to keep moving eternally to survive.

She felt no fear the following morning. The storm was over and the city had been dusted with white powder, as if for a party. It was three weeks before Christmas and the whole town was decked out, covered with lights, shining like a huge mirror. Her husband never rose before nine. It was seven when she left to walk to the office. She was thankful that the weekend would give her a chance to lock herself away and get something done, catch up with her paperwork, dictate instructions without telephone calls, faxes, the jokes of her office mates, the whole New York office ritual, the obligation to be simultaneously indifferent and witty, to have a wisecrack or joke at the ready, to know how to end conversations and phone calls brusquely, to never touch anyone—especially that, to never touch one another physically, never a hug, not even a social kiss on the cheek, bodies at a distance, eyes avoiding eyes . . . Good. Her husband would not find her here. He had no idea . . . He'd go insane calling her, trying to worm his way into her apartment.

That morning, she was a woman who felt free. She'd resisted the outside world. Her husband, too, was now outside her life, expelled from her physical and emotional interior space. She resisted the crowds that absorbed her every morning as she walked to work, making her feel she was part of a herd, individually insignificant, stripped of importance: weren't the hundreds of people walking down Park from 67th to 66th Street at any moment of the morning doing something as important—or unimportant—as what she was doing, or perhaps even more important or less important.

There were no happy faces.

There were no faces proud of what they were doing.

There were no faces satisfied with their jobs.

Because the faces were also working, squinting, gesticulating, rolling their eyes, feigning horror, expressing real shock, skepticism, false attentiveness, mockery, irony, authority. Rarely, she told herself, as she walked rapidly, enjoying the solitude of the snow-covered city, rarely did she show them or they her a true spontaneous face, without the panoply of acquired gestures to please, convince, intimidate, impose respect, share intrigues.

Alone, inviolable, self-possessed, in control of her whole body and soul, inside and out. The cold morning, the solitude, a sure step, elegant, her own person—she was given all that on the walk from her apartment to her office.

The building was full of workers. She'd forgotten. She laughed at herself. The day she'd chosen to be alone in the office was the day they were going to clean the interior glass. They had given advanced warning. She'd forgotten. Smiling, she went to the top floor without looking at anyone, like a bird who confuses its cage for freedom. She walked through the corridor on the fortieth floor—glass walls, glass doors, they lived suspended in midair; even the floors were made of an opaque glass, the tyrant of an architect having forbidden carpeting in his crystal masterpiece.

She entered her office, located between the glass corridor

and the interior atrium. It did not have a view of the street. The polluted air of the street did not circulate here; there was only air-conditioning. The building was sealed, isolated, the way she wanted to feel today. The door opened onto the corridor. But the entire glass wall faced the atrium, and at times she liked to feel that her gaze fell forty stories, transforming on the way into a snowflake, a feather, a butterfly.

Crystal above the corridor. Glass on both sides, so the two offices next to hers were also transparent, obliging her colleagues to be somewhat circumspect in their physical habits while nevertheless maintaining a certain degree of naturalness in their behavior. Taking off their shoes, putting their feet up on the desk—everyone was allowed to do that, but the men could scratch their armpits or between their legs, while the women couldn't. But the women could look at themselves in the mirror and fix their makeup. The men— with some exceptions—couldn't do that.

She looked straight ahead at the atrium and saw him.

4

Lisandro Chávez was alone on the plank they raised to the top floor. They'd asked everyone if they suffered from vertigo, and he'd recalled that he sometimes did—once on a Ferris wheel he'd had the urge to jump into the void—but he'd kept his mouth shut.

At first, busy arranging his mops and cleaning devices, but most of all concerned about making himself comfortable, he did not see her and did not look in. His objective was the glass. Everyone supposed there would be no one working in the building on Saturday.

She saw him first and took no notice of him. She saw him without seeing him. She saw him the way one sees or no longer sees the people fate assigns one when one rides an elevator, gets on a bus, or takes a seat at the movies. She smiled. Her job as an advertising executive obliged her to take planes to meet clients in a nation the size of the universe. She feared nothing so much as a talkative person seated next to her, the kind who tells you his miseries, his profession, how much money he makes—the kind who ends up, after three Bloody Marys, with his hand on your knee. She smiled again. She'd fallen asleep many times with a stranger next to her, both of them wrapped in their airplane blankets like virginal lovers.

When Lisandro's and Audrey's eyes met, she nodded a greeting the way one might, out of courtesy, say hello to a waiter, less effusively, say, than one might to a doorman. Lisandro had carefully cleaned the first window, that of Audrey's office, and as he removed the light film of dust and ash, she had begun appearing, distant and misty at first, then gradually closer, approaching without moving, thanks to the increasing clearness of the glass. It was like focusing a camera. It was like making her his.

The transparency of the glass restored her face. The light in the office illuminated the woman's head from behind, giving her blond hair, which fell like a rope down her neck, the smoothness and movement of a wheat field. The light was concentrated on her nape and, as she pushed aside the soft white hair, it emphasized the blond waves of each strand rising from her back like a handful of seeds to find their earth, their thick, sensual fertility, in the mass of braided hair.

She was working with her head bent over her papers, indifferent to him, indifferent to the work of the others, servile, manual work so different from her own, from her efforts to come up with a nice catchy slogan for a Pepsi commercial. He was uncomfortable, afraid of distracting her with the movement of his arms over the glass. If she raised her head, would she do it angrily, annoyed at the intrusion of a worker?

What kind of expression would she have when she looked at him again?

Christ, she thought to herself. They warned me workers were coming. I hope this man isn't spying on me. I feel spied on. I don't like this. It's distracting.

She raised her eyes and found Lisandro's. She wanted to get mad but couldn't. There was something in that face that amazed her. At first, she didn't note the physical details. What seized her attention was something else. Something she never found in a man. She struggled to find a word—she who was a professional with words, slogans—for the attitude, the face of the worker washing the office windows.

It came to her suddenly. Courtesy. What there was in this man—in his attitude, his distance, his way of nodding his head, the strange mixture of sadness and joy in his eyes—was courtesy, an incredible absence of vulgarity.

This man, she said to herself, would never telephone me frantically at two in the morning, begging me to forgive him. He would restrain himself. He would respect my solitude, and I his.

What would this man do for you? she immediately asked herself.

He would invite me to dinner and then take me to my apartment. He wouldn't let me go home alone in a taxi.

Fleetingly he glimpsed her large, deep chestnut eyes as she looked up, and he became upset, lowering his own. He went on with his work but immediately recalled that she had smiled. Had he imagined it or had it really happened? He dared to look at her. The woman smiled, very briefly, very courteously, before averting her eyes and going back to her work.

That glance was sufficient. He didn't expect to find melancholy in the eyes of a gringa. He'd been told that Yankee women were strong, very sure of themselves, very professional, very punctual—not that Mexican women were weak, insecure, slapdash, and slow, no, not at all. The point was that a woman who came to work on Saturdays had to be anything but melancholy, perhaps tender, perhaps passionate. That Lisandro saw clearly in the woman's expression. She had a sorrow, she had a yearning. She yearned for something. That's what her expression told him: I want something I lack.

Audrey lowered her head farther than necessary in order to lose herself in her papers. This was ridiculous. Was she going to fall in love on the rebound, with the first man to come along, just to make the definitive break with her husband, to teach him a lesson? The worker was handsome, that was the bad part; he had that attitude of unusual, almost insulting gentlemanliness, totally inappropriate, as if he were taking unfair advantage of his inferiority. But he also had shining eyes in which moments of sadness and joy were projected with equal intensity, he had a smooth complexion, olive-toned and sensual, a short, pointy nose, trembling nostrils, black, curly young hair, a thick moustache. He was the complete opposite of her husband. He was—she smiled again—a mirage.

He returned her smile. He had strong white teeth. Lisandro thought he'd avoided all the jobs that would have humiliated him in the eyes of the people he knew when he was a boy with ambition. He'd taken work as a waiter in Focolare, and the situation had became painful when he'd had to serve a table of his old friends from high school. All of them had prospered except him. He embarrassed them, they embarrassed him. They didn't know how to address him, what to say to him. Remember the goal you scored against the Simón Bolívar team? That was the nicest thing he heard, followed by an embarrassed silence.

He was no good as an office worker. He'd left high school after his third year and didn't know shorthand or how to type. Being a taxi driver was even worse. He envied those of his fares who were richer and disdained those who were poorer, Mexico City and its tangled traffic drove him insane, infuriated him, made him shoot his mouth off, curse people out, be everything he didn't want to be. Store clerk, gas station attendant—whatever there was, sure. Unfortunately, not even those jobs existed. Everyone was out of a job; even professional beggars were officially classified as "unemployed." He was thankful for this job in the United States. He was thankful for the eyes of the woman who was now looking directly at him.

He didn't know that she wasn't simply looking at him. She was imagining him. She was one step ahead of him. She imagined him in all kinds of situations. She bit her pencil. What sports would he like? He looked very strong, very athletic. Movies, actors—did he like film, opera, some television program, what? Was he one of those people who tell how pictures end? Of course not. That you could see immediately. He smiled directly at her. She wondered if he was the kind of man who could put up with a woman like her, who couldn't resist telling the man she was with how the picture turned out, how the murder mystery ended, everything but her personal story—no one knew how that would turn out.

Perhaps he guessed something of what was going on in her mind. He wished he could tell her frankly, I'm different.

Don't judge by appearances, I shouldn't be doing this, I'm not this, I'm not what you imagine. But he couldn't speak to the glass, he could only fall in love with the light of the windows, which most certainly could penetrate her, touch her; they shared the light.

He wanted badly to have her, touch her, even if only through the glass.

Distressed, she got up and left the office.

Had something offended her? Some gesture? Had some sign he'd made been inappropriate, had he gone too far because he didn't know gringo manners? He was angry with himself for feeling so much fear, so much disappointment, so much insecurity. Perhaps she had gone away for good. What was her name? Was she wondering about his? What did they have in common?

She came back with her lipstick in her hand.

She held it there, open, pointing upward, and stared at Lisandro.

They spent several minutes looking at each other that way, in silence, separated by the crystal frontier.

Between the two of them an ironic community was being created, a community in isolation. They were recalling their own lives, imagining each other's lives, the streets they walked, the caves where they took refuge, the jungle that their cities, New York and Mexico City, were—the dangers, the poverty, the menace of their towns, the muggers, the police, the beggars, the thieves, the horror of two big cities full of people like them, people too small to defend themselves from so many threats.

I'm not this man, he said to himself stupidly, not knowing that she wanted him to be himself, like this, as she had discovered him that morning when she woke up and said to herself, My God, whom have I been married to? How is it possible? Whom have I been living with? And then she found him and attributed to him everything that was the opposite of her husband—courtesy, melancholy, indifference when she told him how pictures ended.

He and she alone.

He and she, inviolable in their solitude.

Separated from the others, she and he face-to-face on an unusual Saturday morning, imagining each other.

What were their names? Both had the same idea. I can give this man the name I like best. And he: Some men have to imagine the woman they love as a stranger; he was going to have to imagine a stranger as a lover.

It wasn't necessary to say yes.

She wrote her name on the glass with her lipstick. She wrote it backward, as if in a mirror: YERDUA. It looked like an exotic name, the name of an Indian goddess.

He hesitated to write his, such a long name, so unusual in English. Blindly, without reflecting, stupidly perhaps, full of uncertainty—he doesn't know even today why he did it— he wrote only his nationality: NACIXEM.

She made a gesture as if to ask for more, two hands held apart, open—something more?

No, he shook his head, nothing more.

From down below they began to shout to him, What's taking you so long up there, aren't you finished, don't be so lazy, hurry up, it's already nine o'clock, we have to get on to the next building.

Something more? asked the gesture, Audrey's silent voice.

He placed his lips on the glass. She didn't hesitate to do the same. Their lips united through the glass. Both closed their eyes. She didn't open hers for several minutes. When she did, he was no longer there.

THE BET

To César Antonio Molina

Stone country. Stone language. Stone blood and memory.
If you don't escape from here, you're going to turn to
stone. Get out quick, cross the border, shake off that stone.

They arranged to meet him at the hotel at 9:00 a.m. in
order to get to Cuernavaca and back the same day. Just three
passengers. A tourist from the United States—you could tell
a mile away—blond, pale, dressed in a Tehuana costume or
something folkloric like that. A Mexican who kept holding
her hand, a low-class boor, dark, with a big moustache and
a purple shirt. And a woman he couldn't place, white, a bit
dried out, skinny, wearing low heels, a wide skirt, and a
hand-knit wool sweater. Her hair was tied back, and if she
hadn't been so white, Leandro would have sworn she was a
maid. But she spoke up for herself, loudly and aggressively
and with a Spanish accent.

As a tourist driver, Leandro Reyes was used to all kinds,
and this combination was neither better nor worse than all

the others. The Spanish woman sat up front with him, and the couple, the Mexican and the gringa, cuddled together in back. The Spanish woman winked at Leandro and nodded her head significantly toward the rear. Leandro refused to take her lead. He was arrogant with all his passengers—no one was going to think they were dealing with an obsequious, submissive little Mexican. He did not return the Spaniard's wink.

He took off like a shot, more quickly than he intended, but the strangled traffic in Mexico City made him slow down. He put a tape in his player and announced that it gave cultural descriptions of Mexican tourist sites—the pyramids at Teotihuacán, the beaches of Cancún, and of course Cuernavaca, where they were going this morning. He provided, he also announced, first-class service, for discerning clients.

The voices, the theme music, the exhaust from the buses, the polluted air of the city put all of them to sleep except him. And as soon as they got onto the highway to Cuernavaca, he accelerated and went faster and faster. He looked at the couple, the gringa and the yahoo, in his rearview mirror and got mad, as he always did when a dark guy like that took advantage of the chickadees who came looking for the exotic, for romance, and ended up in the hands of sons of bitches like this, crude, disgusting assholes no woman here would give a nickel for. The least he could do was scare the shit out of them.

He drove quickly and began to repeat the descriptions on the tape out loud, until the squatty body in back got riled up and started saying, Careful on the curve here. Listen, don't repeat what the tape says. You think I'm deaf? And the gringa laughed—how exciting!—and only the Spanish lady next to him showed no emotion. She looked at Leandro with a scornful smile and Leandro said to them, This is not a simple tourist trip. It's a cultural trip. That's what they told me at the hotel. If you want to make out, you should have picked another driver.

The dark man in back sank down; the gringa gave him a kiss, and the asshole plunged his circus-clown face—What does this guy think he is, a soap opera star or something?—into the blond hair and didn't make another squawk. But the Spanish lady said, Why do you work at a job you don't like?

Lucky you weren't born stupid. Look at Paquito, the village idiot. Look at how he goes out to the plaza to get some sun, smiling at the sun and the people. You can just see how he wants people to like him. But here in your village that doesn't work. What right does that jackass have to feel happy just because he's alive and the sun shines on his fingernails, on the three or four teeth he's got left, on his almost-always-opaque eyes? Take a good look a him. As if he himself knows that his happiness can't last long, he scratches his head of short hair, perplexed. His hair's not combed and not messed up, because it's so short that the only important thing is knowing if it grows or not. It grows forward, as if invading his narrow and perpetually worried, perpetually furrowed forehead. This morning, the shine of his always-dead eyes contrasts with his wrinkled brow. He looks toward the arches of the plaza. What will happen to him today? He turns off that idea, pushes it shut like an old, dusty drawer. But there is nothing more immediate than the threat. He's defenseless. He realizes he's in the middle of the plaza at noon, under the blazing sun, exposed, with nothing to protect him from the eyes of other people. He raises a hand to his eyes, closes them, hides, disguises himself, and with every passing minute becomes more and more conspicuous. Even people who never notice him are looking at him now. Paquito closes his eyes so no one will look at him that way. He feels terrible pains in his head. If he closes his eyes, the sun will die. He opens them and looks at the stone. Stone plaza. If you don't leave here, you will turn to stone.

The Spanish woman observed him carefully and astutely. First, he wanted to pass for a cultured driver who would show foreigners the beauties of Mexico. It bothered him that instead of him another Mexican was making love to a gringa. It bothered him that they were giving each other sloppy kisses instead of listening to what the cultural tapes said about the Indian ruins. He wanted to get them upset, scare them, drive 120 miles an hour and give his air of culture an edge of savage physical violence. The Spanish woman felt sorry for this little man over forty with the ruddy, almost carrot-colored complexion that she'd noticed in a number of Mexicans in the city, a mixture of blonds and Indians. A sulphur color, really. His carroty reddish-colored hair was obviously dyed, and he wore a blue shirt, a tie, and a suit that was brilliant and silvery, just like the Iberia plane that had brought her to Mexico as the winner of the contest for best tourist guide at the Asturias caves.

Everyone went nuts because she won, but that's what luck's all about—you can't do anything about it.

This man didn't know the two of them did the same kind of work. Still, she couldn't figure him out and amused herself watching the faces he made, all of them so phony it was laughable, angry, disdainful the whole time but know-it-all one minute, fearlessly, savagely macho the next, driven nuts by the couple he envied in the backseat. But more put out, the Spanish woman concluded, because she was smiling at him, staring at him, and not reacting to his driving.

"Why are you looking at me?" he finally blurted out as they got to Cuernavaca. "Do I have two heads or something?"

"You never answered my question. Why do you work at a job you don't like?"

"Hey, since when do we know each other? Who gave you the right to speak familiarly to me?"

"In Spain, we're not that formal."

"Right. But we're not in Spain now. Around here we respect one another."

"So, respect yourself first."

He looked at her, angry and uneasy. What should he do: punch her, kick her out of the car, abandon her in Tres Marías? He couldn't. Would they fire him? Instantly. He always worried about that, though the fact was that people always put up with his nastiness. He banked on it: Be daring, demand respect, don't chicken out, Leandro, risk being fired, and you'll see that people will almost always cave in—they don't want complications, they'll put up with your coarse language. Some won't, and then you play for keeps, you make them get out right in the middle of the Guerrero mountains, you challenge them to walk to Chilpancingo, go ahead. They say they'll complain to the hotel, you speak up about your code of dignity. Who doesn't have run-ins with these arrogant goddamn tourists? If you want, I'll take the matter up with the union—they'll back me up. Want a drivers' strike that will affect not only this lousy hotel but every hotel in town? They calm you down, agree with you: These people are abusive, don't respect a driver's work. Right away they treat us like common cabbies, which we aren't, we're drivers for cultured tourists. With the Europeans, the Japanese we never have problems, we respect them, they respect us, we give high-class service—the fights only happen with the gringos and these Mexican upstarts.

But this woman was Spanish and he didn't know how to deal with her. If he were alone with the gringa and pretty boy here with the moustache studying anatomy in the backseat and ignoring the cultural explanations, treating him like the wild cabbie from Borneo, a wild man behind the wheel, and not giving him the respect he was due . . . Did she give him any respect? She watched him with a smile on her face that was more insulting than a curse, God knows why, and he watched her, feeling she liked being watched that way, not understanding her, as if she too were a mystery, more a mystery to him than he was to her.

"Come on," the Spanish woman said brusquely, "you and I do the same work. I'm a tourist guide too. But it seems I like my work and you do nothing but get mad. Why do you do it if you don't like it? Don't be a jerk. Take up another line of work, you fool, there are lots of ways to make a living."

He didn't know what to say. Thank God the gas station was in sight. He stopped and quickly got out. He put on a show with the attendants, hugging them, exchanging wisecracks, gesturing obscenely. They poked one another in the belly and made jokes full of double entendres. Was he carrying a decent load? the attendants wanted to know. He winked, they squinted suggestively at the passengers. What kind of load was he carrying? He winked, they told him to help himself, tourists were all assholes but they had cash— why them and not us, right? Come on, buddy, have a shot of rotgut to make the trip more enjoyable . . .

The Spaniard poked her head out the window and

shouted at Leandro, "You take a drink and I'll turn you in personally and we'll get out right here, you crook. Why don't you stop trying to be a fucking he-man and do your job, you son of a bitch!"

The attendants laughed their heads off, grabbing their guts, slapping their thighs, holding onto one another for dear life, everyone patting everyone else's ass. Holy shit, Leandro, what'd you do, get married? Or is that your mother-in-law? They sure have you on a short leash, don't they? Better not come around here anymore, son, they've got you yoked up like an ox . . .

He took off, his face bright red.

"Why did you have to embarrass me like that, lady? I treat you with respect."

"First off, my name is Encarnación Cadalso, but my friends call me Encarna. We're going to get along just fine. Just screw up your balls. Let me show you how to get along. You can't fool me, you fucker. All you are is an insecure man in a macho suit. You fuck everyone else over and all you do is end up bitter. Let's get to Cuernavaca, which they tell me is a nice place."

Stone plaza. Eyes of stone. The idiot looks over at the group of thugs sitting in the café. You're with them. They look at Paquito. They make bets. If we start hitting him, will he fight back or not? If he doesn't, will he stay or go? If he stays, will it be so we can hit him some more? Does this asshole like to suffer? Or is he just trying to tire us out so we'll leave him alone? Country of stone: everything here is a matter of bets. Will it rain or not? Will it be hot or cold? Who's going to win, Atlántico or Real Madrid? Does Espartaco get the ears or does he get gored? Is what's-her-name a virgin or not? Is so-and-so a fag or not? Does Doctor Centeno dye his hair? Does Jacinta have false teeth? Did the pharmacist get her tits done? How many bets? Who in this town dares to leave their doors unlocked? How many brave men are there who leave them open? How many bets?

Holding hands and giggling like idiots, the happy couple, the gringa and the boor, gave themselves over to contemplating the gorge from the terrace of Cortés's palace. Encarna and Leandro were studying Diego Rivera's murals of the conquest of Mexico instead, and she said, Were we Spaniards really that bad? Leandro didn't know what to say, he wasn't there to make value judgments, that's how the painter saw it. Well, why do you speak Spanish and not Indian if you're so sorry for the Indians? she said.

"They were really brave," said Leandro. "They had a great civilization and the Spaniards destroyed it."

"If that's the case and you love them so much, you should treat them well today," Encarna said in her hard, realistic manner. "The way I see it is they're being treated worse than ever."

Then they stopped in a room where Rivera had painted everything Europe owed Mexico: chocolate, corn, tomatoes, chiles, turkey . . .

"Hold it right there," exclaimed Encarna. "If he'd put everything Mexico owes Europe, all the walls in this palace wouldn't be enough."

Leandro ended up laughing at the uninhibited Spaniard's wit, and when they sat down in the café opposite the palace to have a couple of icy beers, the driver let his guard down and began to tell her how his father had been a waiter in the restaurant of an Acapulco hotel, how when he was just a little kid he had to sell candy on the streets of the port. How he felt more dignified with his box of candy on the streets than his father, stuffed into that monkey suit, having to take care of every damn fool who came in to eat.

"It hurt me every time I saw him in that waiter's jacket with a napkin over his arm, arranging chairs, always bent over, always bent over—that's what I couldn't stand, his head always bent over. I told myself that wasn't for me, I'd be anything but I wouldn't bend my head."

"Listen, maybe your father was just a courteous man by nature."

"No, what he was was servile, submissive, a slave, like almost everybody else in this country. A few people can do everything, very few; the majority is fucked over forever and can't do anything. A handful of fuckers enslave millions of servile jerks. That's how it's always been."

"It's hard to make something of yourself, Leandro. I admire your effort. But don't make yourself bitter in the process. You can't just waste your time saying, Why them and not me? Don't let your own opportunities pass you by. Grab them by the tail—you know opportunity doesn't knock twice."

She asked him why his name was Leandro.

"Encarnación is a pretty name. Who gave it to you?"

"God himself, my boy. I was born on the feast of the Incarnation. What about you?"

"I was named after Leandro Valle. A hero. I was born on the street named after him."

He told her how as a teenager he stopped selling candy and became a caddie at an Acapulco golf course.

"Know something? At night, I stayed behind to sleep on the fairway. I never had a softer bed. Even my dreams changed. It was then I decided that someday I'd be rich. That soft grass lulled me, it was like a cradle."

"Did your father help you?"

"No, that's the point. He didn't want me to better myself. You're going to take a tumble, he'd tell me. I found out from my pals at the hotel where he worked that he never told me about offers people made to him for me because I was his son—chances to study, drive a car. All he wanted was for me to be a waiter like him. He didn't want me to be more than he was. That's the thing. I had to make my own opportunities. Caddie. First I drove golf carts, then I became a real driver. Bye-bye, Acapulco. I never saw my father again."

"I understand you. But you don't have to be foulmouthed just because your father was a courteous waiter. You have to serve. Both of us do. What do you get by saying all day I have to do this but I don't like it. Don't get even by offending your clients. It just isn't something a gentleman should do."

Leandro blushed. For a time he said nothing. And then the gringa and her leading man appeared among the laurel trees, motioning that they wanted to go back to the city. It was time.

Leandro got up and stood behind Encarnación. He slid out her chair so she could get up. She was shocked. No one had ever done that for her before. She was even afraid. Was he going to hit her? But not even Leandro knew why he'd performed that act of courtesy.

They returned to Mexico City in silence. The couple fell asleep in each other's arms. Leandro drove at a normal speed. Encarna observed the landscape: from the tropical aroma to the frozen pines to the smog of the highlands, pollution trapped by imprisoning mountains.

When they reached the hotel, the vulgarian didn't even look at Leandro, but the American tourist smiled and gave him a good tip.

Alone, Leandro and Encarna looked and looked into each other's eyes, each of them knowing no one had looked at them that way in a long time.

"Come on up with me," she said. "My bed is softer than a golf course."

One night they checked all the houses, door after door, to see who would win the bet about the open doors. They found all of them either locked or bolted; only the idiot's door was open, the door to the shack where Paquito slept, and the idiot was asleep on a plank bed, asleep for one second, awake the next, rubbing his eyes, perplexed, as always. The only door without a lock and another lost bet: Paquito's room wasn't a pigsty, it shone with cleanliness, it was neat as a pin. That bothered them, so they doused it with Coca-Cola and walked out laughing and shouting. The next day the moron avoided looking at you and your friends, let himself be loved by the sun, and all of you bet again: If he just sunbathes, we'll leave him in peace, but if he walks around the plaza as if he were the lord and master, we'll beat him up. An idiot can't be the master. We're the masters and we can do whatever we like. Who says we can't? Paquito moved, squinting, looking at the sun, and all of you shouted your mockery and began to bombard him first with dough balls, then with stale rolls, then with bottle caps, and the idiot protected himself with his hands and arms, only repeating, Leave me alone, leave me alone, look, I'm a good boy, I'm not hurting you, leave me in peace, don't make me leave town, my father's going to come take care of me, my father's very strong . . . Shit, you say to them, we're just pelting him with dough balls, and something exploded inside you, something uncontrollable. You got up from the table, the chair fell over, you lurched out of the shadows of the plaza and started punching the idiot, who screamed, I'm a good boy, stop hitting me, through his rotten teeth and bleeding mouth. I'm going to tell my father. But all the time you knew that what you really wanted was to punch your friends, the thugs, your guards, the ones who held you prisoner in this stone jail, in this shitty town. You'd like to make them bleed, punch them to death, not this poor devil you take out your sense of injustice on, your violated fraternity, your shame . . . Get out, get out. Bet you're going to leave.

It was a very beautiful night. Both of them enjoyed themselves, found each other, then lost each other. They agreed it was an impossible love, but it had been worth it. As Encarna said, You've got to grab opportunity by the tail because it doesn't knock twice and—poof!—it disappears as if by magic.

They wrote each other during the first months. He didn't know how to express himself very well, but she gave him confidence. He'd had to build his self-assurance himself, the way you build a sand castle at the beach, knowing that it's fragile and may be washed away by the first wave. Now that he knew Encarna he felt he was leaving behind everything false and phony in his life. But there was always the risk that he would go back to being the way he'd always been if he lost her, if he never saw her again. It was a pain in the ass having to serve, to fight with stupid, arrogant clients who didn't even look at you, as if you were made of glass. His bad habits came back, his insolence, his obscenities. His foul humor came back. When he was a kid, he kicked the fire hydrants in Acapulco, furious that he was what he was and not what he wanted to be. Why them and not me? The other night, outside a luxury restaurant, he'd done the same thing, he couldn't control himself, he began to kick the fenders of the cars parked there. The other drivers had to restrain him. Now he was in big trouble—this car belonged to Minister X, that one belonged to a big deal in the PRI, a third belonged to the guy who bought the privatized business Z . . .

What luck that at that moment the northern millionaire and ex-minister Don Leonardo Barroso left the restaurant looking for his driver and the man in charge of valet parking told him the man had felt sick and had gone home, leaving the keys of Mr. Barroso's car. Now it was Barroso's turn to throw a fit—This country is populated by irresponsible fools!—and suddenly he saw himself reflected in poor Leandro, in the rage of a poor tourist driver parked there waiting for fares and kicking fenders, and he burst out laughing. He calmed down as a result of that encounter, that comparison, that sense of identification. He also calmed down because on his arm he had a divine woman, a real piece with long hair and a cleft chin. The woman had Mr. Barroso under her spell—you could see it with your eyes shut. She had him by the nuts, no question.

Don Leonardo Barroso asked Leandro to drive him and his daughter-in-law home, and he liked the driver's style, as well as his discretion and appearance, so much that he hired him to drive in Spain in November. He had business there and needed a driver for his daughter-in-law, who would accompany him. Leandro, distrustful after his initial delight faded, wondered if this tall, powerful man, who could do whatever he damn well pleased, saw in him a harmless eunuch who presented no danger driving his "daughter-in-law" around while he took care of his "business." But how could Leandro turn down such an offer? He overcame his diffidence, telling himself that if his bosses had confidence in him, why shouldn't he feel that way about them?

His bosses. That was different from driving around tourists. It was a step up, and you could see Mr. Barroso was a strong man, a boss who inspired respect and made quick decisions. Leandro didn't have to be asked twice—it would be possible to serve someone like that with dignity, with pleasure, without humbling himself. Besides—he wrote instantly to Asturias—he was going to see Encarna again.

They'd bet that the person who gave Paquito a good beating would win a round-trip bus ticket from town to the ocean. And even though Portugal was closer to Extremadura, Portugal was Gallego country, where you couldn't trust people and they talked funny. On the other hand, Asturias, even though it was farther away, was a Spanish sea and, as the anthem said, it was "dear homeland." It turned out that the uncle of one of your thug friends was a bus driver and could do you a favor. He was Basque and understood that the world revolved around betting, around betting alone. Even the wheels of the bus—he said with a philosopher's air—revolved around the bet that accidents were possible but unlikely. "Unless one driver bets another he'll race him from Madrid to Oviedo," said the thug's uncle, laughing. It didn't surprise you that to find the uncle and ask him to help you out no one thought to use the telephone or send a telegram; instead a handwritten note with no copy was sent without an envelope via a relay of bus drivers. Which is why so much time passed between the beating you gave Paquito and the promised trip to the sea. So much time passed, in fact, that you almost lost the bet you won because there were other bets—around here, they live by betting. One hundred pesetas says Paquito doesn't turn up in the plaza again after the beating you gave him. Two hundred says he will and, if he doesn't, a thousand pesetas says he left town, two thousand that he died, six *perras* that he's hiding out. They went to the door of the shack where the idiot slept. Nothing but silence. The door opened. An old man came out, dressed in black with a black hat pulled down to his huge ears, his gray whiskers, three days' worth. He was scratching at the neck of his white, tieless shirt. His earlobes were so hairy they looked like a newborn animal. A wolf cub.

You kept the comparison to yourself. Your pals didn't like that stuff, your comparisons, allusions, your interest in words. Language of stone, fallen from the moon, in a country where the favorite sport was moving stones. Heads of stone: may nothing enter them. Except a new bet. Bets were like freedom, were intelligence and manliness all in one. Why is this old man in mourning coming out of the shack where Paquito used to live? Did Paquito die? They looked at one another with a strange mix of curiosity, fear, mockery, and respect. How they felt like betting and ceasing to have doubts! Just for once, your friends' ways of looking were all different. This imposing man, full of authority despite his poverty, aroused in each one of you a different, unexpected attitude. Just for once, they weren't the pack of young wolves eating together at night. Laughter, respect, and fear. Did Paquito die? Was that why this old man of stone who appeared in the idiot's house was dressed in mourning? They remained silent when you told them that the bet was pointless—it was impossible to know if Paquito didn't go to the plaza anymore because he'd died and in his house they were dressed in mourning because around here everyone was always dressed in mourning. Didn't they realize that? In this town, mourning is perpetual. Someone's always dying. Always. And there are going to be more, the old man in mourning thundered. Let's see if you only know how to beat up a defenseless child. Let's see if you're little machos of courage and honor or, as I suspect, a bunch of faggy shitass thugs. The old man spoke and you felt that your life was no longer your own, that all your plans were going to fall apart, that all bets were going to combine into one.

Encarna never expected to see him again. She hesitated. She wasn't going to change her looks or her way of life. Let him see her as she was, as she was every day, doing what she did to earn her daily bread. "*Pan de chourar*," the bride's bread, she reminded herself, was the "bread of tears" in these parts.

He already knew where to find her. From nine to three, April to November. The rest of the time, the cave was closed to prevent the paintings from deteriorating. Breath, sweat, the guts of men and women, everything that gives us life takes it away from the cave, wears it away, rots it. The cave's pictures of deer and bison, horses painted in charcoal, oxide, and blood are locked in mortal combat with the oxide and blood of living people.

Sometimes Encarna dreamed about those wild horses painted twenty thousand years ago, and during the winter, when the cave was closed to the public, she imagined them condemned to silence and darkness, waiting for spring to gallop again. Insane with hunger, blindness, and love.

She was a simple woman. That is, she never told her dreams to anyone. To the tourists she would only say, tersely, "Very primitive. This is very primitive."

It was raining hard that November day just before the cave would close for the season, and to walk there Encarna had put on her galoshes. The road from her house to the cave entrance was a steep clay path. The mud came up to her ankles. She covered her head with a scarf, but, even so, strands of dripping hair covered her forehead and she had to close her eyes and continuously wipe her hand across her face as if she were crying. The jacket she had on wasn't waterproof; it was wool, with a rabbit collar, and it didn't smell good. Her full skirts, covering a petticoat, made her seem like a well-protected onion. She wore several pairs of wool stockings, one on top of another.

No one came that morning. She waited in vain. Soon the cave would close; people were no longer coming. She decided to go in alone and say good-bye to the cave that would soon be taking its winter siesta. What better way to bid farewell than to put her hands over a mark left in the stone by another hand thousands and thousands of years before. It was strange: the handprint was flesh-colored, ocher, and exactly the same size as the hand of Encarnación Cadalso.

It moved her to think those things. She enjoyed the realization that centuries might pass but the hand of a woman fit perfectly in the hand of another woman, or perhaps that of a man, a husband, a son, dead, but alive in the heritage of the stone. The hand called her, begged Encarna for her warmth so it wouldn't die altogether.

The woman screamed. Another hand, this one alive, hot, calloused, rested on top of hers. The ghost of the dead person who had left his handprint there had come back. Encarna turned her face and in the faint light found that of her Mexican boyfriend, her boyfriend, that's right, Leandro Reyes, taking her by the hand in the very spot where not only she but her nation, her past, her dead lived and pulsated. Would he accept her as she was, far from the glamour—she repeated the word she read so often in magazines—of a tourist trip to Mexico?

It's not that he had to force them. They were all prepared to take a bet—you already knew that. That's how you grew up. That's how you and your friends lived. But this almost supernatural being who received them so unexpectedly in the shack where Paquito lived, raised the stakes very high, he held their lives and honor up to question with his challenge. It was as if all the years of childhood and now of adolescence were hurtling over a waterfall, unexpected, desperate, effacing everything that came before, and all their insolence and mockery, the cruelties they had inflicted on one another, but most of all the cruelties inflicted by the stronger on the weaker had fused in a single silver blade, sharp and blinding. Not another step on earth—the man with a collar but no tie, the man dressed in mourning, was saying—unless you first take the mortal step I'm proposing to you.

One of the thugs tried to jump him; the man with the hairy ears picked him up like a worm and smashed him against the wall. The heads of another two who challenged him he knocked together with a hollow, stony bang that left them dazed.

He said he was Paquito's father and wasn't to blame for his son's idiocy. He offered no explanations. He was also the father of one of them, he said soberly but so as to startle them. One by one, he looked at the nine thugs, two of them unconscious, one flat on his back. He wasn't going to say which—he showed the two or three long yellow teeth he had left—because he was going to choose only one, the one who attacked Paquito. He was going to distinguish that one. He was going to challenge him like a man.

"Bet if you like: which of your mothers did I sleep with one day? Think about it carefully before you dare lay a hand on my son Paquito, before you dare to think he's the brother of one of you, believe me."

He didn't say whether the idiot was dead or alive, seriously wounded or recovered, and he rejoiced to see the faces of the nine sons of bitches who would still want to bet on all the possibilities. He shut them up with a glance that also demanded, Let's see the one who beat up Paquito step forward.

You took that step with your arms folded over your chest, feeling how your chest hairs poked through your grimy buttonless shirt, how they'd sprouted quickly and become a macho forest, a field of honor for your nineteen years.

The big man didn't look at you with hatred or mockery but seriously. He'd left jail the week before—he rendered himself unarmed when he said that, but he unarmed them too—and he had three things to tell them. First, that it was useless to turn him in. They were stupid but they shouldn't even think about it. He swore to eliminate them like flies. Second, that in his ten years in jail, he'd accumulated the sum of two hundred thousand pesetas from his property, his military pension, his inheritance. A nice sum. Now he was betting it. He was betting it all. Everything he had.

Your buddies looked at you. You felt their idiotic, trembling eyes behind your back. What was the bet? They envied you it. Two hundred thousand pesetas. To live like a king for a long time. To live. Or to change your life. To do whatever you damn well felt like doing. Behind you they all accepted the bet even before hearing what it involved.

"We're going to go through the tunnel at Barrios de la Luna. It's one of the longest. I'm going to take off from the north end and you—he glanced at you with mortal disdain—from the south end. Each one driving a car. But each one driving straight into the oncoming traffic. If we both come out unhurt, we split the money. If I don't come out of the tunnel, you get it all. If you don't come out, I get it all. If neither of us comes out, your friends divide it up among them. Let's see what luck has in store for us."

Leandro delicately removed her scarf, ruffled her damp hair, greedily kissed her wet mouth. She wore no lipstick and her mouth looked more lined than it had in Cuernavaca, but it was her face and now it was his.

Later, resting in Encarna's rickety bed, hugging each other to keep out the delightful November cold that demands the closeness of skin to skin, lying under a thick wool blanket in front of a burning fire, they confessed their love, and she said she loved her work and her land. She expected nothing, she admitted it. The truth was—she laughed—that for some time now no one had turned to give her a second look. He was the first in a very long while. She didn't want to know if there would be another. No, there wouldn't be. Before, she'd had her affairs—she wasn't a nun. But real love, true love, only this once. He could be sure of her faithfulness. That's why she told him these things.

More and more, in Encarna's arms, Leandro felt there was nothing to pretend; he'd left insecurity and bravado behind. Never again would he say, "We're all screwed." From now on he'd say, "This is how we are, but together we can be better."

She told him the dream about the cave, which she'd never

told anyone before, how sad it made her to leave those horses alone, dying of cold in the darkness between November and April, galloping nowhere. He asked her if she would dare to leave her land and come to live in Mexico. She said yes again and again and kissed him between each yes. But she warned him that in Asturias a bride's bread was the bread of tears.

"You make me feel different, Encarnita. I'm not fighting it out with the world anymore."

"I thought that if you found me here, barefaced, in the middle of the mud, you'd no longer like me."

"Let's grow old together, what do you say?"

"Okay. But I'd rather we always be young together."

She made him laugh without shame, without machismo, without anxiety, without resentment or skepticism. She took his hand tenderly and said, as if intending never to speak of the other Leandro again, "All right, I've understood it all."

She feared that he'd be disillusioned seeing her here, in her own element, as she was now, with the blanket over her shoulders, her wool stockings on, wearing thick-soled shoes to go stoke the fire. She remembered the sweetness of Cuernavaca, its warm perfumes, and now she saw herself in this land where people wore galoshes and houses rose on stilts, right here where she lived, a granary built on stilts to keep out the moisture, the mud, the torrential rain, the "hecatomb of water," as she called it.

He invited her to spend the weekend in Madrid. Mr. Barroso, his boss, and Michelina, Mr. Barroso's daughter-in-law, were flying to Rome. He wanted to take her around, show her the Cybeles fountain, the Gran Vía, Alcalá Street, and the Retiro park.

They looked at each other and didn't have to declare their

agreement out loud. We're two solitary people, and now we're together.

The old man dressed in black, his black hat pulled down to his hairy ears, is driving the van and doesn't ever look at you; he just wants to be sure that you're next to him and that you'll carry out your part of the bet.

He doesn't look at you but he does talk to you. It's as if only his voice recognizes you, never his gaze. His voice makes you afraid; you could bear his eyes better, however terrible, imprisoned, righteous they are. Inside your chest, something unthought until this moment is talking to you, as if there, in your held breath, you could speak with your jailer, the prisoner who, having finished serving his sentence, has come out into the world and immediately made you his prisoner.

You and your friends also didn't look at one another. They were afraid of offending one another with a glance. Eye contact was worse, more dangerous than the contact of hands, sexes, or skin. It had to be avoided. All of you were manly because you never looked at one another; you walked the streets of the town staring at the tips of your shoes and always you gave other people ugly looks, disdainful, challenging, mocking, or insecure. But Paquito did look at you, looked directly at you, frightened to death but direct, and you never forgave him that—that's why you beat him up, beat the shit out of him.

A hundred, two hundred deer the color of ripe peaches pass, running toward Extremadura, as if seeking the final reinforcement of their numbers. The old man sees the deer and tells you not to look at them, to look instead at the buzzards already circling in the sky, waiting for something to happen to one.

"There are wild pigs too," you say, just to say something, to start up the conversation with the father, the executioner, the avenger of the idiot Paquito.

"Those are the worst," the old man answers. "They're the biggest cowards."

He says that, before coming down to drink, the old wild pigs send the piglets and females, the young males and females, that, guided by the wind and their sense of smell, communicate to the old hog that the path to the water is safe. Only then will the old hog come down.

"The young males that go first are called squires," the old man says seriously before he is gradually overcome by laughter. "The young squires are the ones that get hunted, the ones that die. But the old hog knows more and more just because he's old. He lets the piglets and the females be sacrificed for him."

Now indeed, now indeed he looks at you with a red burning gaze like a coal brought back to life, the final coal in the middle of the ashes that everyone thought were dead.

"When they're old they get gray. The hogs. They only come out at night, when the young have already been hunted or have come back alive to say that the path is clear."

He laughed heartily.

"They only come out at night. They get gray with time. Their tusks twist around. Old hog, twisted tusk."

He stopped laughing and tapped a finger against his teeth.

He hired you a car on this side of the tunnel. He didn't have to tell you he was counting on your sense of honor. He left you alone to drive to the other side. It took exactly fourteen minutes to cross the tunnel of Barrios de la Luna. He would start counting the minutes as soon as you pulled away. After fifteen minutes, you would turn around to enter the tunnel again and he, the old man, would begin to drive in the opposite direction.

"Good-bye," said the old man.

Surrounded by smoke from the power station and mist from the high mountains, they were leaving the highway that ran by abandoned coal pits slowly healing in the earth. Kids were playing soccer. Old women were bent over their gardens. The concrete, the poles, the blocks of cement, and the retainer walls progressively split the earth to make way for the highway and the succession of tunnels that penetrated the Sierra Cantábrica, conquering it. It was a splendid highway and Leandro drove his boss's Mercedes quickly, with one hand. With the other he squeezed his Encarna's, and she asked him to slow down, Jesus, not to scare her—let's get to Madrid alive. But no matter how she softened him, he had his macho habits and responses he wasn't going to give up over night; besides, the Mercedes was purring like a cat, it was a pleasure to drive a car that slid over the highway like butter over a roll. He smiled as they entered the long tunnel of Barrios de la Luna, leaving behind a landscape of snowy peaks and patchy fogs. Leandro turned on lights like two cats' eyes. Behind him was an old van driven by a man dressed in black, his black hat pulled down to his huge ears and his gray whiskers prickling the top of his white collarless shirt. He scratched the lobe of his hairy ear. He took care not to change lanes or pass on the left and risk a crash. Better to follow at a distance, safely, follow that elegant Mercedes with Madrid license plates. He guffawed. Honor was for assholes. He was going to avenge his poor son.

You were doing sixty miles an hour, ashamed to think you were doing it so a highway patrolman would pull you over and keep you from entering the tunnel, which was coming up. The rapid transition from the hard sun to the blast of smoke, the breath of black fog inside the tunnel, made you dizzy. With great assurance, you took the left lane, driving against traffic, telling yourself that you were going to leave that village of stone, that language of stone. It was better to go to America—that was the real thing—to be yourself, take a risk to win a bet, and what a bet, two hundred thousand pesetas in one shot. You were risking your life, but with luck you'd be rich in one shot. Now you'd see if luck was protecting you. If you didn't put everything on the line now, you never would—luck was destiny and everything depended on a bet. It was like being a bullfighter, but instead of the bull what was rushing toward you was a pair of headlights, blinding you, two luminous horns. You took the bet: would it be the old son of a bitch, the father of his faggot sons? Who was the person, who were the people you were going to give a great embrace of stone, you with your shining bull horns, like the starry ones that support the virgin, all the virgins of Spain and America? You thought about a woman before smashing into the car coming in the opposite direction, the right direction; you thought about the bread of the virgins, the bride's bread of the whole world, *pan de chourar*, the bread of tears transformed into stone.

RÍO GRANDE, RÍO BRAVO

To David and Laanna Carrasco

*fathered by the heights, descendant of the snow, the ice of
the sky baptizes the river when it bursts forth in the San Juan
mountains, breaks the virginal shield of the cordillera,
abruptly becomes young, youthfully challenges the canyons
and open cuts of land so that the stormy waters of May can
pass on to sleepy June tides
it then loses altitude but gains the desert, wastes its maturity
generously leaving liquid alms here and there amid the mesquite, parcels out its luxurious old age in fertile farmlands,
and bequeaths its death to the sea
río grande, río bravo,
let me ask you:
did the thick aromatic cedars grow with you, since the dawn
of creation, and then become the wood for your cradle? did
the plants that roll across the desert merely announce your
arrival, always defending you from the spines and bayonets*

of yucca and palo verde? were your loves always perfumed by the incense of the pine nut? did the white poplars always escort you, the spruces disguise you, the olive-colored waves of your immense pastures always rock you? was your death avoided by the nervous nursing of wild thistles, did the black fruits of the juniper announce it, the willows not weep your requiem? río grande, río bravo, did the creosote, the cactus, the sagebrush not forget you, thirsty for your passage, so obsessed by your next rebirth that they have already forgotten your death?

the river of shifting floors now travels back to its sources from the coastal plains, their fertile half-moon a cape of swamps; the valley drops anchor between the pine and the cypress until a flight of doves raises it again, carrying the river up to the steep tower from which the earth broke off the very first day, under the hand of God:

now God, every day, gives a hand to the río grande, río bravo, so it may rise to his balcony once more and roll along the carpets of his waiting room before opening the doors to the next chamber, the step that brings the waters, if they manage to scale the enormous ravines, back to the roofs of the world, where each plateau has its own faithful cloud that accompanies it and reproduces it like a mirror of air:

but now the earth is drying and the river can do nothing for it but plant the stakes that guide its course and that of its travelers, for everyone would get lost here if the Guadalupe mountains were not there to protect the river and drive it back to its womb, río grande, río bravo, back to the nourishing cave it never should have left for exile and death and the blinding hurricane that awaits it again to drown the river again and again . . .

BENITO AYALA

Stopped for the night by the river's edge, Benito Ayala was surrounded by men who looked like him, all between twenty and forty years old, all wearing straw hats, cheap cotton shirts and trousers, sturdy shoes for working in a cold climate, short jackets of various colors and designs.

They all raise their arms, spread them in a cross, clench their fists, silently offer their labor on the Mexican side of the river, hoping someone takes note of them, saves them, pays them heed. They prefer to risk being caught than not to advertise themselves, declare their presence: Here we are. We want work.

They all look alike, but Benito Ayala knows that each of them will cross the river with a different bagful of memories, an invisible knapsack in which only their own memories fit.

Benito Ayala closed his eyes to forget the night and to imagine the sky. Through his head passed a place. It was his village, in the mountains of Guanajuato. Not very different from many other Mexican mountain villages. A single street through which the highway passed. On both sides, houses, all one-story. And the shops, the hardware stores, the restaurant, the pharmacy. At the entrance to town, the school. At the end, the gas station with the best bathrooms in town, the best radio, the best chilled soft drinks. But to use the bathroom you've got to arrive by car. The staff knows the people from the vicinity. They order them to shit in the woods, they laugh at them.

Behind the houses, vegetable gardens, flower gardens, the creek. All the walls painted over with beer ads, propaganda for the PRI, announcements of the next or last elections. All things considered and despite everything, a good little town, a sweet village, a village with history and with what the past bequeaths its descendants to make a good life.

But the town didn't live off any of that.

Benito Ayala's village lived off the workers it sent to the United States and off the money they sent back.

The old and young, the few businesspeople, even the political powers became accustomed to living off that. The money was the principal, perhaps only income the village had. Why look elsewhere? The income represented hospital, social security, pension, maternity benefits all in one.

His eyes closed, his arms spread, and his fists clenched, Benito Ayala, stopped for the night on the Mexican side of the river, was remembering the generations of this village.

His great-grandfather, Fortunato Ayala, was the first to leave Mexico, fleeing the revolution.

"This war is never going to end," he declared one day just before the battle of Celaya, fought there in Guanajuato. "The war is going to last longer than my life. When we all united against the tyrant Huerta, I stuck it out. But now that we're going to be killing our own brothers, I think it's better I leave."

He went to California and tried to open a restaurant. The problem was that the gringos didn't like our food. Putting chocolate into chicken nauseated them. The restaurant folded. He looked for a factory job because he said that if he was going to bend over to pick tomatoes he'd be better off in Guanajuato. But no matter where he went, the answer was always the same, as if they'd learned a catechism lesson.

"You people weren't made for factory work. Look at you. You're short. You're close to the ground. Bend over, pick fruit and greens. That's what God made you for."

He rebelled. He made his way as best he could (mostly by hiding in freight cars and not paying) to Chicago, where he didn't give a damn about the cold, the wind, the hostility.

He found work in steel. Almost half the workers in the steel mill were Mexicans. He didn't even have to learn English. He sent his first few dollars to Guanajuato. In those days, the mail service still worked and an envelope containing dollars reached its destination at the district capital of Purísima del Rincón, where his family went to pick it up. Twenty, thirty, forty dollars. A fortune in a country devastated by war, where every rebel faction printed its own money, the famous *bilimbiques.*

Before mailing his dollars, Fortunato Ayala would stare at them a long time, caressing them with his eyes, imagining them made of satin or silk instead of paper, so shiny and smooth. He held them up to a light and stared again, as if to assure himself of their authenticity and even of their green beauty, presided over by George Washington and the God's eye of the Huicholes. What was the sacred symbol of Mexican Indians doing on the gringo dollars? In any case, the triangle of the divine eye meant protection and foresight, although fatality as well. George Washington looked like a protective grandma with his cottony little head and false teeth.

But no one protected Great-grandfather Fortunato when U.S. unemployment led to his and thousands of other Mexicans' deportation in 1930. Fortunato departed in sorrow, too, because in Chicago he left behind a pregnant Mexican girl to whom he'd never offered anything but love. She knew Fortunato had a wife and children: all she wanted was his name, Ayala, and Fortunato, resigned to being generous, gave it to her, though somewhat fearfully.

He left. He established a tradition: the town would live off the money sent by its emigrant workers. His son, also named Fortunato, managed to get to California during World War II. He was a farmhand. He had entered legally, but his bosses told him his situation was precarious. He was just a step away from his own country. It would be easy to deport him if things started going badly. It was good he had no interest in becoming a citizen. It was good he loved his own country so much and wanted only to return to it.

"It's good I'm a worker and not a citizen," Fortunato the son answered, and that did not please his bosses. "It's good I'm cheap and reliable, right?"

Then his bosses commented that the advantage of the Mexican worker was that he did not become a citizen and did not organize unions or go on strike, the way European immigrants did. But if this Ayala guy started getting uppity, he'd have to be isolated, punished.

"All of them get uppity," said one of the employers.

"After a while they all find out about their rights," said another.

It was for that reason that, when the war was over and the bracero program with it, Salvador Ayala, the young grandson of old Fortunato, found the border closed. Workers were no longer necessary. But the little village near Purísima del Rincón had got used to living off them. All its young men left to look for work up north. If they didn't find any, the town would die, just as an infant abandoned in the hills by its parents would die. It was worth risking everything. They were the men, they were the boys. The strongest, the cleverest, the bravest. They went. The children, the women, the old folks stayed behind. They depended on the workers.

"Here there are men alive because there are men who leave. Nobody can say that there are men who die here because no one leaves."

Salvador Ayala, Benito's father, the son and grandson of the Fortunatos, became a wetback who crossed the river at night and was caught on the other side by the Border Patrol.

It was a gamble for him and the others. But it was worth the risk. If the Texas farmers needed man power, the wetback was brought back to the border and left on the Mexican side. From here he would immediately be admitted—his back now dry—onto the Texas side, protected by an employer. But every year the doubt was repeated. Will I get in this time or not? Will I be able to send a hundred, two hundred dollars home?

The information made the rounds in Purísima del Rincón. From the little plaza to the church, from the sacristy to the tavern, from the creek to the fields of prickly pears and brambles, from the gas station to the tailor's shop, everyone knew that at harvest time the laws were meaningless. Orders are given to deport no one. We can go. We can cross. The police don't go near the protected Texas ranches even though they know all the workers there are illegal.

"Don't worry. This thing doesn't depend on us. If they need us, they let us in, with or without laws. If they don't need us, they kick us out, with or without laws."

No one had a worse time than Salvador Ayala, Benito's father and the grandson of the first Fortunato. He caught the worst repression, expulsions, border cleanup operations. He was the victim of brutal whims. It was the boss who decided when to treat him as a contracted worker and when to hand him over to Immigration as a criminal. Salvador Ayala had no defense. If he alleged that the boss had given him work illegally, he implicated himself without having proof against his boss. The boss could manipulate the phony documents to prove that Salvador was a legal worker, if necessary. And to make him invisible and deport him, if necessary.

Now was the worst time. Benito—grandson of the younger Fortunato and the son of Salvador, descendant of the founder of the exodus, the first Fortunato—knew that any period is difficult, but this more than any other. Because there was still need. But also hatred.

"Did they hate you too?" Benito asked his father, Salvador.

"The way they're going to hate you? No."

He didn't know the reasons, but he felt it. Stopping for the night on the Mexican side of the Río Bravo, he felt the fear of all the others and the hatred on the other side. He was going to cross, no matter what. He thought about all those who depended on him in Purísima del Rincón.

He stretched his arms in a cross, as far as he could, clenching his fists, showing that his body was ready to work, asking for a little love and compassion, not knowing if he was clenching his fists out of anger, as a challenge, or in resignation and despondency.

this was never the land without men: for thirty thousand years the people have been following the course of the río grande, río bravo, they cross the straits from Asia, they descend from the north, migrate south, seek new hunting grounds, in the process they really discover America, feel the attraction and hostility of the new world, don't rest until they explore it all and find out if it's friendly or unfriendly, until they reach the other pole, land that has a placenta of copper, land that will have the name of silver, lands of the hugest migration known to man, from Alaska to Patagonia, lands baptized by migration: accompanied, America, by flights and images, metaphors and metamorphoses that make the going bearable, that save the peoples from fatigue, discouragement, distance, time, the centuries necessary to travel America from pole to pole:
I will not speak their names, only those who know how to listen to silence know them,

I will not recount their deeds, only the dusty stars of the paths repeat them,

I will not recall their sufferings, the hurricane of birds shouts them,

I will not mention their calendars, they are all a river of ashes,

only the dog accompanied them, the only animal friendly to the Indian,

but then they tired of traveling so long, let loose their dogs in ferocious wild packs, and they stopped, decided that the center of the world was right here, where their feet were planted that instant, this was the center of the world, the land of the río grande, río bravo:

the world had sprung forth from the invisible springs of the desert waters: the underground rivers, the Indians say, are the music of God,

thanks to them the corn grows, the bean, the squash, and cotton, and each time a plant grows and yields its fruits, the Indian is transformed, the Indian becomes a star, oblivion, bird, mesquite, pot, membrane, arrow, incense, rain, smell of rain, earth, earthquake, extinguished fire, whistle in the mountain, secret kiss, the Indian becomes all this when the seed dies, becomes child and grandfather of the child, memory, bark, scorpion, buzzard, cloud, and table, broken vessel of birth, repentant tunic of death,

becomes a mask, ladder, rodent,

becomes a horse,

becomes a rifle,

becomes a target:

the Indian dreams and his dream becomes a prophecy, all the dreams of the Indians become reality, incarnate, tell them they are right, fill them with fear and for that reason make them suspicious, arrogant, jealous, proud but horrified of

always knowing the future, suspicious that the only thing
that becomes reality is that which should be a nightmare: the
white man, the horse, the firearm,
oh, they had stopped moving, the great migrations were
over, the grass grew over the roads, the mountains separated
the people, languages were no longer understood, the people
decided not to move anymore from where they were, from
birth to death, but to weave a great mantle of loyalties, ob-
ligations, values in order to protect themselves
until the river caught fire and the earth moved again

DAN POLONSKY

Thin and pale but muscular and agile, he bragged that even though he lived on the border he never exposed himself to the sun. He had the pale complexion of his European ancestors, immigrants who were badly received, discriminated against, treated like garbage. Dan remembered his grandparents' complaints. The savage discrimination to which they were subjected because they spoke differently, ate differently, looked different. They smelled different. The Anglos covered their noses when they passed those old people who were young but looked old, with their beards and black clothes smelling of onion and sauerkraut. But the immigrants persisted, assimilated, became citizens. No one would defend their nation better than they, Dan thought as he stared across to the Mexican side of the river.

"Seen *Air Force* yet?" his grandfather Adam Polonsky asked, and since Dan was too young to have seen World War II pictures, the old man gave him a video so he'd see how the air force was made up of ethnic heroes, not only Anglos but descendants of Poles, Italians, Jews, Russians, Irish. Never a Japanese, it's true; he was the enemy. But never a Latino, a Mexican. A few blacks; they say the blacks did go to war. But never Mexicans. They weren't citizens. They were cowards, mosquitoes that sucked the blood of the USA and ran back home to support their lazy countrymen.

"Seen *Air Force* yet? John Garfield. His real name was Julius Garfinkle. A kid from the ghetto, like you, the son of immigrants, Danny boy."

They gave their lives in two world wars and also in Korea and Vietnam. They almost equaled the sacrifices of the Anglo-Saxon generations of the previous century, the conquerors of the West. Why didn't anyone ever say so? Why did they still feel shame at having an immigrant past? Dan felt proud looking at a map and seeing that the USA had acquired more territory than any other power in the last century. Louisiana. Florida. Half of Mexico. Alaska. Cuba. Puerto Rico. The Philippines. Hawaii. The Panama Canal. A stream of little islands in the Pacific. The Virgin Islands. The Virgin Islands! That's where he'd like to go on vacation. Just for the name, so seductive, so sexy, so improbable. And for the challenge. To take a vacation in the Caribbean and not get a tan. To come back as white as his grandparents from Pomerania. To conquer color. Not let himself blacken for any reason, not by contact with a Negro or a Mexican, not by the sun.

He requested night duty for that secret reason, which he communicated to no one—he was afraid of being ridiculed. There was a cult of the tan. A man with such white skin even seemed suspect. "Are you sick?" another officer asked, and the only reason he didn't punch him was because he knew the consequences of attacking an officer and Dan Polonsky did not want for anything in the world to lose his job—it satisfied him too much. From the moment when they positioned the equipment to detect the nighttime passage of illegal immigrants across the Río Grande, Dan requested and was granted assignment to the details that saw the night world illuminated through movie-style robot glasses, night-scopes that spotted illegals as if they glowed, heat detectors that picked up the warmth of the human body . . . The bad thing was that so many Border Patrol agents, even if they were Texans, were of Mexican origin and Polonsky some-times made mistakes; looking through his infrared goggles he would spot someone dark-skinned and it would turn out the person was carrying Border Patrol ID, even if he had the face of a wetback . . . The good thing was that it was easy to sucker those Tex-Mex agents, exploit their divided loy-alties, demand they prove—Let's see—that they were good Americans and not Mexicans in disguise . . . Polonsky laughed at them. He felt pity for them but manipulated them like laboratory rats.

One thing that did bother him, though, was the need to insist that the USA was always moral and innocent. Why did the politicians and the journalists pretend that they had no ambitions or personal interests, that they were always moral, innocent, good? That exasperated Dan Polonsky. Everybody had personal interests, ambitions, malice. Everybody wanted to be somebody. He stared intently through his night-vision glasses, which rendered the dry, hostile landscape of the river clear without the sun; he stared at an intoxicating red land-scape, like a glass of Clamato and vodka. For Dan, the United States had saved the world from all the evils of the twentieth century: Hitler, the kaiser, Stalin, the Communists, the Japanese, the Chinese, the Vietnamese, Uncle Ho, Castro, the Arabs, Saddam, Noriega . . .

His list of enemies ran out, and all he was left with was one central, angry justification. It was necessary to save the southern border. The enemy was entering through there. To-day the nation was being protected there, just as it was at

Pearl Harbor or on the Normandy beaches. It was all the same.

There they were, provoking him indecently, grouped up on the Mexican side, showing their arms open in a cross, clenching their fists, saying to the other side: You need us. We come to the border because without us your crops would rot. There is no one to harvest them, there is no one to help in hospitals, take care of children, serve in restaurants unless we lend you our arms. It was a challenge, and Dan's wife told him so with a brutal joke: "Listen, I need a nanny for the kid. Don't tell me you're going to turn Josefina in? Don't be stubborn. The more workers that enter, the safer your job is, buster . . . I mean, darling."

When his wife, Selma, became tedious, Dan would invent a trip to the state capital in Austin to lobby for more money and influence for the Border Patrol. He wanted to convince the legislators: If you don't give us money, we can't protect the country against the invisible Mexican invasion. He focused his night-vision glasses. There they were. Incapable of taking off their hats, as if even at night the sun were shining. He felt a furious need to urinate. He unzipped his fly and looked at himself in the phosphorescent light. His liquid was white, too, without color, like a flow of Chablis. He disliked the idea that grapes ripen and harden under the sun. But he consoled himself thinking of the farmworkers who harvested them in California.

He tried to resolve his contradiction. He wasn't a man of contradictions. He detested the illegals. But he adored and needed them. Without them, damn it, there would be no budget for helicopters, radar, powerful infrared night lights, rocket launchers, pistols . . . Let them come, he said, shaking his penis to rid himself of the last pale drops. Let them keep on coming by the millions, he begged, to give

meaning to my life. We have to go on being innocent vic-
tims, he said, absolutely certain that no matter how many
times he shook the thing the last drop inevitably fell in his
shorts.

the horse, the hog, the cattle came
steel and gunpowder came
the bloodhounds came
terror came
death came: fifty-four million men and women lived in the
vast continent of the migrations, from the Yukon to Tierra
del Fuego, and four million north of the río grande, río
bravo,
when the Spaniards came
fifty years later, only four million lived
on the whole continent and the lands of the river almost
turned into what they said they had always been:
the land where man never was
or almost ceased to be, decimated by smallpox, measles, ty-
phus,
where the survivors took refuge in the highlands, seeking
help and a will to resist
when Francisco Vázquez de Coronado came one fine day with
three hundred Spaniards, including a mere three women,
poorly rationed, six Franciscans, fifteen hundred horses, and a
thousand Indian allies brought from the lands of Cohahuila
and Chihuahua, in search of the cities of gold, the passage to
the fabulous orient, another Mexico and Peru:
they found nothing but the death that preceded them, but
they left their sheep and goats, chicken and burros, plums,
cherries, melons, grapes, peaches, and grain, scattered like
their Castilian words, with the same facility, with the same
fertility, on both banks of the río grande, río bravo

MARGARITA BARROSO

Every day she crossed the border from El Paso to Juárez to supervise the workers in a plant where television sets were assembled. Sometimes she wished she could talk about something else, but the job sucked out her brain, as her grandma Camelia said, and Margarita had long since decided that her only salvation was work. She found her dignity, her personality, in work; she respected herself and made herself respected. She had developed a hard, intransigent character: sure, there were nice girls, sweet, even sentimental, and also serious, professional workers, but all you needed was one bitch—and there was always more than one—to screw everything up and force the supervisor to be mean, put on a sour face, say harsh words . . .

Now, at night, she returned. It was Friday and all the women were going out to have fun. Margarita wouldn't miss it—it was her only concession to relaxation, okay, to probable abandon, when she could look less uptight and go to the discos with the girls. After all, she could mix with the crowd there, where women were allowed to exercise some fantasy in their outfits. You saw them all: Rosa Lupe with her mania for making vows and dressing like a Carmelite, Marina, who was dying to see the ocean, the fool, as if any of them after they get here ever see their dreams come true— what illusions!—Candelaria, who must think she's Frida Kahlo or something, dressed like a perfect peasant, and the one who didn't dance anymore, Dinorah, mourning her kid who strangled himself because there was no one to take care of him—who asked her to be an unwed mother, the idiot, and live way the hell out in Buenavista? Better to cross the river every day, live in a suburban house in El Paso, even if it was in a black neighborhood. At least you were assimilated there. Let them see that she was assimilated—she didn't want to be seen as a Mexican or a Chicana. She was a gringa, she lived in El Paso; in Chihuahua her name was Margarita but in Texas she was Margie. From her school days in El Paso on, she was told, Listen, you're white, don't let them call you Margarita, make them call you Margie. Pass for white—who's going to find out?—don't speak Spanish, don't let them treat you like a Mexican, a *Pocha*, a Chicana.

"How do you get along with your family?"

"They're unbelievable. I can't go out on a date without my mother chasing after me asking, Is he from a good family? Is he from a good family? It makes me want to go out with a black so they have a fit."

"Don't be a jerk. Just go out with blonds. Never admit you're Mexican."

She rebelled by fighting to be a majorette at her high school. She told her parents that she was joining the school band, that they were going to play at the football games. But when they saw her in the fall wearing skimpy shorts, her legs bare, showing her thighs—thighs nothing!—showing her ass, the thing I sit on, said Grandma Camelia—she never said *ass*—showing you know what and tossing around a baton that looked like a phallus, they knew they'd lost her. She left home, and they warned her, No decent boy will want to marry you, you show your fanny in public, slut. But she didn't have time for boyfriends, she didn't think about them, she only went on Fridays to the Excalibur to dance the *quebradita* with men who were all the same—they all danced with their white hats on, they were ranchers, rich or poor—how could you tell when they were all identical?—and the longhaired guys who wore bands tied around their heads and fringed vests, those were tough guys or pimps, no one took them seriously. It was all just a respite, a way to lose

yourself and forget the grandfather who didn't make it, paralyzed in his wheelchair, sweet Grandma Camelia who never
said *ass*, her parents who were around there someplace, her
father working in Woolworth's, her mother in another assembly plant, her brother making burritos at a Taco Bell,
and her powerful, incredibly rich uncle, the self-made man
who doesn't believe in family charity. I'm supposed to support that pack of lazy relatives? Let them work the way I
work, make their own fortune. What are they, crippled or
something? Money only tastes good if you earn it, not when
someone gives it to you, or as the gringos say, There's no
such thing as a free lunch. She, Margarita Margie, she was
ambitious, disciplined, and what did it get her? Stuck there
on the border, trying to get through that mess of a demonstration that's interrupted everything, eager to leave Mexico
every night, bored crossing over to Juárez every morning past
iron skeletons, cemeteries of skyscrapers left half-built because of Mexico's repeated bad luck: money's all used up,
the crisis has arrived, they've locked up the investor, the government functionary, the top dog, but not even then does the
corruption stop, fucked-up country, screwed country, desperate country like a rat running on a wheel, deluding itself
into thinking it's going somewhere but never moving an
inch. There's nothing to be done though—that's where her
job is and she's good at her job, she knows the assembly line
from A to Z, from the chassis to the soldering to the auto-
matic test to the cabinet to the screen to the warm-up to see
if all the parts work and to make sure there's no infant mor-
tality, as the Italian assistant manager jokingly calls it. She
knows about the alignment that insulates the television set
and keeps the earth's magnetic field from causing interfer-
ence, what do you think of that? She tries that one out on
her dance partners, who immediately lose the beat be-

cause she knows more than they do. They don't like her and leave her to herself because she talks about testing the TV in front of mirrors, about the plastic case, the Styrofoam packing, and the final shipping box, the television set's coffin, all ready for Kmart. The whole process takes two hours, eleven thousand TVs per day, not bad, huh? Does this chick know her shit or what? And if it was her job that day to check that each phase was carried out correctly, sticking green stars on the TVs with problems and blue stars on those with none, she deserved a great big gold star on her forehead, right on her forehead, like the good girls in nuns' schools, like the drum majorettes who twirled their batons and showed their panties when they marched and disguised themselves as colonels to lead the parades and were whistled at by the boys, who called her Margie and said she's not *Pocha*, not Chicana, not Mexican, she's like you and me . . .

the shipwrecked, the defeated, the man dying of hunger and thirst, the man in rags,
from whom if not that man could come the impossible dream of the wealth of the river, disposable wealth as in Eden, golden apples within easy reach of hand and sin: who but a delirious shipwrecked man could make such an illusion about the río grande, río bravo believable?
Alvar Núñez Cabeza de Vaca of Extremadura, fleeing from the sleepless stone as most of the conquistadors fled (Cortés from Medellín, Pizarro and Orellana from Trujillo, Balboa from Jerez de los Caballeros, De Soto from Barcarrota, Valdivia from Villanueva de la Serena, men from the borderland, men from beyond the Duero), wanted, as they did, to transmute the stone of Extremadura into the gold of America, took ship at Sanlúcar in 1528 with an expedition of four hundred men bound for Florida, of whom forty-nine re-

mained after a shipwreck in Tampa bay, wading through the swampy lands of the Seminoles, painfully marching along the Gulf coast to the Mississippi river, building boats to try the sea once again, squeezed in so tight they couldn't move, now attacked by a storm from which only thirty escape alive, this new shipwreck in Galveston, the march west to the río grande, río bravo, defending themselves from Indian arrows, eating their horses and sewing up the hides to carry water, until they reach the lands of the Pueblo Indians north of the river,

but the distance, their ignorance of the land and the people are nothing compared with the hunger, the thirst, the exposure, the nights without cover, the days without shade, their bodies more and more naked, darker, until the fifteen Spaniards left can't be told from the Pueblos, the Alabamas, and the Apaches:

only the black servant, Estebanico, is darker than the others, but his dreams are luminous, golden, he sees the cities of gold in the distance while Alvar Núñez Cabeza de Vaca looks at himself in the mirror of his memory and tries to see himself reflected there as the hidalgo he was, the Spanish gentleman he no longer is; the only mirror of his person are the Indians he finds, he has become identical to them, but he misses the chance to be one of them, he is equal to them but does not understand the opportunity he has to be the only Spaniard who could understand the Indians and translate their souls into Spanish:

Cabeza de Vaca cannot understand a history of wind, an endless migratory chronicle that takes the Indian from the hot hunt of the plains to the tepee of the snows, from the tanned and naked body of summer to the body wrapped in blankets and skins of winter,

he does not want to rule over this world; nomadism attracts

*him but he denies it because here no one moves to conquer
but simply to survive,*

*he does not understand the Indians, the Indians don't un-
derstand him: they see the Spaniards as shamans, witch doctors, sorcerers, and Cabeza de Vaca acts out the only role
assigned him, he becomes a cut-rate medicine man, he cures
by means of suction, blowing of breath, laying on of hands,
Our Fathers, and abundant signs of the cross,*

*but in reality he fights, horrified, against the loss, layer by
layer, of the skin and clothes of his European soul, he clings
to it, pays no heed to the advice of his internal voice: God
brought us naked to know men identical to ourselves in their
nakedness . . .*

*which God? Cabeza de Vaca wanders the corridors and bed-
rooms of the great houses of the Pueblos, sees a god he
doesn't recognize fleeing from floor to floor up hand ladders
that at night it pulls up in order to isolate itself as it pleases
from the moon, death, the stranger . . .*

*eight years of wandering, of involuntary pilgrimage, until he
finds the compass of the río grande, río bravo and takes
again the road from Chihuahua to Sinaloa and the Pacific
and inland to Mexico City, where he and his comrades are
received as heroes by Viceroy Mendoza and the conquistador
Cortés:*

*only four survivors are left of the four hundred who departed
Sanlúcar for Florida—Cabeza de Vaca, Andrés Dorantes,
Alonso del Castillo Maldonado, and the black servant, Es-
tebanico:*

*they are celebrated, they are questioned: where did you go,
what did you see, what do you promise?*

*Cabeza de Vaca, the two Spaniards, and the black tell not
what they saw but what they dreamed,*

they were saved to tell a mirage,

they were given turquoises and sumptuous skins torn from
the backs of the strange gray cattle of the plains, the buffalo,
they glimpsed the seven cities of gold of Cibola,
they heard word of the incalculable wealth of Quivira, they
propagate the illusion of Eldorado, another Mexico, another
Peru, beyond the río grande, río bravo,
an immortal dream of wealth, power, gold, happiness that
compensates for all our sufferings, for the thirst, the hunger,
and the shipwrecks and the Indian attacks,
they survived in order to lie,
death would have fused them with the truth of the desert,
poor, hostile, underpopulated lands,
life gave them the opulent wealth of lies,
they can fool everyone because they survived:
río grande, río bravo, frontier of mirages from then on
where men survive so that they can lie

SERAFÍN ROMERO

Mr. Stud, that's what they called him from the time he was
a kid because of his shiny black hair like patent leather and
his long eyelashes, but he called himself Mr. Shit because
that's how he always felt, growing up surrounded by the
mountains of garbage in Chalco, dedicated since childhood
to digging around in the disfigured mass of rotten meat,
vomited beans, rags, dead cats, scraps of unrecognizable existence, giving thanks when something kept its form—a bottle, a condom—and could be brought home. An acrid cloud
accompanied Serafín from his earliest days, and when he left
the cloud of refuse, the smell was so sweet, so pure, that it
made him dizzy and even a little nauseated: his country was
the mud streets, the puddles, the children with screwed-up
knees, unable to walk properly, stray dogs fucking, affirming

their lives, telling us in barks that everything can survive despite everything, despite the pushers who get eight-year-old kids started on drugs, despite the extortionist cops who kill at night and then turn up by day to count the bodies and add them to the gigantic rolls of urban death, forever overcome by the fertility of the bitches, the rats, the mothers. Everything can survive because the government and the party organize corruption, allow it to flourish a bit, and then organize it as improvement so everyone will accept the notion that it's the PRI or anarchy, which do you prefer? By the time hair had sprouted in Serafín's armpits, he already knew everything about the evil of the city, no one could teach him anything. The problem was survival. How do you survive? By giving in to the masters of thievery, voting for the PRI, attending meetings like a jerk, seeing how the kings of the garbage got rich—what the fuck—or by saying no and joining a rock band that dares to sing about what a pisser it is to live in Mexico, D.F., in an underground network of rebel kids, or by speaking up even louder, refusing to vote for the PRI, and running the risk, as he and his family did, of having to take refuge in a half-built school, almost a thousand of them huddled together there, their shacks demolished by the cops, their miserable possessions stolen by the cops, all because they said, We're going to vote the way we feel like voting?

At the age of twenty, Serafín headed north. He told his people, Get out of here, this country is beyond salvation, the PRI alone is more than enough reason to leave Mexico. I swear I'll figure out a way to help you up north. I've got relatives in Juárez, guys, you'll hear from me . . .

On this night of clenched fists and arms opened in a cross, Serafín, now twenty-six, expects nothing from anyone. He's spent two years organizing the gang that crosses the border almost every night, thirty armed Mexicans who pile up wooden boxes, old scrap iron, roof tiles, and abandoned car bodies on the tracks of the Southern Pacific in New Mexico, change the switches, stop the train, steal everything they can to sell it in Mexico, then fill the cars with Mexican illegals. How many nights like this does Serafín Romero remember as he drives off in his truck from the train stopped in the desert, the truck filled with stolen goods, the train filled with peasants who need work, the stolen goods all brand-new, still in their packages, shiny—washing machines, toasters, vacuum cleaners, all brand-new, none turned yet to garbage that will end up on a mountain of trash in Chalco . . . Now he really is Mr. Stud, now he really has stopped being Mr. Shit. And Serafín Romero thought, leaving the stopped train behind, that the only thing missing for him to be a hero was a whinnying stallion . . , and oh yes, the night air of the desert was so dry, so clean.

no one lives more opulently in opulent Mexico City than Juan de Oñate, son of the conquistador Cristóbal of the same name, who discovered the Zacatecas mines, infinite hives of silver, a man who reached the Villa Rica de la Veracruz without a doubloon and now is able to bequeath to his son one of the greatest fortunes in the Indies, an inexhaustible vein of silver that allows Juan de Oñate to be named price regulator in the capital of New Spain, to roll through that city in the best carriages, surrounded by the best women, the best pages, to be attended in his palace by squads of majordomos and priests praying all the livelong day so Oñate will end up in heaven:
why does this man leave all his luxury, shake off his indolence, and go off to the unknown territories of the río grande, río bravo?

was he so stuffed with old silver that he wanted new gold?

did he want to owe nothing to his father?

did he want to begin like him, poor and defiant?

or did he want to show that there is no greater wealth than that which we cannot attain?

look at Juan de Oñate plant his black boot on the brown bank of the río grande, río bravo:

he's fat, bald, moustachioed, a turtle with an iron shell and Dutch lace frills at his neck and wrists, a robust potbelly and weak feet and between the two the indispensable sac of his scrotum so he can pee whenever he pleases amid the conquests and battles, his indispensable silver helmet, topped off with a crest, proclaims:

he comes to the río grande with a hundred and thirty soldiers and five hundred settlers, women, children, servants:

he founds El Paso del Norte and claims Spanish dominion over all things, from the leaves on the trees to the rocks and sand in the river: nothing stops him, the founding of El Paso is merely the springboard for his grand imperial dream,

fat, bald, moustachioed, fortified by steel and softened by lace, Juan de Oñate is a private contractor, a businessman who believed Cabeza de Vaca's lies and paid no heed to the expeditions of Fray Marcos de Niza or to the death of the ill-fated, stubborn black Estebanico, who disappeared in a quest for his own lie, the cities of gold: Oñate came not to find gold but to invent it, to create wealth, to discover what's left to discover of the new world, the mines yet to find, the empires yet to be founded, the passage to Asia, the ports in both oceans: to realize his dream he embarks on a campaign of death, he reaches Acama, the center of the Indian world (center of creation, navel of the universe), and there he destroys the city, kills half a thousand men, three hundred women and children, and takes the rest captive: the boys

between twelve and twenty will be servants: the twenty-five-year-old men will have a foot chopped off in public:
this is a matter of founding, in truth, a new world, of creating, in truth, a new order, where Juan de Oñate rules as he pleases, capriciously, not owing anyone anything, intent on losing everything as long as he's infinitely free to impose his will, to be his own king and perhaps his own creator:
here there was nothing before Oñate arrived, here there was no history, no culture: he founded them
but here there was distance, enormous distance, and distance, after all was said and done, defeated him

ELOÍNO AND MARIO

Polonsky told Mario that tonight more illegals than ever would try to cross the river, taking advantage of the squabble about the bridge, but Mario knew very well that as long as a poor country lived next to the richest country in the world, what they, the Border Patrol, were doing was squeezing a balloon: what you squeezed here only swelled out over there. There was no solution, and even though Mario was amused by his job at first, almost as if it were a kids' game like hide-and-seek, exasperation was starting to get the better of him because the violence was increasing and because Polonsky was implacable in his hatred of Mexicans. If you wanted to stay on his good side, it wasn't enough to act professionally; you had to show real hate and that was hard for Mario Islas, the son of Mexicans, after all, even though he was born on this side of the Río Grande. But that fact aroused the suspicion of his superior, Polonsky. One night Mario caught him in the tavern saying that Mexicans were all cowards, and he was on the verge of punching him. Polonsky noticed. It's likely he had deliberately provoked him, which is why he then took the chance to say, "Let me be frank, Mario, you Mexicans who serve in the Border Patrol have to show your loyalty more convincingly than we real Americans do—"

"I was born here, Dan. I'm as American as you. And don't tell me the Polonskys came over on the *Mayflower*."

"You'd better watch your mouth, boy."

"I'm an officer. Don't call me boy. I respect you. You respect me."

"I mean, we're white, Europeans, savvy?"

"Spain isn't in Europe? I'm of Spanish descent, you're of Polish descent, we're Europeans . . ."

"You speak Spanish. The blacks speak English. That doesn't make them English or you Spanish."

"Dan, this conversation doesn't make any sense." Mario smiled, shrugging his shoulders. "Let's just do our job well."

"Not hard for me. For you it is."

"You see everything like a racist. I'm not going to change you, Polonsky. Let's just do our job well. Forget that I'm as American as you."

During the long nights on the Río Grande, Río Bravo, Mario Islas told himself that maybe Dan Polonsky was right to have his doubts about him. These poor people only came looking for work. They weren't taking work away from anyone. Was it the Mexicans' fault the defense plants were closed and there was more unemployment? They should have continued the war against the evil empire, as Reagan called it.

These doubts passed very quickly through Mario's alert mind. The nights were long and dangerous and sometimes he wished the whole Río Grande, Río Bravo really were divided by an iron curtain, a deep, deep ditch, or at least a simple fence that would keep the illegals from passing. Instead, the night was filling with something he knew only too well, the trills and whistles of nonexistent birds, the sounds the coyotes, the men who guided illegals across, used to communicate with one another. Though they gave themselves away, sometimes it was all a trick and the coyotes used their whistles the way a hunter uses a decoy duck; the real crossing was taking place elsewhere, far from there, with no whistles at all.

Not this time. A boy with the speed of a deer came out of the river, soaked, dashed along the shore, and ran right into Mario—into Mario's chest, his green uniform, his insignia, his braid, all his agency paraphernalia—hugging him, the two of them hugging, stuck together because of the moisture of the illegal's body, because of the sweat of the agent's. Who knows why they stayed there hugging like that, panting, the illegal because of his race to avoid the patrol, Mario because of his race to cut him off . . . Who knows why each rested his head on the other's shoulder, not only because they were exhausted but because of something less comprehensible . . .

They pull apart to look at each other.

"Are you Mario?" said the illegal.

The agent said he was.

"I'm Eloíno. Eloíno, your godson. Don't you remember? Sure, you remember!"

"Eloíno isn't a name you can forget," Mario managed to say.

"The son of your pals. I know you from your photos. They told me that if I was lucky I'd find you here."

"If you were lucky?"

"You're not going to send me back, are you, Godfather?" Eloíno gave him an immense white smile like an ear of corn shining in the night between his wet lips.

"What do you think, you little bastard?" said Mario, furious.

"I'll be back, Mario. Even if you catch me a thousand times, I'll be back another thousand times. And one more for luck. And don't call me a bastard, bastard." He laughed again and again hugged Mario, the way only two Mexicans know how to hug each other, because the border guard couldn't resist the current of tenderness, affiliation, machismo, confidence, and even trust that there was in a good hug between men in Mexico, especially if they were related . . .

"Godfather, everybody in our village has to come to work over the summer to pay their debts from winter. You know it. Don't be a pain."

"Okay. Sooner or later you'll go back to Mexico the way all of you do. That's the only advantage in this thing. You can't live without Mexico. You don't stay here."

"This time you're mistaken, Godfather. They told me it's going to be harder than ever to get in. This time I'm staying, Godfather. What else is there to do?"

"I know what you're thinking. Once upon a time all this was ours. It was ours first. It will be ours again."

"Maybe you think that, Godfather, because you're a man of sense, my mother says. I'm here so I can eat."

"Get going, Godson. Just figure we never saw each other. And don't hug me again, it hurts . . . I'm hurt enough already."

"Thanks, Godfather, thanks."

Mario watched the boy he'd never seen in his life run off. He was no godson or goddamn anything else, for that matter, this Eloíno (what was his real name?). He'd read Mario's name on his badge, that's how he knew it, no mystery there; the enigma lay elsewhere, in the question of why they lived that fiction, why they accepted it so naturally, why two complete strangers had lived a moment like that together . . .

but the territories were lost even before they were won
the lands did not grow
the population did not increase
the missions grew
the long whip of the Franciscans grew, the whip of implacable colonizers moved by the philosophy of the common good above individual liberty, the letter arrives with the whip, the word of God is written in blood, faith arrives as well,
whip for the Pueblos because the brothers previously used it on themselves, doing penitence and inflicting it: but
the rebellions increased,
Indians against Indians, Pueblos against Apaches,
Indians against Spaniards, Pimas against whites,
until they culminated in the great rebellion of the Pueblos in 1680, it took them two weeks to liberate their lands, to destroy and sack, to kill twenty-one missionaries, burn the harvest, expel the Spaniards, and realize they could no longer live without them, their crops, their shotguns, their horses:
Bernardo de Gálvez, a little more than twenty years old and with the energy of more than twenty men, established peace by means of a ruse:
the technique for subjugating the wild Indians of the Río Grande is to give them rifles made of soft metal with long, flimsy barrels so they'll depend on Spain for their replacement parts, "The more rifles, the less arrows," says the young, energetic Río Grande peacemaker and future viceroy of New Spain, Gálvez of Galveston,
let the Indians lose the ability to shoot arrows, which kill more Spaniards than badly used rifles:

"Better a bad peace than a pyrrhic victory," says Gálvez for the ages,
but just plain peace requires inhabitants, and there are only three thousand in the río grande, río bravo, they invite families from Tenerife, they give them land, free entry, the title of hidalgo, fifteen families from the Canary Islands come to San Antonio, exhausted by the voyage from Santa Cruz to Veracruz, colonists come from Málaga, exhausted by the voyage to the Río Grande,
and the first gringos arrive:
the territories were lost before they were won

JUAN ZAMORA

Juan Zamora had a nightmare, and when he woke up to find that what he'd dreamed was real, he went to the border and now he's here standing among the demonstrators. But Juan Zamora doesn't raise his fists or spread his arms in a cross. In one hand he carries a doctor's bag. And under each arm, two boxes of medicine.

He dreamed about the border and saw it as an enormous bloody wound, a sick body, mute in the face of its ills, on the point of shouting, torn by its loyalties, and beaten, finally, by political callousness, demagoguery, and corruption. What was the name of the border sickness? Dr. Juan Zamora didn't know and for that reason he was here, to relieve the pain, to give back to the United States the fruits of his studies at Cornell, of the scholarship Don Leonardo Barroso got for him fourteen years earlier, when Juan was a boy and lived through some sad loves . . .

On his white shirt, Juan wears a pin, the number 187 canceled by a diagonal line that annuls the proposition approved in California, denying Mexican immigrants education and health benefits. Juan Zamora had arranged an invitation to a Los Angeles hospital and had seen that Mexicans no longer went there for care. He visited Mexican neighborhoods. People were scared to death. If they went to the hospital—they told him—they would be reported and turned over to the police. Juan told them it wasn't true, that the hospital authorities were human, they wouldn't report anyone. But the fear was unbearable. The illnesses too. One case here, another there, an infection, pneumonia, badly treated, fatal. Fear killed more than any virus.

Parents stopped sending their children to school. A child of Mexican origin is easily identified. What are we going to do? the parents asked. We pay more, much, much more in taxes than what they give us in education and services. What are we going to do? Why are they accusing us? What are they accusing us of? We're working. We're here because they need us. The gringos need us. If they didn't, we wouldn't come.

Standing opposite the bridge from Juárez to El Paso, Juan Zamora remembers with a grimace of distaste the time he lived at Cornell. He doesn't want his personal sorrows to interfere with his judgment about what he saw and understood then about the hypocrisy and arrogance that can come over the good people of the United States. Juan Zamora learned not to complain. Silently, Juan Zamora learned to act. He does not ask permission in Mexico to attend to urgent cases, he leaps over bureaucratic obstacles, understands social security to be a public service, will not abandon those with AIDS, drug addicts, drunks, the entire dark and foamy tide the city deposits on its banks of garbage.

"Who do you think you are? Florence Nightingale?"

The jokes about his profession and his homosexuality stopped bothering Juan a long time ago. He knew the world,

knew his world, was going to distinguish between the su-
perficial—he's a fag, he's a sawbones—and the necessary—
giving some relief to the heroin addict, convincing the family
of the AIDS victim to let him die at home, hell, even having
a mescal with the drunk . . .

Now he felt his place was here. If the U.S. authorities
were denying medical services to Mexican workers, he, Florence Nightingale, would become a walking hospital, going
from house to house, from field to field, from Texas to Arizona, from Arizona to California, from California to
Oregon, agitating, dispensing medicines, writing prescrip-
tions, encouraging the sick, denouncing the inhumanity of
the authorities.

"How long do you plan to visit the United States?"

"I have a permanent visa until the year 2010."

"You can't work. Do you know that?"

"Can I cure?"

"What?"

"Cure, cure the sick."

"No need to. We've got hospitals."

"Well, they're going to fill up with illegals."

"They should go back to Mexico. Cure them there."

"They're going to be incurable, here or there. But they're
working here with you."

"It's very expensive for us to take care of them."

"It's going to be more expensive to take care of epidemics
if you don't prevent diseases."

"You can't charge for your services. Did you know
that?"

Juan Zamora just smiled and crossed the border.

Now, on the other side, he felt for an instant he was in
another world. He was overwhelmed by a sensation of vertigo. Where would he begin? Whom would he see? The truth

is he didn't think they'd let him in. It was too easy. He didn't expect things to go that well. Something bad was going to happen. He was on the gringo side with his bag and his medicines. He heard a squeal of tires, repeated shots, broken glass, metal being pierced by bullets, the impact, the roar, the shout: "Doctor! Doctor!"

the gringos came (who are they, who are they, for God's sake, how can they exist, who invented them?)
they came drop by drop,
they came to the uninhabited, forgotten, unjust land the Spanish monarchy and now the Mexican republic overlooked,
isolated, unjust land, where the Mexican governor had two million sheep attended by twenty-seven hundred workers and where the pure gold of the mines of the Real de Dolores never returned to the hands of those who first touched that precious metal,
where the war between royalists and insurgents weakened the Hispanic presence,
and then the constant war of Mexicans against Mexicans, the anguished passage from an absolutist monarchy to a democratic federal republic:
let the gringos come, they too are independent and democratic,
let them enter, even illegally, crossing the Sabinas River, wetting their backs, sending the border to hell, says another energetic young man, thin, small, disciplined, introspective, honorable, calm, judicious, who knows how to play the flute: exactly the opposite of a Spanish hidalgo
his name is Austin, he brings the first colonists to the Río Grande, the Colorado, and the Brazos, they are the old three hundred, the founders of gringo texanity, five hundred more

follow them, they unleash the Texas fever, all of them want land, property, guarantees, and they want freedom, protestantism, due process of law, juries of their peers,

but Mexico offers them tyranny, catholicism, judicial arbitrariness

they want slaves, the right to private property,

but Mexico abolished slavery, assaulting private property,

they want the individual to be able to do whatever the hell he wants

Mexico, even though it no longer has it, believes in the Spanish authoritarian state, which acts unilaterally for the good of all

now there are thirty thousand colonists of U.S. origin in the río grande, río bravo, and only about four thousand Mexicans,

conflict is inevitable: "Mexico must occupy Texas right now, or it will lose it forever," says the Mexican statesman Mier y Terán,

Desperate, Mexico seeks European immigrants,

but nothing can stop the Texas fever,

a thousand families a month come down from the Mississippi, why should these cowardly, lazy, filthy Mexicans govern us? this cannot be God's plan!

the pyrrhic victory at the Alamo, the massacre at Goliad: Santa Anna is not Gálvez, he prefers a bad war to a bad peace,

here are the two face-to-face at San Jacinto:

Houston, almost six feet tall, wearing a coonskin cap, a leopard vest, patiently whittling any stick he finds nearby,

Santa Anna wearing epaulets and a three-cornered hat, sleeping his siesta in San Jacinto while Mexico loses Texas: what Houston is really carving is the future wooden leg of the picturesque, frivolous, incompetent Mexican dictator

"Poor Mexico, so far from God and so close to the United States," another dictator would famously say one day, and in a lower voice, another president: "Between the United States and Mexico, the desert"

JOSÉ FRANCISCO

Sitting on his Harley-Davidson on the Yankee side of the river, José Francisco watched with fascination the unusual strike on the Mexican side. It wasn't a sit-down but a raising up—of arms displaying the muscle of poverty, the sinew of insomnia, the wisdom of the oral library of a people that was his own, José Francisco said with pride. Perched on his bike, the tip of his boot resting on the starter, he wondered if this time, with the fracas going on on the other side, both patrols might stop him because he looked so weird, with his shoulder-length hair, his cowboy hat, his silver crosses and medals, and his rainbow-striped serape jacket. His only credible document was his moon face, open, clean-shaven, like a smiling star. Even though his teeth were perfect, strong, and extremely white, they, too, were disturbing to anyone who didn't look like him. Who'd never been to the dentist? José Francisco.

"You must go to the dentist," he was told in his Texas school.

He went. He returned. Not a single cavity.

"This child is amazing. Why doesn't he need dental work?"

Before, José Francisco didn't know what to answer. Now he does.

"Generations of eating chiles, beans, and tortillas. Pure calcium, pure vitamin C. Not a single cherry Lifesaver."

Teeth. Hair. Motorcycle. They had to find something suspicious about him every time in order to admit he wasn't odd, simply different. Inside he bore something different but he could never be calm. He bore something that couldn't happen on either side of the frontier but can happen on both sides. Those were hard things to understand on both sides.

"What belongs here and also there. But where is here and where is there? Isn't the Mexican side his own here and there? Isn't it the same on the gringo side? Doesn't every land have its invisible double, its alien shadow that walks at our side the same way each of us walks accompanied by a second 'I' we don't know?"

Which is why José Francisco wrote—to give that second José Francisco, who apparently had his own internal frontier, a chance. He wanted to be nice to himself but wouldn't allow it. He was divided into four parts.

They wanted him to be afraid to speak Spanish. We're going to punish you if you talk that lingo.

That was when he started singing songs in Spanish at recess, until he drove all the gringos, teachers and students, insane.

That was when no one talked to him and he didn't feel discriminated against. "They're afraid of me," he said, he said to them. "They're afraid of talking to me."

That was when his only friend stopped being his friend, when he said to José Francisco, "Don't say you're Mexican; you can't come to my house."

That was when José Francisco achieved his first victory, causing an uproar in school by demanding that students—blacks, Mexicans, whites—be seated in the classroom by alphabetical order and not by racial group. He accomplished this by writing, mimeographing, and distributing pamphlets, hounding the authorities, making a pain in the ass of himself.

"What gave you so much confidence, so much spirit?"

"It must be the genes, man, the damn genes."

It was his father. Without a penny to his name, he'd come with his wife and son from Zacatecas and the exhausted mines that had once belonged to Oñate. Other Mexicans lent him a cow to give the child milk. The father took a chance. He traded the cow for four hogs, slaughtered the hogs, bought twenty hens, and with the carefully tended hens, started an egg business and prospered. His friends who'd lent him the cow never asked him to return it, but he extended unlimited credit for as many "white ones" as they liked— out of modesty, no one ever referred to "eggs" because that meant testicles.

There, here. When he graduated from high school they told him to change his name from José Francisco to Joe Frank. He was intelligent. He would have a better time of it.

"You'll be better off, boy."

"I'd be mute, bro."

To whom if not to himself was he going to say, as he gathered the eggs on his father's little farm, that he wanted to be heard, wanted to write things, stories about immigrants, illegals, Mexican poverty, Yankee prosperity, but most of all stories about families, that was the wealth of the border world, the quantity of unburied stories that refused to die, that wandered about like ghosts from California to Texas waiting for someone to tell them, someone to write them. José Francisco became a story collector.

he sang about his grandparents, who had no birth date or last name,

he wrote about the men who did not know the four seasons of the year,

he described the long, luxurious meals so all the families could get together, and when he began to write, at the age of nineteen, he was asked, and asked himself, in which language, in English or in Spanish? and first he said in something new, the Chicano language, and it was then he realized what he was, neither Mexican nor gringo but Chicano, the language revealed it to him, he began to write in Spanish the parts that came out of his Mexican soul, in English the parts that imposed themselves on him in a Yankee rhythm, first he mixed, then he began separating, some stories in English, others in Spanish, depending on the story, the characters, but always everything united, story, characters, by the impulse of José Francisco, his conviction:

"I'm not a Mexican. I'm not a gringo. I'm Chicano. I'm not a gringo in the USA and a Mexican in Mexico. I'm Chicano everywhere. I don't have to assimilate into anything. I have my own history."

He wrote it but it wasn't enough for him. His motorcycle went back and forth over the bridge across the Río Grande, Río Bravo, loaded with manuscripts. José Francisco brought Chicano manuscripts to Mexico and Mexican manuscripts to Texas. The bike was the means to carry the written word rapidly from one side to the other, that was José Francisco's contraband, literature from both sides so that everyone would get to know one another better, he said, so that everyone would love one another a little more, so there would be a "we" on both sides of the border.

"What are you carrying in your saddlebags?"

"Writing."

"Political stuff?"

"All writing is political."

"So it's subversive."

"All writing is subversive."

"What are you talking about?"

"About the fact that lack of communication is a bitch. That anyone who can't communicate feels inferior. That keeping silent will screw you up."

The Mexican agents got together with the U.S. agents to see just what it was all about, what kind of a problem this longhaired guy on the bike was creating, the one who crossed the bridge singing "Cielito Lindo" and "Valentín de la Sierra," his bags filled, they hoped, with counterfeit money or drugs, but no, it was just papers. Political, he said? Subversive, he admitted? Let's see them, let's see them. The manuscripts began to fly, lifted by the night breeze like paper doves able to fly for themselves. They didn't fall into the river, José Francisco noted, they simply went flying from the bridge into the gringo sky, from the bridge to the Mexican sky, Ríos's poem, Cisneros's story, Nericio's essay, Siller's pages, Cortázar's manuscript, Garay's notes, Aguilar Melantzón's diary, Gardea's deserts, Alurista's butterflies, Denise Chávez's thrushes, Carlos Nicolás Flores's sparrows, Rogelio Gómez's bees, Cornejo's millennia, Federico Campbell's *fronteras* . . . And José Francisco happily helped the guards, tossing manuscripts into the air, to the river, to the moon, to the frontiers, convinced that the words would fly until they found their destination, their readers, their listeners, their tongues, their eyes . . .

He saw the demonstrators' arms open in a cross on the Ciudad Juárez side, saw how they rose to catch the pages in the air, and José Francisco gave a victory shout that forever broke the crystal of the frontier . . .

the frontier is not yet the río grande, río bravo, it's the Nueces river, but the gringos say nueces—nuts—to a frontier

that keeps them from carrying out their manifest destiny:
to reach the Pacific, create a continental nation, occupy Cal-
ifornia:
the railroad cars full, the wagons, people on horseback, cities
packed with pioneers, seeking deeds to the new lands, thirty
thousand gringos in Texas on the day of the Alamo, a hun-
dred and fifty thousand ten years later, the day of the War,
Manifest Destiny, dictated by the protestant God to his new
Chosen People, to conquer an inferior race, an anarchic re-
public, a caricature of a nation that owes money to the whole
world, with a caricature army, with only half of the forty
thousand men it says it has, and those twenty thousand, al-
most all of them, Indians marched down from the hills, con-
scripts, armed with useless English muskets, dressed in
ragged uniforms:
"There's a Mexican garrison that hasn't been able to show
itself in Matamoros because the soldiers have no clothes"
was the American army any better?
no, say the enemies of Polk's war, they only have eight thou-
sand men, cannon fodder who have never been in a fight,
disloyal criminals, deserters, mercenaries . . .
let them set us on the gringos, they shout from the Mexican
bank of the río bravo in Chihuahua and Coahuila, we'll beat
them with our natural allies, fever and the desert, with the
freed slaves who join up with us,
do not cross the río grande, say the American enemies of
Polk's war, this is a war to help the slave owners, to expand
the southern territories:
río grande, río bravo, Texas claims it as its border,
Mexico rejects it, Polk orders Taylor to seize the bank of the
river, the Mexicans defend themselves, there are deaths, the
war has begun,

"Where?" demands Abraham Lincoln in Congress, "will someone tell me exactly where Mexico fired the first shot and occupied the first piece of land?"

General Taylor laughs: he himself is the caricature of his army, he wears long white filthy trousers, a moth-eaten dress coat, and a white linen sash, he's short, thickset, as round as a cannonball,

and he laughs seeing how the Mexican cannonballs bounce into the American encampment at Arroyo Seco, only one Mexican cannon shot in a thousand hits the mark: his guffaw is sinister, it divides the very river, from then on everything is a stroll, to New Mexico and California, to Saltillo and to Monterrey, from Vera Cruz to Mexico City: Taylor's army loses the torn trousers of its commander and wins the buttoned-up dress coat of Winfield Scott, the West Point general the only thing that doesn't change is Santa Anna, the man with fifteen nails (he lost five when he lost his leg), the cockfighter, the Don Juan, the man who can lose an entire country laughing if his reward is a beautiful woman and a destroyed political rival,

the United States? I'll think about that tomorrow

he chews gum, buries his leg with full honors, orders equestrian statues from Italy, proclaims himself Most Serene Highness, Mexico puts up with him, Mexico puts up with everything, who ever said that Mexicans have the right to be well-governed?

looted country, sacked country, mocked, painful, cursed, precious country of marvelous people who have not found their word, their face, their own destiny, not manifest but uncertain human destiny, to sculpt slowly, not to reveal providentially: the destiny of the underground river, río grande, río bravo, where the Indians heard the music of God

GONZALO ROMERO

To his cousin Serafín he said, when Serafín turned up still smelling like a garbageman, that here in the north there were jobs for everyone, so Serafín and Gonzalo were not going to engage in a territorial fight, especially as they were cousins and especially as they were working to help their country-men. But Gonzalo warned him that to be a bandit on the other side of the border is another thing, it's dangerous—nobody's tried it since Pancho Villa—but being a guide like Gonzalo, what they call a coyote in California, is a job that's practically honorable, it's one of the liberal professions, as the gringos put it: meeting with his colleagues, some fourteen or so young men like him, around twenty-two years old, sitting on the hoods of their parked cars, waiting for to-night's clients, not those deluded types in the demonstration over at the bridge but the solid clients who will take advan-tage of this night of confusion on the border to cross over then and not by day, as the coyotes recommend. They know the Río Grande, Río Bravo by heart, El Paso, Juárez: they don't go where it's easiest to wade across, the river's narrow waist, because that's where the thieves lie in wait, the junk-ies, the drug pushers. Gonzalo Romero even has a flotilla of rubber rafts to carry people who can't swim, pregnant women, children, when the river really does get grand, really requires bravery. Now it's calm and the crossing will be easy; besides, everyone's distracted by the famous demonstration—they won't even notice. We're going to cross at night, we're professionals, we only get paid when the worker reaches his destination, and then—Gonzalo told his cousin Serafín—we still have to split the profits with drivers and people who run safe houses, and sometimes there are telephone and airplane expenses. You should see how many want to go to Chicago, to Oregon because there's less checking there, less persecution, no laws like Proposition 187. An entire village in Michoacán or Oaxaca chips in their savings so one of them can pay a thousand dollars and fly to Chicago.

"How much do you make out of all this, Gonzalo?"

"Well, about thirty dollars a person."

"You'd be better off in my gang," laughed Serafín. "I swear by your mother: that's the future."

The confusion of the cold, urgent night allows Gonzalo Romero to bring fifty-four workers across. But it was a bad night, and later in his house in Juárez with Gonzalo's children and wife, all weeping, cousin Serafín noted that when everything seems too easy you've got to be on guard, for sure something's going to fuck up, it's the law of life and anyone who thinks everything's going to go right for him all the time is a jerk—meaning no offense to poor cousin Gonzalo.

It was as if that night the Texas employers, stirred up by the raised-arms demonstration and by the sight of the fifty-four people gathered by Gonzalo Romero next to a gas station on the outskirts of El Paso, had agreed to screw the people who'd come across. From their truck, the contractors first said that there were too many, that they couldn't contract for fifty-four wetbacks, although they'd take anyone who would work for a dollar an hour even though they'd said they'd pay two dollars an hour. All fifty-four raised their hands, and then the contractors said, Still too many—let's see how many will come with us for fifty cents an hour. About half said they would, the other half got mad and began to argue, but the employer told them to get back to Mexico fast because he was going to call the Border Patrol. The rejected men started insulting the contracted workers, who in turn called them stinking beggars and told them to hurry up and get out because there was a lot of bad feeling against them in these parts.

Romero began to gather all of them together—no way. He wouldn't charge them, he only charged when he delivered the worker to the boss. That's why he was respected on the border. He kept his word, he was a professional. Listen, he told them, I'm even teaching my kids how to be guides when they grow up—coyotes, as we're called in California—that's how honorable I think my miserable job is . . .

It was then that the desert night filled with the echo of a storm that Gonzalo Romero tried to locate in the sky; but the sky was clear, starry, outlining the black silhouettes of the poplars, perfumed by the incense of the piñons. Was the tremor coming from deep within the earth? Gonzalo Romero thought for an instant that the crust of mesquite and creosote was the armor plating of this plain of the Río Grande and that no earthquake could break it up; no, the roar, the tremor, the echo arose from another armor plate, one of asphalt and tar, the straight line of the highways of the plain, the wheels of the motorcycles calcifying the desert, motors ablaze, as if the bikes' lights were fire and their riders warriors in an unmentionable horde. Gonzalo Romero and the group of workers saw the arms tattooed with Nazi insignia, the shaved heads, the sweatshirts proclaiming white supremacy, the hands raised in the Fascist salute, the fists clutching cans of beer, twenty, thirty men, sweating beer and pickles and onion, who suddenly surrounded them. They formed a circle of motorcycles, screaming, White supremacy, Death to the Mexicans, Let's invade Mexico, might as well begin now, we came to kill Mexicans. And at point-blank range each fired his high-powered rifle at Gonzalo Romero, at the twenty-three workers. Then, when they were all dead, one of the skinheads got off his bike and checked the bleeding head of each body with the tip of his boot. They'd aimed well, at the Mexicans' heads, and one of them put his cap back on his bare head and said to no one in particular, to his comrades, to the dead, to the desert, to the night: "Today I really had the death faucet wide open!"

He showed his teeth. On the inside of his lower lip was tattooed WE ARE EVERYWHERE.

and then disguised as a French lawyer, Benito Juárez sent Santa Anna packing, was attacked by the French, and took refuge in El Paso del Norte because the French left him nothing but that bend in the río bravo, río grande, to defend his Mexican republic:
he arrived with his black coach and his wagons filled with papers, letters, laws, he arrived with his black cape, his black suit, his black top hat, he himself as dark as the most ancient language, like the forgotten Indian language of Oaxaca, he himself as dark as the most ancient time, when there was no yesterday or tomorrow,
but he didn't know that: he was a liberal Mexican lawyer, an admirer of Europe betrayed by Europe who had now taken refuge in the bend of the río bravo, río grande, with no other relics for his exodus than the papers, the laws he'd signed, identical to the laws of Europe,
Juárez looks at the other side of the river, at Texas and its growing prosperity, there where Spain left only the footprints of Cabeza de Vaca in the sand and Mexico, translating that name word for word, was only a cow's head buried in the sand,
gringo Texas founded commercial towns, attracted immigrants from all over the world, crisscrossed its territory with

railroads, increased its wheat and cattle, and received the gift of the devil, oil wells, with no need to make the sign of the cross:

"Texas is so rich that anyone who wants to live poorly will have to go elsewhere, Texas is so vigorous that anyone who wants to die will have to go elsewhere":

look at me, Juárez says from the other side of the river, I have nothing and I even forgot what my grandparents had, but I want to be like you, prosperous, rich, democratic, look at me, understand me, my responsibility is different, I want us to be governed by laws, not tyrants, but I have to create a state that will see to it that laws are respected but that won't succumb to despotism:

and Texas did not look at Juárez, it only looked at Texas, and Texas only saw two presidents cross the bridge to visit and congratulate each other, William Howard Taft, fat as an elephant, seeing him walk on the bridge made everyone fearful the bridge wouldn't hold, immense, smiling, with roguish eyes and ringmaster moustaches, Porfirio Díaz light and thin under the weight of his myriad medals, an Indian from Oaxaca, sinewy at the age of eighty, with a white moustache, furrowed brow, wide nostrils, and the sad eyes of an aged guerrilla fighter, the two of them congratulating themselves that Mexico was buying merchandise and that Texas was selling it, that Mexico was selling land and that Texas was buying it,

Jennings and Blocker more than a million acres of Coahuila, the Texas Company almost five million acres in Tamaulipas, William Randolph Hearst almost eight million acres in Chihuahua,

they didn't see the Mexicans who wanted to see Mexico whole, wounded, dark, stained with silver, and cloaked in

mud, her belly petrified like that of some prehistoric animal,
her bells as fragile as glass, her mountains chained to one
another in a vast orographic prison,
her memory tremulous: Mexico
her smile facing the firing squad: Mexico
her genealogy of smoke: Mexico
her roots so old they decided to show themselves without
shame
her fruit bursting like stars
her songs breaking apart like piñatas,
the men and women of the revolution reached this point,
from here they departed, on the bank of the río grande, río
bravo, but before marching south to fight
they stopped, showing the gringos the wounds we wanted to
close, the dreams we needed to dream, the lies we had to
expel, the nightmares we had to assume:
we showed ourselves and they saw us,
once again we were the strangers, the inferiors, the incom-
prehensible, the ones in love with death, the siesta, and rags,
they threatened, disdained, didn't understand that to the
south of the río grande, río bravo, for one moment, during
the revolution, the truth we wanted to be and share with
them shone, different from them, before the plagues of Mex-
ico returned, the corruption, the abuse, the misery of many,
the opulence of a few, disdain as a rule, compassion the ex-
ception, equal to them:
will there be time? will there be time? will there be time?
will there be time for us to see each other and accept each
other as we really are, gringos and Mexicans, destined to
live together at the border of the river until the world gets
tired, closes its eyes, and shoots itself, confusing death with
sleep?

LEONARDO BARROSO

What had Leonardo Barroso been talking about a minute before? He was almost spitting into the cellular phone, demanding compensation for the losses these gangs of thieves—these end-of-the-millennium Pancho Villas!—attacking trains were causing him, piling up debris outside the terminals, robbing shipments from the assembly plants, smuggling in workers: did Murchinson know what it cost to stop a train, investigate if there were illegals on it, fuck up the schedules, replace stolen merchandise, get the orders to their destinations on time—in a word, to fulfill contracts? What had Leonardo Barroso been thinking about a minute before? The threat had been repeated that morning. Over the cellular phone. Territories had to be respected. Responsibilities as well. In matters related to drug trafficking, Mr. Barroso, only Latin Americans are guilty, Mexicans and Colombians, never Americans: that was the crux of the system. In the United States there can never be a drug king like Escobar or Caro Quintero; the guilty parties are those who sell drugs, not those who buy them. In the United States there are no corrupt judges—they're your monopoly. There are no secret landing strips here, we don't launder money here, Mr. Barroso, and if you think you can blackmail us in order to save your skin and be proclaimed a national hero in the process, it's going to cost you plenty because there's millions and millions involved here—you know that. Your whole way of operating is to invade territories that aren't yours, Mr. Barroso; instead of being content with the crumbs, you want the whole feast, Mr. Barroso . . . and that just cannot happen . . .

What did Leonardo Barroso feel a moment before? Michelina's hand in his as he feverishly sought the girl's familiar

heat without finding it, as if a bird, long caressed and consoled, had suffocated, dead from so much tenderness, tired
of so much attention . . .

Where was Leonardo Barroso a minute before?

In his Cadillac Coupe de Ville, being driven by a chauffeur supplied by his partner Murchinson, he and Michelina
sitting in back, the chauffeur driving slowly to get past the
booths and obstacles U.S. Immigration had set up so immigrants couldn't run through and cause a stampede, Michelina making who knows what small talk about the Mexican
chauffeur Leandro Reyes who crashed in that tunnel in
Spain, crashed into that foolish nineteen-year-old boy driving
in the other direction . . .

Where was Leonardo Barroso a minute later?

Riddled with bullets, shot five times by a high-powered
weapon, the driver dead at the wheel, Michelina miraculously alive, screaming hysterically, clutching her hands to
her throat, as if she wanted to strangle her shouts, immediately remembering her tears, wiping them in the crook of her
elbow, staining the sleeve of her Moschino jacket with mas-
cara.

Where was Juan Zamora two minutes later?

At Leonardo Barroso's side, answering the urgent call—
Doctor! Doctor!—he'd heard as he crossed the international
bridge. He looked for vital signs in the pulse, the heart, the
mouth—nothing. There was nothing to do. It was Juan Zamora's first case in American territory. He didn't recognize
in that man with his brains blown out the benefactor of his
family, the protector of his father, the powerful man who
sent him to study at Cornell . . .

What did Rolando Rozas do three minutes later?

He spoke into his cellular phone to transmit the bare
news—job done, no complications, zero errors—then passed

his sweaty hand over his airplane-colored suit, as Marina called it, adjusted his tie, and began to stroll, as he did every night, through his favorite restaurants, through the bars and streets of El Paso, to see what new girl might turn up.

now Marina of the Maquilas crosses the bridge over the río grande, río bravo, and she's holding the arm of a tiny old lady wrapped in shawls, protecting her, an unreadable old woman under the palimpsest of infinite wrinkles that cross a face like the map of a country lost forever,
Dinorah asked her this favor, take my grandma to the other side of the bridge, Marina, deliver her to my uncle Ricardo on the other side, he doesn't want to come back to Mexico ever again, it makes him sad, makes him afraid, too, that they might not let him back in,
take my grandma to the other side of the río grande, río bravo, so my uncle can take her back to Chicago,
she only came to comfort me on the death of the kid,
she can't do it alone, and not just because she's almost a hundred years old
but because she's spent so much time living as a Mexican in Chicago that she forgot Spanish a long time ago and never learned English,
she can't communicate with anyone
(except with time, except with the night, except with oblivion, except with mongrels and parrots, except with the papayas she touches in the market and the coyotes that visit her at dawn, except with the dreams she can't tell anyone, except with the immense reserve of that which is not spoken today so it can be said tomorrow)
but on the other side, trying to cross the bridge amid great confusion, two naked men approach the immigration kiosks, a fifty-year-old, silvery hair, athletic physique but well-fed,

dragging a scrawny simpleton by the arm, the simpleton screwed up beyond all screwing up, just skin and bones, dark, but the two of them together, pleading, they seem like lunatics, they didn't let us leave through San Diego and come in through Tijuana, or leave through Caléxico and come in through Mexicali, or leave through Nogales Arizona and come in through Nogales Sonora,

where are they going to send us?

to the sea?

are we going to swim our way to Mexico?

with nothing on, stripped, cleaned out?

give us a place to rest, in the name of heaven!

don't you realize that behind us, pursuing us, armed garbage, death with deodorant, is approaching and that toward us is advancing once again the dead earth, the unjust earth, the law that says: Shoot fugitives in the back!

we want to enter to tell the story of the crystal frontier before it's too late,

let everyone speak,

speak, Juan Zamora, bent over, attending a corpse,

speak, Margarita Barroso, showing your uncertain identity so as to cross the border,

speak, Michelina Laborde, stop screaming, think about your husband, the abandoned boy, Don Leonardo Barroso's heir, imagine yourself, Gonzalo Romero, that the skinheads didn't murder you but instead the coyotes that now surround your corpse and the corpses of the twenty-three workers in a circle of inseparable hunger and astonishment,

get pissed off, Serafín Romero, and tell yourself you're going to attack as many damn trains as cross your path so that war can return to the frontier again, so that it's not only the gringos who attack,

adjust your night-vision glasses, Dan Polonsky, hoping that

the strikers dare to take a step forward,
pretend you're stupid, Mario Islas, so that your godson Elo-
íno can run inland, wetback, young, breathless, intending
never to return,
raise your arms, Benito Ayala, offer your arms to the river,
to the earth, to everything that needs your strength to live,
to survive,
toss the papers in the air, José Francisco, poems, notes, di-
aries, novels, let's see where the wind takes the sheets of
paper, let's see where they fall, on which side, this one or
that one,
to the north of the río grande,
to the south of the río bravo,
toss the papers as if they were feathers, ornaments, tattoos
to defend them from the inclemency of the weather, clan
markings, stone collars, bone, conch, diadems of the race,
waist and leg adornments, feathers that speak, José Fran-
cisco,
to the north of the río grande,
to the south of the río bravo,
feathers emblematic of each deed, each battle, each name,
each memory, each defeat, each triumph, each color,
to the north of the río grande,
to the south of the río bravo,
let the words fly,
poor Mexico,
poor United States,
so far from God,
so near to each other